LOST IN AMERICA

BOOK ONE

LAURA FITZGERALD

ALSO BY LAURA FITZGERALD

Veil of Roses
One True Theory of Love
Dreaming in English

CONNECT WITH LAURA

www.laurafitzgerald.com

Facebook Group: **"Laura Fitzgerald Fan Club"**

To Friend on Facebook: **writer.laurafitzgerald**

Goodreads: **Laura Fitzgerald**

Twitter: **@FitzgeraldLaura**

Instagram: **writerlaurafitzgerald**

Tumblr: **LostInAmerica-TheBook**

All social media websites are managed directly by the author.

This book is the first in a series and contains the first three episodes in the series. To be notified when a new episode is available, please sign up at

WWW.LAURAFITZGERALD.COM

LOST
IN
AMERICA

**BOOK
ONE**

LAURA FITZGERALD

This is a work of fiction. Names, characters, organizations, places, events, and incidents are either products of the author's imagination or are used fictitiously.

Published by Cardinal Press, Tucson
First Edition 2015

Edition ISBNs
Trade Paperback 978-1-942656-11-1
E-Book 978-1-942656-12-8

Cover design by Oceana Garceau
Book design by Morgana Gallaway

This edition was prepared for printing by
The Editorial Department
7650 E. Broadway Blvd., #308
Tucson, AZ 85710
www.editorialdepartment.com

Be who God meant you to be and you will set the world on fire.

—Catherine of Siena

EPISODE
ONE

EARLY MORNING FOG BLANKETED THE SAN FRANCISCO AIR- field, and the man was glad to be on the ground again. The flight had been quick and his pilot the best money could buy; none- theless, he'd been uncharacteristically anxious for what turned out to be a textbook-smooth landing. At this point, he'd hate to be undone by something as insignificant yet uncontrollable as fog.

But he knew he wouldn't be. He'd known they would land safely; it was just the niggling fear of his expert pilot being unable to see what was literally right in front of him that had clutched his heart until the plane's wheels hit the tarmac.

He found it disturbing visually. Symbolically. Man was worth- less without his ability to see clearly. That's what this entire situa- tion boiled down to, in fact: People caught up in the happenings of the day as if those happenings actually mattered. Only one thing mattered, and that was *his* vision—*his* ability to see clearly that which others could not.

Very soon, his plan would begin to unfold. Nothing had been left to chance. Everything that could be controlled had been con- trolled, and there would be no twists of fate. His opponents were proving worthless, despite their so-called insight.

"After you, sir," said Russell Hendricks, his bodyguard, who was sitting in the row behind him and across the aisle.

"Take my portfolio and blanket. Bring the blanket with us. Please." Although he was eager to deplane and begin his day's activity, the man's body cringed with pain, and he rose slowly to his feet.

"Of course," Hendricks said and wisely did not offer assistance.

The man was pleased with this bodyguard. In the months he'd worked for him, he'd proven himself to be both competent and unquestioning. He was polite. Had decent grammar, and he demonstrated that all-important military-acquired combination of patience and blind obedience. Really, his biggest flaw was a ghastly tattoo on his left forearm, a coiled snake with the words, *Don't Tread on Me or I Will Strike.*

The man abhorred tattoos, for they bespoke a lack of class, of people desperate to assert their uniqueness but so stupid as to choose a laughably common way to do so. Tattoos were for people who thought small.

The man's own canvas was bigger.

His canvas was the whole damned world.

After he deplaned from the Gulfstream G650 and shook hands with both pilots, he slowly made his way through the executive terminal and to the waiting Town Car, where he was pleased to see the same driver as last time, a thin, blond, long-haired beauty. A good specimen. He'd inquired and learned she was working on her PhD in molecular biology at Berkeley, driving on the side to help pay her mother's medical bills. He liked this, for it showed she had brains and a work ethic. He'd bet anything she didn't have a tattoo.

He appreciated as well that, like Hendricks, she did not question what he was doing or why. On his last trip to the city, he'd first spent several hours at the historical society immersed in the city's rich early history. For the redesign of San Francisco, he'd decided to use the Great Earthquake and Fire of 1906 as the delineator and drew the boundary on the Rand McNally map he'd brought with him. He'd left the airport intact, of course, but any technology companies would have to relocate to within the 1906 city limits. Shouldn't be a problem, as there would be plenty of available office buildings. The population of San Francisco had been four hundred thousand at the time of the earthquake, and would be again—just half of today's population.

From the historical society, they'd driven the 1906 perimeter so he could get a general sense of the size, scope, and scale of the new Old San Francisco. Finally, they'd driven all the interior streets. He'd done a visual inspection, calling out orders to Hendricks. *Cross this out. Circle this. Shade this green. Put a question mark here.* Hendricks dutifully marked up the maps spread across his lap.

The man had then gone back home and thought long and hard for several weeks. He spent a lot of time these days in his zero-gravity recliner, covered in a cashmere blanket, indulging in his favorite thing to do: Think big thoughts.

This late-stage project had occurred to him on a recent visit he'd taken to his childhood home in Santa Ana, where his parents still lived. When he was growing up, ugly tract houses were already replacing the cherished orange groves of his father's youth. His father told yearning tales of how he and his childhood friends played in the groves—throwing oranges at each other, stuffing themselves on sweet navels, and racing through the groves on their dirt bikes, often chased by irritated farmers. The rural childhood sounded idyllic, but now there was only one grove left in the entire city.

He'd realized it didn't have to be that way. With such a huge reduction in population as was coming, all the ugliness that had been erected could be dismantled and the orange groves could return. For his father's old stomping grounds, he'd chosen postwar 1950 as the delineator. Opened in the mid-fifties, nearby Disneyland could stay, but everything around it would return to rural, and the orange groves would reclaim their rightful place in the Southern California landscape, scenting the air. The population of Orange County would go from over three million to the two hundred thousand it had been in 1950, a reduction of more than ninety percent.

Invigorated by his visit to Santa Ana, he expanded his thinking. It was one thing to solve the world's overpopulation nightmare in one fell swoop—a heck of a thing, granted, certainly one for the history books—but he had agreed to take ownership for the project because he was the only one who *could*, not because it was enjoyable. This—designing the world as it would be a hundred years from now—was pure fun.

Of course, he couldn't redesign the *whole* world; after all, he was running out of time. He wouldn't even be alive in a month. With that limitation in mind, he'd declared himself the purveyor of California and left the rest to the other members of the board.

"A beautiful day," he said to his woman driver. As his remaining time dwindled, every day was beautiful, in spite of his increasing weakness and never-ending pain. The woman got him settled in the Town Car and then took her place behind the wheel. Hendricks handed him the blanket, which he tucked around his stick-thin legs. "Turn on the heat," he said, and as an afterthought added, "Please."

"Of course." She complied and did not point out it was a thickly hot June day. "Are we taking another tour of the city today, sir?"

"Just one area," he said. "Take me to the Tenderloin District. We'll start at the Lower Nob Hill side, maybe Geary Street, and work our way down."

He'd thought long and hard about what to do with the fifty-odd blocks that made up the Tenderloin. None of the people in the Tenderloin were worth anything—they were takers, not givers—and the present neighborhood was beyond redemption. All the Southeast Asian crap would go, as would all the liquor stores, strip clubs, druggies, and prostitutes.

"Yes, sir," she said. "I'll just mention the tourist attack that took place there this week. A double homicide. Two college girls from Canada. Shouldn't have been wandering through at night, of course."

"Young people can be so dumb," he said. "It's amazing so many survive to adulthood."

As part of his planning for the Tenderloin, he'd read Dashiell Hammett's Sam Spade detective novels, which took place there. Hammett's descriptions of the theaters and gambling and speak-easies provided inspiration, and he decided to rename the area the Falcon District, after *The Maltese Falcon*. Half would turn into green space, while the other twenty-odd blocks would honor the area's history, albeit in a movie-set sort of way, replete with theaters and speakeasies and jazz clubs but minus the seedy underbelly.

When the man arrived at the Tenderloin that day, the fog had cleared. He no longer saw the neighborhood as it was. Instead, he saw the Falcon District of the future.

His bodyguard didn't see it. His driver didn't see it. But make no mistake: Society was about to be revolutionized. Destroyed and then rebuilt. Sure, the first generation of survivors would be consumed by grief—anger, too, if details of the Great Reset came to light, as they very well might.

But a hundred years from now, rivers would flow cleanly again. Forests would thrive. Food would be plentiful and disease nearly nonexistent. Nature would be in balance. There would be no traffic jams. No smog. No crime. No pollution-induced cancer. Children would once again bike through the Southern California orange groves while their parents raised their glasses in the cleaned-up, trendy Falcon District.

It would be idyllic: The population of the past and the technology of the future.

It would be his final gift to the world.

It would be his most important legacy.

THE STREET IN FRONT OF MICHAEL CUNNINGHAM'S HOUSE was littered with cars waiting for their party-going owners. Ducking through the sprinklers, I cut across the lawn in search of Adam Hanson, my perpetually-angry boyfriend. He was parked a few houses up and was already yanking open the door to his car. He seemed to have forgotten about me altogether.

"Hey, Adam!" I called. "Wait up!" He got in his car, slammed the door, and started the engine. I raced to get to the car and into the passenger seat before he took off without me. "I said wait!"

"I thought you were staying."

"Why *shouldn't* I stay, Adam? You've ignored me all night, and you're constantly in a bad mood. It's getting old."

"I'm sorry I can't pretend to be happy for you."

"I don't want you to pretend," I said. "I want you to *be* happy. I want you to *choose* to be happy. Lots of people go through hard times. It's not an excuse to be a jerk."

"Easy for you to say. You've got a great life."

"My life hasn't always been great, and you know it." The truth was, sometimes I had to work really hard to keep my mood up, but at least I made the effort. Adam didn't even try. "Sometimes I think you like being a jerk."

"Maybe I do," he said. "And maybe you should get out of the car."

"Listen, Adam." I shifted sideways, facing him, and waited for him to look at me. "We need to talk."

"I don't want to talk." He put the car in drive and turned the wheel to the left. "I want to get out of here, so you need to decide if you're in or out. Are you coming or going?"

I glanced back at Michael's house, where Matt Perkins stood watching from the doorway. The easy thing to do would've been to get out of the car and stay, but I knew that as in most cases, the harder thing to do was also the right thing to do.

"I'm in," I told Adam. "But I want to go straight home, and we're going to talk before you drop me off. You know we can't go on this way."

"You're breaking up with me."

"You seem to want me to, based on how you're acting."

I'd always loved his solid blue windows-to-his-soul eyes, but that night all I saw in them was bitterness.

"If you're going to break up with me, just do it now," he said. "Let's not drag it out. I'm not in the mood for any of your drama-queen stuff. I'm getting sick of your nagging, Kendra, to be honest."

"And I'm sick of you being so negative."

"So get out of the car."

"I'm coming with you, and we're going to talk, calmly and maturely."

"Whatever." He shrugged. "It really doesn't matter one way or the other."

"It matters to me."

On that note, he tried to peel out of his parking spot but didn't have enough room, so he had to back up, turn the wheel harder, move forward again, and repeat. When he finally got out of the parking spot, he realized he had a flat tire and sighed.

"Can I not catch one friggin' break?"

Karma, I thought, wanting to laugh, but it would've been too mean.

He pulled ahead a few car lengths to where there was more open space near the curb, then slammed on the parking brake and got out. As he popped the trunk and pulled out a wrench and a jack, I got out, too, and was both glad and nervous when I saw Matt crossing the lawn toward us.

"Need some help?" he called.

"Bastard," Adam muttered.

"He knows everything about cars," I said. "Let him help."

Watching Adam fumble as he attempted to unscrew the lug nuts, I should've suspected he was drunk, but it honestly didn't occur to me. He had plenty of faults, but drinking and driving wasn't one of them, and I'd been with him long enough to know his pattern at parties: He'd have a beer when he arrived and maybe nurse a second, but he'd switch over to Pepsi in plenty of time to sober up before he got behind the wheel. Not because he cared about potentially hurting people—with Adam, it was all about the car.

"Here, I'll get it." Matt reached for the jack. "Why don't you find some rocks to put in front of the tires?"

As Adam went off to get some landscaping rocks, Matt looked at me. "Everything okay?"

"No, but it will be."

"You know you can stay," he said quietly, so Adam couldn't hear. "I can take you home."

I shook my head. "I need to end this tonight or the entire summer's going to suck."

"Can't have that." He grinned, no doubt pleased with my decision to break up with Adam.

"Can't have what?" Adam asked, coming back with the rocks.

"Someone slashed your tire," Matt said and pointed to show him.

"Figures."

Matt had the tire changed in no time. He handed the tools back to Adam and then put the old tire in the trunk. "You're all set."

"Thanks, Matt," I said.

"Yeah, thanks, Matt," Adam said in a sing-song voice, mocking me.

"I'll call you later," I said, mostly because I knew it would annoy Adam.

Matt watched us until we'd turned the corner out of sight. Adam sped to every stop sign and then jerked on the brakes, over and over again, until we were out of the neighborhood and onto the six-lane Mayfair Road, a main drag in our town. Normally, it was fun to cruise down Mayfair Road in the top-down convertible, but convertibles were made for happy people, and I kept thinking how we must have looked—him scowling and me all tense. My arm hurt from gripping the armrest because he was speeding like crazy, aggressively passing every car he caught up to, almost giving them the finger by the obnoxious way he was driving. I'd been in the car with him before when he'd broken the speed limit, but nothing like this.

"SLOW DOWN!" I finally blurted, unable to stand it anymore.

He let up on the accelerator. "I'm sorry, all right? I just—" He glanced over at me. "I'm sorry. I know I shouldn't take out my problems on you."

I knew then that something was seriously wrong, because one thing Adam didn't do in life was apologize. It finally hit me: He was drunk. Before he could stop me, I shoved my Butler smartwatch in his face and ordered it to do a Breathalyzer. The response was instant. *One-point-one, m'lady.*

"Oh, Adam." Moving into kind, gentle, don't-piss-him-off mode, I put my hand on his knee. "You're way over the limit. You don't want to lose your license. You'd better pull over and let me—"

"Argh!" He bolted upright and looked in the rearview mirror. "That guy's totally on my ass!"

He was right. We were in the far left lane, and a motorcycle had suddenly come up behind us and was following us much, much too closely. One touch of the brakes on Adam's part and the guy would be road kill.

"Okay . . . uh, just put on your signal and move to the right and let him pass." I said it calmly, firmly, utterly sober. "After that, pull over."

Instead, Adam accelerated, and it was at that moment I knew: I was going to die.

The motorcycle responded to Adam's acceleration by swerving into the oncoming-traffic lane on his left, across the solid yellow line. He pulled alongside the convertible and looked tauntingly at Adam. Because his helmet had a dark face shield, I couldn't get a look at his face, but it was clear he was looking for trouble.

Suddenly, a semi-truck was in the motorcyclist's path, barreling toward him. If this were a game of high-stakes chicken, the motor-cycle driver surely would lose.

"Slow down!" I yelled. "You need to let him in!"

Adam glanced in his rearview mirror. A car was behind us, and I could tell that although his thinking was drunkenly slow, Adam recognized it would be better to brake and let the car hit us from behind than for the motorcycle driver to be hit head on.

In the meantime, the truck driver must have figured out his own less-worse scenario, because I could see the whites of his terrified eyes as he veered from his own lane . . . and into ours. He was going to hit us, in our unprotected, top-down convertible, in order to avoid hitting the motorcycle.

"Adam!" I yelled as the horrible realization hit me, as my mom's face flashed into my mind's eye. She'd be alone without me, and she'd already lost so much.

I braced for the impact, and then suddenly, weirdly, I was outside the car, lifted up, floating above, watching myself inside it with Adam. It wasn't my physical body floating up there; I thought maybe it was my soul. My physical body was still back in the car, still bracing for impact.

There was the sickening sound of the truck's tires screeching.

Of windshield glass breaking.

Of metal crushing metal.

Of me, screaming down below.

And then there was nothing.

Two Hours Earlier

DAEMON GODWIN WASN'T BEAUTIFUL IN THE CELEBRITY WAY some guys are. You didn't look at him and immediately think, *Oh, he's so hot, he must be self-centered; he's sure to break my heart.* He wasn't a slick beauty like that, although he did have sculpted cheekbones to die for.

Neither was he a wounded beauty, although that's a closer description. He *was* wounded—so badly scarred on the inside it was impossible to get close to him, but you wouldn't know that right away. You wouldn't see it in his dark brown eyes, because all you saw there was exactly what he wanted you to see and nothing more.

Daemon was just matter-of-fact tough. From the beginning, he scared me a little. I sensed he was dangerous, and somehow magical, too.

Case in point: When he touched me, I sizzled.

Literally: Hand on arm. *Sizzle.*

The first sizzle happened at Michael Cunningham's party. I'd driven over with my best friend, Nora Atkins, and we spent the first few minutes together near the door, shaking off the water from the sprinklers that had turned on unexpectedly as we'd run across

Michael's massive front lawn. The silver heels I'd worn had sunk into the grass and were muddy, my grey satin cocktail dress had water streaks, and my white fedora had a little puddle in its center, which I took off so I could shake it at Nora.

"Stop!" she squealed, laughing. With her usual flair for the dramatic, she pulled at her spiky dyed-blond hair, setting it off in new and interesting directions. "I'm already drenched!"

"What if there's a wet T-shirt contest?" I joked. "I'm just trying to help."

"Yeah, thanks." She looked around at the already-crowded house. Michael lived on the rich side of town and threw parties whenever his dad was away. Without fail, they were wall-to-wall packed, loud, and fun. There was flirting. Dancing. Good music. Cheap booze. Beer pong. Pot, if that was your thing. Whatever *your thing* was, you could indulge in it at Michael's parties. "Another great party, I can tell."

"Isn't every party great, by definition?" I said. My thing was just having fun—drinking a little, dancing a little, laughing a lot.

"Carpe the diem," she said.

"Carpe the diem," I agreed. "And the night, too."

We looked at each other and grinned. She'd slept over the previous night, and we'd rolled out of bed at dawn, feeling stuffy in my small bedroom. We'd found our way to my backyard, where we lay barefoot in the dewy grass and half-fell back to sleep, but not fully. We imagined out loud what college would be like—who we'd date, where we'd party. So much was uncertain, but what we did know was that life was good; the future was bright; and we'd take on the world together. We were both moving less than thirty miles to the dorms at the University of Minnesota, where we'd be roommates. Before that, we'd be camp counselors for an Outward Adventure program in the Boundary Waters up north, scheduled to leave in less than a week. Now here we were at the first party of the summer, on the cusp of everything our future might hold.

"What do you want to do?" Nora said. "I think I want to find Christopher."

"Of course you do." Christopher was her ongoing hookup. "I'm going to find Matt."

Matt Perkins was not my hookup. He was my other best friend, in some ways a better friend than Nora, but she was the first friend I'd made in Brookview, which earned her a spot nearly impossible to take away.

"How do I look?" she asked as she brushed the last drops of water from her flouncy pink skirt.

"Predictably unpredictable, as always." Nora was a fashionista of her own funky style. That night, besides the flouncy pink skirt, she wore a white midriff and black combat boots. Her flower barrette was a little lopsided, so I straightened it for her. "See you later, okay?"

We hugged goodbye and went in different directions. Nora headed down to the basement rec room, while I started toward what Michael's family called the study. Granted, it did have a lot of fancy-looking books on floor-to-ceiling mahogany shelves, but they seemed more for decoration than for reading. It was more like a rich dude's man cave, with black leather couches surrounding a stone fireplace, a wet bar, and a pool table, which is where I figured Matt would be. I knew he'd already arrived because I'd seen his vintage yellow Camaro parked out front.

I'd taken about three steps when, out of nowhere, Daemon grabbed my arm, not that I knew his name at the time. The charge was electric, how I imagined a strike of lightning might feel.

"OW!" I yanked my arm back. "What the—?"

"Listen," he said in a low voice. "Whatever you do, don't go home with your boyfriend tonight."

Wincing, I pressed against my still-tingling arm. "Was that supposed to be a pick-up line? Because if it was, it needs some work."

"No, Kendra, it wasn't," he said. "It was a warning."

I got goose bumps but tried to play it cool.

"How do you know my name?"

"I just do."

"What's yours?" I held up my wrist and took a picture of him with my Butler watch so I could find him online later using my Butler's photo facial recognition scanner.

"Daemon Godwin," he said. "But I highly doubt you'll find me online."

"Who do you know at the party, Daemon Godwin? Are you someone's creepy older brother?"

I said that because one thing was clear: He was not one of us.

"I don't know anybody besides you," he said.

We locked eyes in an uncomfortable way—uncomfortable because it felt like he really *did* know me, in a deep-down sort of way. But he was a stranger to me, a tall, dark, and handsome stranger of the sort you read about in romance novels. The dangerous kind.

"Sorry, but you *don't* know me."

He leaned close. "Remember what I said."

"I already forgot."

He looked annoyed by my smart-ass joke. "Don't leave with your boyfriend tonight."

"And you—don't tell me what to do."

I walked away from him then, resisting the urge to look over my shoulder. He'd rattled me, but I didn't want to give him the satisfaction of knowing it.

Matt was indeed in the study shooting pool. His eyes lit up when he saw me.

"Hey, nice dress!" he said. "Very sparkly."

"Thanks. I got drenched crossing the lawn."

"I see." He brushed my bangs, which were apparently still water-damaged. "You okay? Is something wrong?"

"I'm fine." I shook off the confusion I still felt from my encounter with Daemon. "Looks like a good party, huh?"

"Who'd you come with?"

"Nora," I said. "Adam's coming at some point. I think I'm going home with him."

He nodded without replying. Matt was not a fan of Adam. Few of my friends were. Honestly, even I wasn't much anymore, but we'd started seeing each other the first week of swim team senior year, and in the eight months we'd been together, his dad's addiction to painkillers had cost him his job, which led to them nearly losing their house, which they so far had managed to hold onto through selling almost everything they had of value. So their house was practically emptied out of furniture but filled instead with hurtful words and slamming doors and a general sense of failure. I was a good listener and kept things light and understood when Adam was in a bad mood, which was often. I was an easy girlfriend for him, although he was an increasingly difficult boyfriend for me.

Adam knew I was with him mostly out of pity at that point, and I could tell he hated it, but not enough to do the dirty work of ending things himself. Honestly, a large part of me was simply counting the days until summer ended and we went our separate ways to college. We'd already decided not to try the long-distance thing.

"Want to play pool?" Matt asked, gesturing to the pool table. "We can be partners."

"Sure! As long as you don't mind losing."

"Hey, Perkins, you're up."

The voice made my skin crawl. Of all people, Matt was playing against the freakishly tall, skinny, snobby Robert Chiu, the only one in our graduating class going to an Ivy League university. He'd been called gifted his whole life, but as far as I was concerned, the only thing he was gifted at was being a jerk. I'd won my high school's Most Likely to Kill the World with Kindness yearbook vote, but even I found it difficult to be nice to him.

"Here." He offered me his red plastic cup. "Drink the Kool-Aid."

I drank from Matt's cup instead, one generous gulp and then another, beginning my quest for the perfect buzz—enough to make the night dazzlingly fun but not so much that it would turn me into an emotional idiot, which had been known to happen. With me, it was a tricky balance.

I lifted my wrist and spoke to my Butler. "Gerald, tell me if my blood-alcohol level gets to point-five, and make me stop drinking at eleven o'clock no matter what, okay?"

Will do, m'lady, Gerald said.

Robert sneered. "You named your Butler?"

"You didn't?" I said back. "You should, seeing as it's probably your only friend in the world."

Robert was the first and only person I'd ever given myself permission to be rude to, and I had to admit, it was kind of fun.

"You're going to state school, right?" he said. "What are you majoring in, partying?"

"Maybe," I said, although it was far from the truth. I wasn't much of a partier, but around Robert I became argumentative on principle. "Anything wrong with that?"

"For you? No. But some of us aspire to greatness."

I laughed. "You, great? Good luck with that."

"You know what's going to be the next big thing after Butlers?"

"No." I honestly didn't think anything *would* ever come along and replace Butlers—they were that cool. Butlers had changed the world much like personal computers and the Internet and iPods and cell phones had before them.

"Neither do I," Robert said. "But whatever it is, I'm going to invent it."

"Really?" I smiled at Matt, who rolled his eyes at Robert's well-known grandiosity. "Little ol' you?"

There were both wall Butlers and watch Butlers, and they linked together seamlessly. Wall Butlers had pretty much replaced every other electronic device—TVs, desktop computers, laptops, tablets, phones—combining them into one super-cool, tell-it-what-to-do-and-it'll-do-it system, all for cheaper than the fees we paid for everything separately. Until they were invented, if we wanted to watch a particular show, for example, we had to go from Hulu to Netflix to Amazon to see if it was available, and for what price.

Now we only had to say, *Find me Survivor,* and our Butlers found it for us, free if possible. Our Butlers knew our clothing sizes and all our personal information, so if an actress was wearing a shirt we liked, we could just say, *Get me that shirt,* and it would arrive the next day. If there was an ad for pizza, we could say, *I want one, a large,* and it would be at our door in thirty minutes. Our Butlers had our topping preferences, address, and payment information.

Jeff Meyers, the universally-regarded genius who invented Butlers, called them "luxury for the little guy," and they really were like having our own personal butlers. Wall Butlers came first, followed by watches a year later, which not only had screens that folded out, but voice technology so good it made typing unnecessary.

And Robert Chiu thought he could top all that?

"You're up, Bobby." I handed him the pool cue. "You break."

Robert got a decent break, and then Matt banked a nice corner shot, making us solids. He missed his follow-up attempt and handed me the pool cue.

"So, question. Do you see that guy out there?" I asked while waiting for my turn. "The anti-social dude, in the corner?"

Matt scanned the living room. "Yeah, what about him?"

"Do you know who he came with, or why he's here?"

"I have no idea," he said. "But he's staring at you."

"That's the thing," I said. "Do you have any idea why?"

"I'm sure it's because he thinks you're hot."

I scoffed. "I doubt it."

As much as I liked to imagine otherwise, no guys really gave me more than a passing glance at parties. With my long black hair, blue eyes, and super-white skin, I'm what's called Black Irish, which sometimes got people's attention because it's a rare look for

Minnesota, but too many other girls were too much (take your pick): Cuter, taller, bigger-boobed, sluttier.

Mostly sluttier.

I was the nice girl, the one you could safely take home to Mom and she'd approve.

"You have no idea," Matt said, nodding toward the pool table. "Your turn."

Unsurprisingly, I completely biffed my shot, and when I looked up, I was startled by the admiring way I'd caught Matt looking at me. I couldn't help but look back. Sometime in the past year without my really noticing, he'd developed broad shoulders and his skin had cleared up and he'd gone from a shaggy-puppy haircut to a clean-cut one, which suited him very well. I probably hadn't noticed because for so long I'd been hung up on Adam.

But that night?

That night I noticed, and I could tell he was noticing me, too, and it made me feel all fluttery and confused.

"Hey, can I have another sip of your drink?" I asked, trying to distract myself from my weird feelings. He handed me his cup again. "Nice new video, by the way."

His face lit up. "You saw it?"

Matt played classical guitar—never in public, but he posted videos on ButlerTube and had developed a small but steady following. In his newest, he played *Moonlight Sonata*, which I'd never heard on the guitar before, only on the piano.

"Saw it?" I said. "I watched it like a hundred times. I loved it. It was so pretty, it made me want to cry."

That wasn't true. I *had* cried, numerous times, because it was so beautiful and so sad, and because it was *Matt. His* fingers. *His* guitar. *His heart.* Matt, who otherwise spent his life fumbling through school and restoring his car and working at his family's hardware store, a guy's guy through and through. Yet he'd had a little brother who died, and so he knew sorrow, too, and it came through in his music in a way it never did otherwise.

"I'm glad you liked it," he said, and all of a sudden we were there again, trying to read each other's hearts, teetering at the brink of emotions we'd long been avoiding, until we were interrupted by an angry shout from the living room.

"No *way* you're taking my keys!"

And with that, the moment was ruined, because the angry shout was Adam, and now I had to go deal with him. Matt handed off the pool cue he'd been leaning on, and by the time we got to the living room, three guys had pushed the mysterious Daemon Godwin out the front door. Two others were restraining Adam, who would have otherwise gone after him.

I went straight over. The others backed off, except for Matt, who stayed close.

"What was that about?" I said. I didn't know if Adam had started it or not, but I knew he wouldn't take responsibility. With Adam, it was always the other guy's fault. Or mine.

"The jerk wanted my car keys," he said. "Said he'd give them back tomorrow. Who the hell does he think he is?"

"Why would he take your keys?" I peered at him. "You're not drunk, are you?" He gave me a punishing glare. "I'm only asking because he didn't try to take anyone else's keys."

"Who is he?"

"No one we know, and I don't think he knew anybody here, either."

Except me, apparently.

"He probably wanted to steal my convertible."

Adam—unlike me, Nora, and Matt—was from the richer side of town. When he turned sixteen, back before his dad lost his job, his parents had given him a new red convertible for his birthday. They'd since sold his dad's Lexus and his mom's Mercedes and replaced them with used cars of the sort my mom always drove, but Adam had picked up extra shifts at the quarry and had so far managed to keep the convertible.

"Anyway, forget about him. I'm glad you're here." I leaned to kiss him, and he tasted of mint-gum-covering-up-booze, but his kiss was solid, not sloppy, and his blue eyes were clear. He looked like the varsity swimmer he'd been, athletic and strong, and the college athlete he'd be, having won a swimming scholarship to the University of Arizona. I gestured to the back patio, which was the dance floor for the night, complete with a disco ball. "Want to dance?"

"Hell, no," he said and finally acknowledged Matt with a nod. "I'm going to go find Schneider and Dawson. I'll catch up with you later, okay?"

I said sure and watched him walk away. I'll confess I was mostly relieved.

"Come on," Matt said. "I'll dance with you."

We danced for several songs, then talked to some people, then joined a game of barefoot ultimate Frisbee in the expansive backyard, and then danced some more. When a slow song came on, I started to walk off the dance floor, but Matt took my hand.

"Let's keep dancing," he said, although in all the years we'd been friends, we'd never slow-danced before. "There's something I need to tell you."

Matt's eyes changed color based on what he wore, and that night he was wearing a denim shirt, which turned his eyes into the color of perfectly-faded denim. Well, I *loved* perfectly-faded denim, and I was eager to hear what he had to say, even though I suspected it might complicate my life tremendously.

And so I agreed, but as we linked fingers, Adam swooped in. His eyes were hard and his jaw was clenched, and really? I was so over him.

Still, I pulled away from Matt.

"I'm leaving," Adam said. "You coming, or not?"

"Not," I said. "It's still early."

Even though I was eighteen and had graduated high school, I still had a midnight curfew because my mother said nothing good ever happened after midnight—a statement I highly doubted. In any case, it was nowhere near midnight.

Adam's look was accusing. "I thought we were leaving together."

"We were, but I'm having fun, and I'm not ready to go yet. Plus, you've been ignoring me the whole night. If you want to spend time with me, you can spend time with me right here."

"Whatever. Stay and dance with Perkins. I know that's what you really want to do, anyway."

The sneer on his face was quite unattractive, and yet I found myself sucked into my usual pattern of trying not to worsen his already-bad mood.

"Adam, I—"

"I said never mind." With that, he stormed off. Part of my heart went with him, and another part held firm.

"I hate that you let him treat you that way," Matt said quietly.

"He's having a hard time." I said it automatically, out of habit more than conviction anymore. The truth was, I hated that I let him treat me that way, too. "Listen, I'd better go."

Matt took my hand again. "We were going to dance, remember?"

His eyes searched mine as he waited to see what I'd do, and the fact was: I wanted to stay. I wanted to stay and hear what he had to say. I wanted to know why he'd taken my hand like it meant something.

But I didn't.

Instead, I slipped my hand out of his and followed my pissed-off boyfriend out the door, forgetting all about the warning I'd received earlier from the mysterious stranger: Don't go home with your boyfriend tonight.

If only—two of the worst words in the English language.

If only, if only.

If only I'd stayed behind.

WHEN I CAME TO, THE FIRST THING I SAW WAS A BIG WHITE
sign on the wall that said in red letters, *Did You Get Your Flu Shot Yet?*

The next thing I saw was faded-pink wallpaper and stained ceiling tiles, and I knew then I was at Brookview General Hospital. I'd been there once before when I fell off the monkey bars as a kid and needed eight stitches on my scalp, and I recognized the wallpaper and ceiling-tile stains after all those years.

I blinked awake and fought to get to the surface, desperate but unable to lick my dry, thirsty lips. My mom was beside me, smiling bravely although pale with worry.

"Maddie!" I managed to say. "We've got to help Maddie!"

"Shhh, Kendra. You're dreaming. Everything's fine." She smoothed back my hair as tears brimmed in her eyes. "You're going to be just fine."

"But no, Mom. Maddie needs help!"

I struggled to sit up, but it took too much energy so I fell back against the pillow.

"Maddie who?" my mom said. "Honey, I don't know what you're talking about, but you're in the hospital. You were in an accident, but you're going to be okay. You have a slight injury to your leg, but it's nothing we can't manage. It's nothing time and a little physical therapy won't heal."

"But no, Mom, listen. Maddie Meyers needs our help."

"Maddie *Meyers*, you said? Why on earth would you be dreaming about her?"

I fell back into unconsciousness before I could answer, and this is what I saw, the same thing I'd seen immediately before gaining consciousness a few moments earlier.

· · ·

It's a beautiful, barely-breezy summer day, all blue skies. It must be California, because that's where she lives. She and a dark-haired girlfriend, both carrying Starbucks drinks, walk down the street to Maddie's shiny white pickup truck. In the back are two surfboards and Maddie's golden retriever, who wags her tail eagerly at their approach. Maddie's blond hair is in a ponytail. She's wearing cut-off jean shorts and a simple white tank top with a bikini underneath. You'd never know from looking at her how absurdly rich she is.

It happens so fast.

From different directions, four men, all wearing sunglasses and Hawaiian shirts, swoop in and surround the girls. The men are smiling, and it almost seems friendly, but it's only made to look that way so as not to draw attention to the fact that they force the girls into a waiting tinted-window black SUV. Maddie's friend screams. One of the men shoves a red bandana over her mouth, and whatever substance is in it makes her pass out.

Maddie stares, wide-eyed.

Her dog barks in alarm.

The SUV speeds away.

No one but the dog has noticed.

Maddie Meyers, the beloved and famous daughter of Jeff Meyers, CEO of Butler Systems and one of the richest men in the world, has been kidnapped.

* * *

I jolted back awake.

"We need to help her! She's been kidnapped!" I grabbed my mom's wrist, barely noticing I was hooked up to an IV drip. "Mom, we have to help Maddie! No one knows they took her!"

"Dr. Ridgeway?" My mom's tone had a worried strain as she turned to the doctor standing nearby. "What do you think? Why is she saying this? She's all right, isn't she? You don't think this is a head injury, right? It's just a dream?"

"They're driving a black SUV," I said before the doctor could reply. "And they took her friend, too!"

The middle-aged doctor stepped forward. He was dark-haired and handsome and he had the sort of straight-backed posture my mom always admired, but his eyes were a spooky shade of green. He came to my side and smiled down at me like I was a good friend he hadn't seen for awhile.

"Hi, Kendra. I'm Dr. Ridgeway." He glanced at the monitor, where my heart rate registered at a high 110 beats per minute. "Please try not to be afraid. I know you must be very scared right now."

"Maddie Meyers has been kidnapped!"

Dr. Ridgeway smiled. "You're on some pretty heavy painkillers, and they've got you kind of agitated, which isn't at all unusual—"

"Listen to me!" I insisted. "Maddie Meyers was kidnapped and nobody saw it. You need to tell the police right away. I think it was in California, on a street that was, like, one of the main shopping streets in the—"

He nodded to the nurse in the room, who did something to adjust my IV drip.

"Do you even know what day it is, Kendra?" he asked. I shook my head. "I didn't think so. Let's start from there. Today's Saturday. Last night, you were in a very serious car accident. You got thrown from the car, and—"

I grabbed his arm. "MADDIE MEYERS JUST GOT KIDNAPPED."

"Kendra, stop! Enough!" He pulled out of my grasp and pressed my arm firmly to my side. "I don't want to have to restrain you. Your poor mother has been waiting all night for you to wake up, and now you have, but can't you see you're upsetting her? She's been so worried. Let's show her you're okay, all right?"

"SOMEBODY NEEDS TO HELP MADDIE!"

Before Dr. Ridgeway could say anything, my mom leaned forward.

"You're talking about *the* Maddie Meyers, Kendra?" she asked. "Jeff Meyers' daughter?"

"Yes, of course!"

There was no other Maddie Meyers.

A couple years earlier, Maddie, who was my age, had been biking to school and got hit by a car. Besides a bunch of broken bones, she suffered a head injury, and at first no one knew if she'd have permanent brain damage. It was right after Butlers were invented, and because her dad was so famous—the next Steve Jobs, they were calling him—it was all over the news. The doctors injected her with some kind of saline mixture and lowered her body temperature to freeze her vital organs while they operated on her brain. She was in a coma for several days, but eventually she healed from her brain injury and regained full mobility, although now she sometimes had seizures.

But rather than letting it ruin her life, she started a foundation called The Lemonade Foundation (because you've got to take life's lemons and make lemonade) for kids with traumatic brain injuries and diseases like Down syndrome, epilepsy, and autism, and it gave them the opportunity to do things like surf and water ski and play golf and try things that weren't typically or easily available for people like them. She started summer camps and adventure trips, and you'd never know from seeing how hard she worked that she enjoyed one of the most privileged lives imaginable.

Literally the entire country had followed her progress; I, like many, adored Maddie Meyers, and so I had to make them take me seriously.

"Listen," I begged. "They came in black SUVs, and the SUVs had tinted windows. There were four men, and they all wore Hawaiian shirts. Maddie was coming from Starbucks with a friend, and they were on a busy street with an American Eagle on it, and—"

Whoosh. A cool liquid coursed through my veins.

"There." Dr. Ridgeway smiled, having pushed whatever button caused my wooziness. "You'll calm down soon. This sort of anxiousness is not at all uncommon, given the medication you're on."

Frantic, I grabbed my mom's arm.

"Police," I mumbled through rubbery lips. "Please, Mom, call the police."

"Don't worry, Mrs. Sinclair," Dr. Ridgeway said. "She'll fall asleep in a few seconds, and if the drugs do their job, she won't remember a thing about this when she wakes up again."

He was right.

When I woke up next, I'd forgotten it all—much to the frustration of the police detective waiting in the room, desperate for me to tell him more.

I SPENT A FEW DAYS IN AND OUT OF CONSCIOUSNESS AFTER that, according to how much Dr. Ridgeway lightened my sedation. When I finally and fully opened my eyes, Matt was at my bedside, playing his guitar for me.

"Hey, sleepy girl!" He smiled. "Welcome back."

"I thought maybe I was in heaven, that music was so pretty." Matt was a sight for sore eyes. "I kept hearing it, and it was so beautiful."

"Nope, you're still with us. You're going to be for a long, long time."

I reached for his hand. "I'm glad you're here."

He squeezed my hand. "Back at you."

"What about me?" Nora pushed up against him and leaned in to kiss me. "It's about time you woke up, chickie-poo! I've had no one to gossip with for four whole days!"

Four whole days?

"I'm chopped liver, apparently," Matt said.

I lay still for a moment, feeling woozy but grateful. *These guys,* I thought. *These guys are the best.* They both had pasty-white faces from being indoors breathing sickly-sterile hospital air for far too long.

"You two don't look so good."

"You should talk," Nora said. "You're all black and blue."

"I feel puffy."

"You look puffy." She kissed me again. "I guess that happens when you get thrown out of a convertible going at a high rate of speed. Speaking of which, I'd better get your mom. There's a cop waiting to talk to you."

"A cop?" I said. "Why?"

"How much do you remember about your accident?" Matt asked, and Nora paused at the doorway long enough to hear my answer.

I tried to think back. "Accident?"

"I guess that answers that," he said.

"I remember dancing with you at Michael's party," I said. "And Adam had a flat tire, right?"

Matt and Nora exchanged a glance.

"What about Maddie Meyers?" Nora said. "Do you remember any dreams you had about her?" When I shook my head, she continued in a singsong voice, "Larson's going to be pissed!"

"He won't be pissed," Matt said. "He'll just be disappointed."

"Who's Larson?" I said.

"Ridgeway shouldn't have kept her doped up for so long if he wanted her to remember things," Nora said.

"It's okay if she doesn't remember. All's well that ends well." Matt looked at me. "Larson's the detective assigned to your case."

"You said my mom's here?"

"I'll go get her," Nora said and left.

I looked around. The room was full of plants and flowers, but underneath their fragrance I could still smell hospital. There was a huge oak tree outside my window, and I was on a floor high enough that I saw into its branches, where birds and squirrels hung out.

I looked back to Matt. "Adam's dead, isn't he?"

Matt sighed heavily, but before he said anything, Nora came back into the room with my mom and two men, making the small room feel claustrophobically crowded. My mom rushed to my bedside.

"Oh, sweetie! It's so good to see you awake!"

Her hand felt warm on my arm, her lips warm on my forehead. Her touch felt like home. "Adam's dead, isn't he?"

"I'm sorry, baby," she whispered, enfolding me in her arms. "His injuries were too severe."

"He died instantly, so he didn't suffer," Matt said. "He didn't feel a thing. That's something to be grateful for."

I should be crying, I thought. *Why am I not crying?*

My eyes caught those of a man who I knew instinctively must have been Larson. For one thing, he wasn't the doctor, who wore a white lab coat. For another, he had a holstered gun and a badge flashed from his belt. In addition, his red polo shirt had the logo of the Brookview Police Department. He gave me a sad, closed-mouth smile of sympathy. I quickly looked away.

"When's his funeral?" I asked.

"It's today," my mom said. "Right now, actually."

"I should be there," I said. "They should have waited for me. *You* should be there, all of you. Why aren't you there?"

"We're with you," Nora said. "You're our priority."

"Our parents are there, Nora's and mine," Matt said. "And I went to the wake last night."

"I didn't," Nora said.

"Sorry to interrupt, but I've got some questions for Kendra, and there are people waiting on the answers."

"Yeah, we know," said Nora, none too nicely. Since she'd gotten her driver's license, she'd been in two accidents that had been her fault and had gotten pulled over at least half a dozen times. Somewhere along the way, she'd lost her manners when it came to talking to the police. "We already know the questions you're going to ask. You've been asking them the last four days!"

"Nora, it's okay," I said. "You don't have to be rude."

"Sometimes you do," she said.

My mom beckoned Larson closer. "Kendra, this is Detective Larson. Do you remember meeting him?"

"Should I?"

"Hi, Kendra. I'm Bob Larson. I'm very sorry for your loss." He had sandy hair, blue eyes, and pale skin like most Minnesotans. The skin around his eyes crinkled when he smiled, and his eyes looked friendly, but what I noticed most of all was how he looked at me like I was a creature from another world. "We've spoken several times over the last few days. I have more questions for you, if that's all right."

"That's fine," I said, but before he could ask me anything, the doctor came around the side of the bed and shined a little penlight in both my eyes.

"I need to run a few tests," he said. "I'll have you all wait in the hallway."

"Can't I stay, Dr. Ridgeway?" My mom put her hand on my arm. "I'm sure Kendra would like me to stay with her."

"It won't take long," he said curtly and gestured to the elderly nurse in the room, who then shepherded everyone out, Larson last of all, who frowned at the doctor even though his back was turned, like they had a history together and it wasn't a good one. Once they'd left, Dr. Ridgeway ran through a routine of asking me a bunch of questions like how I felt, could I wiggle my toes, could I follow his finger. After I answered his questions and did what he asked, he pulled up a chair.

"I feel I should warn you about Detective Larson," he said. "He's been hanging around far more than necessary. It's like he hasn't got anything better to do."

"Well, he needs to ask me about the accident, I guess, right?"

"The facts of the accident are pretty clear-cut," said Dr. Ridgeway. "Your boyfriend drank too much and drove too fast, which as you know is a deadly combination. Your car was already traveling at a high rate of speed when a semi-truck crossed the centerline and smashed into your convertible. The driver admitted to falling asleep behind the wheel. He'd been driving for sixteen hours—well beyond what he was legally supposed to. As your friend mentioned, your boyfriend died instantly from the impact, but a passing motorcyclist was able to perform CPR on you until the paramedics arrived."

"CPR?" I said. "Does that mean—?"

"It means you weren't breathing when he got to you."

My heart pounded. "I guess I'm pretty lucky."

"You're a survivor, that much is sure." Dr. Ridgeway leaned closer. "Kendra, listen. When Larson comes back, he's going to ask you about a dream you had. Do you recall dreaming about Maddie Meyers?"

"Nora told me I did, but—" I shook my head. "I don't remember. Does it matter?"

"It doesn't," he assured me. "Only, Larson's obsessed with it. I'm going to run interference for you, but don't feel you need to tell him anything at all. In fact, tell him nothing. Tell him to move on and find someone else to harass."

It wasn't the kind of thing I'd ever say. "Why would he care about a dream I had?"

"Like I said, he seems to have nothing better to do. Maybe they're overstaffed at the Brookview PD."

"I'm going to be okay, right?" I said. "I'm going to walk again and everything?"

"You'll have a full and complete recovery, absolutely," said Dr. Ridgeway. "You'll need some physical therapy for your leg—I had to put some titanium screws in there for you—but time will work its magic and soon you'll be as good as new."

He nodded to the nurse, who then let the others re-enter the room. Matt and Nora hung back, but my mom came around the side opposite Dr. Ridgeway and took my hand. Larson stood at the foot of my bed with a notepad and pen at the ready and gave me another forced smile. I ignored him and pulled my mom close.

"I'm sorry," I said. "I didn't realize he was drunk until it was too late."

Larson cleared his throat. "I have some questions for you about Maddie Meyers, and they really can't wait any longer."

"I'm sorry, but I don't remember anything about any dream I had." I glanced, just barely, at Dr. Ridgeway. "Nora and Dr. Ridgeway told me I had a dream about Maddie, but I don't remember it at all."

"It wasn't just a dream you had," Larson said. "It was a premonition of some sort. A vision of the future."

"A premonition!" I looked to my mom, then to Matt, then to Nora, expecting one or all of them to join me in laughing at such a ridiculous idea. None did. "I don't have premonitions. I don't believe in them!"

"Leave the girl alone." Dr. Ridgeway glared at Larson. "She's been through a great trauma."

"I'm not leaving until I talk to her," Larson said. "You've kept her drugged up for days hoping I'd go away, but I won't. I'm not leaving until I've had a chance to ask my questions."

"You've already asked them," Nora said. "A million times. She doesn't remember."

My mom smoothed back my hair. "Honey, Maddie Meyers was kidnapped three days ago, in broad daylight on a public street in Santa Monica."

I gasped. "Oh, no! Poor Maddie!"

"She's okay," Larson said. "Thanks to you, she's fine."

"Mom, what's he talking about?"

My mom gestured to Larson that he should explain, and that I should listen. He gave her a nod of appreciation.

"You told us it was going to happen," Larson said, while behind him a furious Dr. Ridgeway listened with pressed lips, trying to hold in his anger. "After your accident, you woke in an agitated state, panicked about this kidnapping, which you described in some detail. You made your mom promise to tell the police, which she did, and out of an abundance of caution I put in a call to the Santa Monica PD, which in turn contacted the family's security team. Turns out, Maddie had slipped past her bodyguards that morning, which apparently she does fairly often. I got through at the perfect moment—any later, and it would have been too late. As it was, the girls had been grabbed and thrown into a vehicle, but before they could get away, the security team blocked them in. Thanks to you, Maddie and her friend were released unharmed. If not for you and your insistence the police be told, the story might have had a very different ending." He glanced back at Ridgeway. "The doctor here tried to prevent your mom from calling us."

Ridgeway bristled. "Because I was sure she was simply hallucinating from the medication she was on."

"Right, but now you know better." Larson studied him. "Now you know there's more going on, and I don't understand why you're so stubbornly insisting on sticking to the same impossible theory. Hallucinations aren't premonitions, by definition. And *you know* she saw the future. *You know* her premonition came true."

"I know no such thing," Ridgeway said. "And neither do you."

"Yes, you do!" Larson looked like he wanted to physically attack Ridgeway, who merely smiled at him dismissively. "You're being deliberately obtuse about this whole thing."

"Welcome to the pissing contest," Nora said to me.

"No kidding," I muttered.

"None of us understands how it happened." My mom used her gentle, smoothing-things-over tone. "But, Kendra, I was right here. I saw it happen. You woke up and insisted Maddie and her friend were being kidnapped *right then*, and we needed to stop it. And it happened exactly as you described, only Maddie was okay in the end. In your dream—or whatever it was—she wasn't."

"Kendra, you've got a superpower!" Nora's eyes gleamed. "You can see the future! Isn't that completely cool?"

Cool? Hardly.

Impossible? Yes.

"Matt, what do you think?" I said.

"I think we've been having this same conversation for the past few days, and I still don't know *what* to think." He shrugged. "I'm just glad you're okay."

But was I?

I looked out the window, away from them all. The leaves from the giant oak tree waved at me. Streaks of hot summer sunlight shimmered at me. An airplane flying by dipped its wings at me. Every color outside was super-saturated, and suddenly, I understood.

"This is the dream, isn't it?" I looked at each of them in turn. "This moment right now—this is the dream. I'm dreaming I woke up and you all told me I had a dream about Maddie getting kidnapped and I saved her . . . which means Adam might still be alive, too, because you telling me he wasn't is only part of my dream."

"This isn't a dream, honey," my mom said.

"But we don't believe in premonitions," I said desperately. "Right? We don't believe in them."

"I never used to," she said, and I knew we were both thinking back to the same memory. "But now? I guess maybe I do."

MY DAD DIED IN A PLANE CRASH, A VERY FAMOUS PLANE crash.

Flight 93 on September 11, 2001.

Yes, *that* Flight 93. The *let's roll* Flight 93, where the passengers, including my dad, rushed the terrorists and prevented them from crashing the plane into their intended target. (Or so we've been told.)

We lived in New Jersey back then, and September 11 is actually my birthday. My mom was supposed to bring cupcakes to my preschool, but she didn't come at circle time when she said she would, or any other time, either. A lot of parents picked up their kids early that day, but I was one of about ten kids left in my class when school ended.

Neither was she waiting when the dismissal bell rang like she always, always was. At the time, she didn't work, and except for the worst part of winter, she walked the five blocks from our house to pick me up at school and waited with the other parents by the big oak tree out front.

That day when my mom didn't show up, my teacher brought me to the office to call my house. Within seconds, she burst into tears. Then she drove me home herself and came inside and stayed while my mom, surrounded by her best friend and some neighbors and a few people I didn't know, told me my dad had been in an accident—an airplane crash—and he'd died and wasn't ever coming home.

Being that I was so young, she left out the hijacking part, the terrorist part, the bad-guys-flew-planes-into-tall-buildings part. I learned all that later, of course, but at the time she simply called it an accident, which was already beyond my ability to comprehend.

Growing up, I was the only kid I knew who hated her birthday.

Shortly after 9/11, a woman showed up at our house and said she'd had a vision of her husband in which he told her he was still alive, and so was Jack. She didn't know who Jack was, but after the seating charts were released from the airline, she realized her husband had been seated on Flight 93 next to my dad.

•   •   •

My dad's name was Jack.

Jack Sinclair, and he would have been very pleased to learn he had not, in fact, died in the plane crash that so obviously had killed him.

It was a moment I'd never forgotten: Me in pigtails, standing next to my mom right inside our doorway while that lady told her story. As she talked, I slipped my hand into my mom's. The more the lady talked, the more my mom crushed my hand, but I didn't dare pull away.

You can't come here and give us false hope, my mom said firmly after the lady got to the punch line of her story. *You can't make this into something it's not.*

But they're alive! Tears rolled down the lady's face. *Our husbands are alive! Don't you want to find your husband?*

He's dead, my mom said firmly. *And the passengers didn't bring the plane down. That's just a story they're telling us to make us feel better. The military shot the plane down, and that's okay. It's what they should have done; only the government doesn't want people to know they killed their own citizens, so they're giving us this other story. Maybe they did rush the cockpit, but the military still shot the plane down.*

No, the woman insisted. *The plane wasn't shot down. It was diverted. Our husbands are still alive. They're being held on an island somewhere, waiting for us to find them.*

They're not.

But I had a dream, the woman said. *It was so real. It was realer than real!*

You're grieving and you're grasping at straws, but my daughter and I don't believe in that sort of thing, my mom said. *We're going to accept what happened and go on with our lives. I suggest you do the same.*

Hand shaking, she pointed to the door and ordered the woman out.

• • •

Soon after, we moved to Brookview, my mom's hometown. I was enrolled in kindergarten. I got my puppy, Huckleberry, as a present for my next birthday. My mom opened a Pilates studio the year after that. I met Nora in the third grade. My mom's Pilates studio closed a couple years after that, and she reinvented herself yet again, this time becoming a chef. Over time, my memories of my dad faded and sometimes I forgot about him altogether, but every so often his face was shown on the news, and I remembered all over again that he was gone.

I don't know if I agree with my mom's version of what happened, that the plane was shot down by the military.

I don't know if it's good to question the official story.

All I know is I don't have a dad anymore.

A FEW DAYS PASSED. DETECTIVE LARSON STOPPED HANGING around my hospital room once he realized I wasn't going to remember anything about Maddie Meyers, and the rest of us put what happened with Maddie out of our minds, deciding it was simply a freak occurrence that wouldn't be repeated.

I had physical therapy every day, which I hated because it was difficult and painful but appreciated because it was difficult and painful enough I didn't have time to think about Adam while I was doing it.

His parents came to visit me. Part of me was furious with them for making such a mess of their lives that it affected Adam the way it had, and part of me even blamed them for what happened, but the largest part of me simply felt bad for them. They looked so broken. I shared some of my better memories of Adam and told them how much he'd meant to me. I know it made *them* feel better, but their visit made me feel worse.

Eventually, Nora left for the Outward Adventure program, where we were supposed to have been counselors together. She said she didn't want to go, that her parents were making her, but part of me suspected she couldn't wait to get away and get a break from the hospital and all the sadness, and I couldn't blame her—I would have loved to get away from it, myself. But it still hurt to have her leave. Had the situation been reversed, I wouldn't have gone, and it's not a good feeling to know you're a better friend to someone than they are to you.

Matt, on the other hand, was awesome. His parents covered for him at the hardware store, and besides when he went home to sleep or shower, he was either with me or bringing us food or running errands for my mom. We played cards for hours at a time. We watched movies. He let me talk about Adam and never said a bad word about him. He went with me to physical therapy, was a shoulder to cry on when I needed it, and played his guitar for me whenever I asked him to.

Lots of friends from school and swim team came by, but as was the case with Adam's parents, I spent most of my time trying to make *them* feel better, which was exhausting. I couldn't stop them from coming, but after a few such visits, Matt and my mom made sure no one stayed longer than a few minutes.

My favorite visitor turned out to be someone I didn't even know.

A man showed up one day shortly after I'd gotten back from physical therapy. Matt was off getting lunch, and I was playing Hearts with my mom when someone knocked on the closed door. She answered it, and I knew right away I'd seen him somewhere before, but I couldn't think where. He had a super-white, perfect smile and wore an expensive suit, and I thought maybe I'd seen him on the news, although I rarely watched the news. In one hand, he held a bouquet of flowers, and in the other he held a medium-sized white box.

"Forgive me for intruding, but I'm here to see Kendra. Kendra Sinclair?" He handed my mom the flowers, then pointed at me. "I'm guessing that's you?"

He had the kind of smile that made you smile back.

"It is," I said.

"I'm Bill Rhodes. It's an honor to meet you. I've heard some pretty fascinating things about you recently, and I had to come see for myself."

"*Governor* Bill Rhodes, right?" my mom said. "We met not too long ago, although you probably don't recall."

"You do look familiar." He extended a hand for my mom to shake. "When did we meet?"

"I'm Susan Sinclair, and I'm a chef at the Franklin downtown. You were in not too long ago with a group of people, and I prepared your dish. You asked for me to come out. You liked my—"

"Roasted lamb with mint sauce! I remember!"

"I'm glad it made such an impression."

"Trust me, it did. I asked my personal chef to try and duplicate the recipe, but it didn't come close to yours." The governor stepped further into the room, leaving behind in the hallway two well-muscled men who I assumed were bodyguards. "So, Kendra, I wonder if you could guess who called me today."

"I doubt it," I said, not in the mood for guessing games.

"I'll give you a hint. He invented something a few years ago so brilliant none of us can live without it anymore, and it seems you rescued his daughter from quite a dangerous situation."

"Jeff Meyers?" I said. "*You* talked to Jeff Meyers? About *me*?"

"I did." His smile broadened. "He asked if I'd stop by and thank you personally, on his behalf, for saving his daughter's life—the story of which, I've got to say, is fascinating and a little . . . well . . . let's just leave it at fascinating. I've never heard of something like this before, certainly not involving legitimate, ordinary, non-crackpot individuals." He laughed. "Call me a skeptic, but if the authorities weren't involved and if I hadn't heard it from someone as indisputably well-regarded as Jeff Meyers, I almost certainly wouldn't have believed what I was hearing."

"Kendra doesn't believe it herself," my mom said. "She doesn't remember any of it."

"This is the only time something like this has happened?"

She nodded. "We're considering it some kind of weird, crazy fluke. A hiccup of the universe."

Governor Rhodes laughed. "I like that," he said. "In any case, Jeff said he would have come in person to thank you himself, but he's not leaving his daughter's side at the moment. However, he did ask me to give you this."

He handed me the box. It was light and shaped very similarly to the box my Butler watch had been in when I received it.

"Is this what I think it is?" I said, excited because my Butler had gotten lost in the accident somehow.

"Open it and find out," he said.

I tore open the box. Not only was it a Butler watch, it was the *new* Butler watch not even on the market yet.

"It's so thin and light!" I held it up for them to admire. "And look, the fold-out screen is nearly twice as big as the old one. I can't wait to show Matt. He's going to be so jealous."

"I heard it gives you biometric feedback," Governor Rhodes said. "Supposedly it can tell you if you're running a fever, and it can measure your blood sugar if you're diabetic, from your sweat glands or something. It's going to eliminate the need for diabetics to be pricking themselves all the time. That's the rumor, anyway."

Guessing the new features for each Butler update was something of a national pastime, but I was surprised even the governor was in on the speculation.

"Go ahead and set it up," he said. "Jeff asked that after you put it on, you call him. He put an app on there that will allow you to connect with him directly."

"*Me* talk to Jeff Meyers?" The idea struck me as ludicrous, him so famous and brilliant and me so . . . not. "What would I say?"

"Thank him for the watch and ask how Maddie's doing," my mom said.

I took out the instruction booklet from the box, as well as a long, slim pin that looked like a sewing needle, and a crisp white note card designed with the elegant simplicity for which Jeff Meyers was known.

I read it out loud.

Hello! I'm your new Butler and I will help you navigate through life in several important new ways. To log on, you must do two things. First, look directly at the white smiley face on the watch and press the button on my side. Go ahead, I'll wait.

"So cute," my mom said.

"What's it for?" I wondered, as I did as instructed.

"It's eyeball recognition for security," said Governor Rhodes. "It takes a print of your iris and uses it much like a fingerprint. It's apparently an excellent technology. My wife keeps recommending I get it for my office."

"What's the benefit over fingerprints?" my mom asked.

"That I don't know," he said.

The smile on the smiley face got bigger and turned a happy shade of green. I looked back to the direction card.

Mission accomplished? Great! Now, take the enclosed pin and prick a fingertip. A miniscule amount of blood is all you'll need to press onto the smiley face. Hold your finger there until you hear the beep.

"Yuck." I disliked needles of any kind. "Do I have to?" I flipped over the card, but it was blank. Apparently, it wasn't optional.

"It's only a little pin prick, honey," my mom said. "It won't hurt."

"Still, it seems . . ."

"Incredibly invasive?" said Governor Rhodes.

"Exactly," I agreed.

"That's why I don't even own a Butler," he said. "But this new one takes it quite a few steps further, doesn't it?"

I did as the card instructed. After about a minute, the watch beeped and a message appeared where the smiley had been. *Almost done. Please speak your full name.*

Perfect, Kendra! my new Butler said after I'd done that. *Your biometric data will be available within twenty-four hours, and in the meantime, you have one new message: Jeff Meyers is awaiting your call. Shall I connect you?*

"Yes! And I'm going to name you Gerald Two, if that's okay."

That's fine, m'lady. Would you like to see your guest on the wall via the system's built-in projector, or on the Butler screen?

Only then did I notice the super-tiny projector on the top edging of the watch face. *So cool.* "I guess the wall!"

Within seconds, Jeff Meyers was live, full size, projecting against the wall of my hospital room where I'd aimed the little projector. Even Governor Rhodes, who surely must have met famous people somewhat regularly, seemed in awe, or maybe he was in awe of the technology.

"Hello, all." Jeff waved from a seated position on an extremely comfortable-looking couch with a view of what I assumed was the Pacific Ocean behind him, considering he lived in Malibu. Tall and bony, he wore his trademark white oxford shirt with jeans. "You must be Kendra and family."

"This is Kendra and her mother and their governor," said Governor Rhodes, waving. "I'm Bill Rhodes. We spoke earlier today."

"Good to meet you, Bill. Thanks so much for visiting Kendra on my behalf."

"It's my pleasure," said Governor Rhodes. "She's a lovely young woman. About your daughter's age, I believe."

My mom waved next. "I'm Susan Sinclair, Kendra's mom."

"Good to meet you, Susan. You've got quite an amazing daughter."

"Thank you," she said. "So do you."

He smiled at me. "So, Kendra, what do you think of the new Butler? Pretty exciting, isn't it?"

"I love it! Thank you so much. I actually lost mine in the accident, and I'm not used to being without it. I didn't like having to prick myself—" I laughed to let him know I was mostly joking. "But it's awesome! I can't wait to play around with it and see what all it can do, but even this is really amazing to be able to talk to you when you're life-sized like this."

"Sorry you had to prick yourself," he said. "My daughter's squeamish about that, too, but I promise it's for a good cause. We've got what we call a CODIS system built in—basically, you're assigned a specimen identification number, which will contain information about your entire genetic makeup—your race, your gender, your health, your disease history. It'll even be able to tell you if you're predisposed to certain diseases. And then, in addition to the DNA information, the biometric analyzer we've created is going to revolutionize healthcare, just you watch. For instance, a person may one day get a message telling him he's in the early stages of a heart attack, and what to do next—before he feels any symptoms himself. The analyzer runs in the background until it needs to alert you you're mixing medications dangerously, or you're running a fever, or your heart rate's too high, or your blood sugar's crashing. There are sensors on the back of the watch face that enable all this to happen, once we have your basic genetic profile."

"That *is* revolutionary," my mom said. I nodded, although it wasn't something I cared much about. I was more concerned with music and movies and whatever its social features might be.

"When will it be out?" I asked.

"It's a surprise. I'd tell you, but then I'd have to . . . just kidding." He smiled. "Enough about me. Kendra, I can't thank you enough for what you did for my daughter. I'll be forever grateful."

"It was really my mom who did it," I said. "I don't even remember what happened. I only know what I've been told, but my mom was the one who told the police about my dream, so she's the one who saved Maddie."

"It was all Kendra," my mom insisted. "She might not remember now, but I wouldn't have done anything had she not demanded I call the police. We thought it was just a dream, but Kendra somehow knew better."

"I'm glad Maddie's okay," I said. "She is, isn't she? She wasn't hurt or anything?"

"She's fine. My daughter takes everything in stride," he said. "She says to tell you your dream reminded her of the crystal ball from *The Wizard of Oz*. Remember how the Wicked Witch of the West had that magic crystal ball that allowed her to see what was happening in other parts of Oz? She says it was like that."

It was as good an explanation as any I'd heard.

"I hope she doesn't really think I'm the Wicked Witch of the West!" I joked.

He smiled. "Well, that's only Maddie's unscientific explanation. How does your doctor explain it?"

"He doesn't," I said.

"He thinks Kendra had some sort of hallucination from the painkillers she was on," my mom said. "But the fact is, nobody knows how it happened."

"Is Maddie there?" I asked. "Could I maybe say hi?"

"Unfortunately not," he said. "But I'll tell you what—once you're released from the hospital, why don't I send a plane for you, and you can come out here and meet her? You could take in some fresh California sun and spend some time at the ocean. Just what the doctor ordered, am I right? Would that be okay with you, Mom?"

"Oh!" she said, surprised. "Um . . ."

Neither my mom nor I had gotten on an airplane since 9/11 and had no plans to ever do so, but we didn't usually tell people that. And yet, I'd love to meet Maddie—him, too.

"We might go on a road trip," I said, which was something we'd actually talked about but hadn't gotten past the wouldn't-it-be-fun stage. "Maybe we'll try to get out there."

"Please do. We'd love to have you. In the meantime, keep an

eye on the news. We're making a big announcement soon having to do with my fiftieth birthday."

"Thanks so much for the watch," I said. "It was really nice to meet you."

"You, too," he said. "Take care and don't be a stranger. If I can ever help you with anything, anything at all, please let me know. You've got that app on your Butler now— please don't hesitate to use it."

With that, he pressed a button on his own watch and waved as he faded away, taking the summer ocean day along with him.

"I think we should go visit him, Mom," I said.

She smiled. "I think you're right."

● THE BIRDS ARE STILL SILENT. IT'S NOT EVEN DAWN. A MAN *lies asleep in his bed, a woman by his side. The man is around forty; the woman is notably younger. There's a baby in a crib by the window.*

The bare-chested man jolts awake and sits up. On his left arm is a tattoo of a coiled snake along with the words, Don't Tread on Me or I Will Strike.

He's heard something, someone, on his property, maybe in his house. He fixes on the picture on his nightstand of himself in uniform not that many years ago and remembers: You don't mess with a Delta.

The man slips out of bed, grabs a rifle from the closet, and, wearing only his pajama bottoms, makes his way stealthily down the dark hall like he did so many times in so many houses in Iraq, Afghanistan, North Africa. There is no question: He will shoot to kill whatever bastard is putting his family in danger. And if that doesn't work, he'll slit the guy's throat, and if that *doesn't work, he'll twist the guy's neck straight around. He's done all three many times before.*

Rifle at the ready, he follows his instincts and inches along. To the kitchen, no one there. The living room, no one there. The entry closet, nothing. But he heard something, he knows he did. He slides open the front-door lock, reaches for the knob, and pulls open the door.

Bam.

Bam bam bam bam. Bam bam bam.

Numerous bullets strike him, even though the first one went straight through his temple, straight through his brain, killing him instantly.

Bam bam bam. They don't stop shooting.

Why won't they stop?

•   •   •

I woke up screaming.

"Stay awake! Kendra!" Detective Larson had hold of both my arms and shook me, trying to break into the dream I was having. "Talk to us! Look at me!"

"Detective Larson?" I latched onto his eyes. I hadn't seen him in days, and I couldn't say I'd missed him, but in that moment I was glad he was there. "Why are *you* here?"

"Your mom called when she suspected you might be having another premonition like the one you had about Maddie," he said. "That time, too, you kept waking in a panic and falling back into the same dream."

I looked around. It was still light out. "How long have I been out?"

"About two hours, honey," said my mom. "You fell asleep after your call with Jeff Meyers. It's been about an hour since you started waking up in a panic about someone—a man—being killed. We haven't been able to keep you awake until now. Until Detective Larson got here."

I felt woozy, in a whoosh-of-painkiller sort of way, which was strange because besides aspirin, I hadn't taken any pain medication for the last few days. Also in the room were Dr. Ridgeway and the not-very-friendly nurse, Olivia, who seemed to have no other patients besides me, considering how much time she spent in my room not doing much of anything.

"The soldier!" I said, suddenly remembering. "We've got to help him!"

Escalating heart rate, said Gerald Two. *172 beats per minute. Take immediate action to lower heart rate. Get help.*

"They've surrounded his house, and they're going to kill him, and he has a new baby! We've got to—"

Before I could say more, the nurse squirted the contents of a syringe into my mouth.

"Hurry up," she said. "Swallow it."

I did, and within seconds I was vomiting. Olivia shoved a bedpan at me. Dr. Ridgeway ordered the others to give me room. As they stepped aside, he examined my pupils.

"What did you give her?" Larson demanded. "What the *hell* did you just give her?"

"He has a tattoo!" Retch. Puke. Vomit. "The man being killed, he has a tattoo, and—!"

"Don't try to talk," Dr. Ridgeway said. "Just rest until you feel better."

"On his left arm," I continued. "It's a snake with the words, *Don't Tread on Me or*—"

The hovering nurse quickly aimed another fluid-filled syringe down my throat without consulting Dr. Ridgeway. My retching commenced anew.

"What are you giving her?" my mom asked, repeating Larson's earlier question.

"Just something for the anxiety," Olivia said.

Ipecac detected in bloodstream, said Gerald Two. *Alert a medical professional if you suspect you have ingested poison. Do not self-treat.*

"Poison!" my mom said. "What's happening?"

"Why would you give her ipecac?" Larson yelled. "What kind of quack—"

"Mom!" I gripped her arm. "We have to help him! A bunch of men in—"

"Kendra, quiet!" Dr. Ridgeway took my wrist as if to measure my heart rate, but in reality he pressed hard enough against my vein to cause pain. It also felt deliberate. "Let us help you."

Carbon dioxide levels abnormally low, said Gerald Two, which did not lessen my panic. *Heart rate 155 beats per minute. Take immediate action to lower heart rate and increase oxygen. Seek medical help now.*

My mom stood frozen with her hand covering her mouth, wearing an expression of complete terror.

"Everyone needs to leave the room," Dr. Ridgeway announced. "Immediately."

"I'm not going anywhere," Larson said.

"He's a soldier," I said to him, who nodded to let me know he was listening. "Or at least he was, and—"

"Out!" Dr. Ridgeway ordered, physically putting himself in between Larson and me. "Nurse, show them out."

"I'm not going anywhere," Larson said. "She wants me to stay."

I nodded, and it was about to turn into a showdown.

"Doctor, Kendra needs an MRI, don't you think?" Olivia said. She tapped her wrist. "Think about it. We should measure what's happening in her brain right now. As it's happening."

"No MRI," I said.

Olivia handed me a cup of water and a little green pill. "Here, swallow this. It'll make you feel better."

"What is it?" Larson asked.

"Patient-doctor confidentiality," Ridgeway snapped. "I suppose you've heard of it? Now, I asked you to wait in the hallway. Do I need to call security? Because I will."

I swallowed the pill, and my nausea ended as quickly as it began. I sank back onto my pillow, exhausted.

"Better?" Dr. Ridgeway asked. I nodded. "Now, Kendra, we're going to take you for an MRI. Do you know what that is? It's going to take a picture of your brain that—"

"No MRI," I said. "But listen. So this guy's at his house, and I don't know where that is, but he was definitely in the military. He thought of North Africa, Iraq, and—"

Dr. Ridgeway clamped his hand over my mouth. "I need you to be quiet."

"Do *not* do that." Larson started to grab Ridgeway's arm, but the arrival of two beefy, black-clad men in the doorway shifted his attention. "You're not hospital security. Who are you?"

They eyed Ridgeway, but addressed Larson. "Can we speak to you, sir?"

Larson moved toward them. As he did, Ridgeway leaned closer.

"Don't tell Larson anything. You got it?"

I nodded, and he removed his hand from my mouth.

"I don't want an MRI." I'd seen those tube-things in the movies and they reminded me of being trapped in a coffin. "Please."

"I need you to trust me on this, Kendra. I'll explain everything in a little while," he said. "Right now, we've got to get you out of here. It's life or death, Kendra. Life or death."

Olivia began readying my bed for transport. Larson had moved out of earshot into the hallway and continued talking with the security men, glancing at me occasionally. I felt like I had the night of the accident when I was trapped in the car with Adam, knowing something bad was about to happen. I hadn't acted quickly enough to get myself out of that situation; this time had to be different.

"You need my permission to do an MRI, don't you? Don't I have to sign something? Because I won't. I'm eighteen. You need my consent, and I refuse to give it."

"You'd like to get released from the hospital eventually, wouldn't you, Kendra?" Olivia asked. I nodded. "Then shut your mouth and do what the doctor tells you, or you'll be stuck here forever."

Her threat stunned me into silence, and I remained quiet as they moved me from my room.

"I need to take Kendra down for an MRI," Dr. Ridgeway told my mom in the hall. "I'm concerned she might have some bleeding in her brain that we missed the first time around, or some sort of brain injury we didn't recognize earlier."

"Oh, no," my mom said. "Please, God, no."

"He's lying," I said, finally breaking out of my stupor. "He's just trying to shut me up. He's trying to get me away from you so I can't tell you about my premonition."

"As you can see, she's showing increasing signs of paranoia," said Dr. Ridgeway, smirking at me. "We need to rush. I'm afraid time is of the essence."

"Detective Larson, please!" I pleaded, crying. "Help me!"

"What did you give her?" Larson asked. The security men flanked him, and his voice was strained, as if he was holding back, following protocol but not agreeing with what was happening.

"Her Butler indicated it was ipecac, which is used to make someone vomit if they've ingested something toxic, but Kendra hadn't, so why would you give her ipecac?"

Ridgeway's expression was chilly. "Detective, I enjoy watching crime dramas as much as the next guy, but that doesn't mean I'm qualified to do a police investigation—and just because you've seen a few medical dramas doesn't make you qualified to debate with me over the course of Kendra's treatment. Now, excuse me."

He and the nurse moved me toward the elevator. I grabbed for my mom, who was out of reach.

"Mom, I don't need an MRI, please! The soldier's going to get killed! Please—he's got a snake tattoo on his arm, and it says—"

"We'll be awhile," said Olivia. "This might be a good time to run some errands or—"

"We're not going anywhere, Kendra," Larson assured me, but really addressing Dr. Ridgeway. "We're going to get to the bottom of what's going on with Dr. Ridgeway and your course of treatment, because it's highly unorthodox. I'm going to pull his medical license and take it from there. I'd like to know who gave him privileges to practice in this hospital."

"You do that," Dr. Ridgeway said, but once we were in the elevator, he turned to Olivia. "I have to go back and talk to them. I don't want Larson doing anything stupid to complicate things."

"Tell them this is only a precaution," Olivia said. "Tell them you're sure she's going to be fine and that you'll probably be able to release her in the next day or so. That should settle them right down. Because you're right—we *don't* want anyone else involved."

Olivia held the elevator door while Dr. Ridgeway went back to talk to them.

"Don't even think of calling out to them," she muttered to me. "Or you'll never get out of here."

"Why are you *doing* this?" I said, tears streaming down my face. I watched in horror as my mom listened and nodded and got talked into whatever Dr. Ridgeway was telling her. From the doorway of my room, she waved cheerfully to me.

"It's okay, honey," she called. "Just do whatever the doctor tells you!"

At that point, it felt like very bad advice.

Dr. Ridgeway came back, and the elevator door closed. None of us spoke on the ride down. Once we got off, they rolled me down a long hallway that must have been below ground, because there were no windows.

We passed through a doorway that identified the room as an MRI Scan Room. It felt like a forgotten dungeon. They brought me right up to the low, sleek tube they intended to slide me into. It had the same tubular shape as an airplane.

Tears streaked down my face as they moved me onto the extended MRI table that I knew would slide forward and trap me in the narrow tube.

"Please don't do this," I begged.

"Kendra, relax," he said as the nurse fixed the headpiece in place and adjusted the little mirror so I could see them from inside. "I promise this will be painless. The key is not to move, to hold entirely still so we can get good pictures of your brain. After we're done, we'll go somewhere and have a talk. Everything will make a lot more sense once we do."

As the part I was laying on began moving into the tube, my

left arm started to feel pulled toward the tube with an increasing intensity that made me feel it might rip my arm from its socket.

"Wait!" I said. "Something's not right—wait! My watch! It's going to get ruined!"

At the same moment, Gerald Two beeped urgently. *Strong magnetic pull determined. Measuring 3.0 Tesla. Danger! Will damage Butler's magnetic encoding system. Danger!*

I could feel it trying to pull away from my skin into the depths of the MRI machine.

"Please, stop! My watch! It's getting ruined!"

They heard me; I know they did because I looked at them in the mirror, and I saw how they looked at each other and smiled.

"DO YOU KNOW THE STORY OF ALICE IN WONDERLAND?" DR. Ridgeway asked me about twenty minutes later.

He'd sent Olivia back to my hospital room to tell my mom I was fine. This, after he'd ruined my new Butler, given to me personally by the man who'd invented it. While in the MRI machine, it had broken off my wrist and virtually disintegrated from the machine's magnetic pull. Then he'd helped me into a wheelchair and taken me to an empty hospital room on the floor beneath mine. He rolled me inside, closed the door behind us, and then left me by the door while he went and looked out the window. He'd looked out the window a long time, until he came up with the Alice-in-Wonderland question.

"I only know the story of how you're such a jerk," I said.

He smiled. "I ask because ever since your accident, you're like Alice. You've gone down the rabbit hole and entered a strange, almost fantastical new world, one where nothing's like it used to be and nothing makes any sense at all. I don't envy you what you're going through, Kendra. I really don't."

"What don't you envy?" I said. "The fact that my doctor

basically kidnapped me inside the hospital and won't take me back to my room? Is that what you don't envy?"

"Those things you've been calling dreams," he said. "The one about Maddie and the new one about the man with the snake tattoo. They're not dreams."

"I know they're not dreams," I said. "But they're not hallucinations, either."

"You're right, they're not," he said. "They're actually called Insights."

I recoiled at the word. "Insights? That's really . . . deep."

"Please lose the sarcasm," he said. "We really don't have time for it."

"I really don't have time for *this*," I said. "Take me back to my mom. Right now!"

He approached me at a rapid clip, sharply jolted the wheelchair to face him directly as he sat on the edge of the hospital bed, and looked at me for a too-intense minute.

"I get it, okay?" he said. "I get that I pissed you off, and I ruined your special watch, and life in Kendra-Land is not so great at the moment. I get it all, I promise you. You've made your point. But you need to know a few things. For one, you're not the only person who has Insights. There's a whole group who has them. And you're not going to stop having them, either. You're going to have them for the rest of your life, and with that comes new responsibilities."

He spoke with a certainty I found absolutely terrifying, and I had to look away from his too-green eyes because the clarity in them only made it worse. It was my turn to look out the window.

"You need to release me soon," I said faintly. "I'm missing the entire summer."

"Kendra, look at me."

I don't want to, I thought. *I never want to see your face again or listen to you talk or let you touch me.*

"Kendra."

I looked back at him slowly, sullenly. "What?"

"Please tell me about the Insight you just had."

"I'm not going to tell you anything," I said. "I tried to tell you, and you wouldn't listen. And that was back when I liked you, but I don't anymore, and I'm not going to tell you a thing. *Just take me back to my room.*"

"I ruined your Butler because it can be used to spy on you. It's also why I couldn't let you tell me about your Insight back in your hospital room. I didn't know who else was listening."

"Oh, geez. You're one of those people." I laughed rudely, no longer feeling any obligation to be polite. "You're a conspiracy freak, huh? How's that working for you? Couldn't you have just *asked* me to take off my watch? You don't think I would have preferred that over you ruining it like you did?"

"Tell. Me. Your. Insight." He grabbed my wrist and squeezed hard. "I get that you're mad. I get that I'm the devil incarnate to you right now. But do you really want to be responsible for that man's death to prove a point? Didn't you say he had a new baby? Do you want to leave that child fatherless?"

It was a low blow, as I was fatherless myself and wouldn't wish it on anyone, as Dr. Ridgeway probably knew.

"Let go of me," I snarled. "I don't have to do anything."

He let go, but not without giving me his best take-me-seriously narrowing of his eyes. I put my hands in my lap to make it harder for him to grab me again and then took a few deep breaths and ordered myself to be calm.

"Anything you want to say to me, I want you to say it in front of my mom and Detective Larson," I said. "I don't trust you anymore, and I'm not comfortable being alone with you, and because of that, I'm not going to tell you anything."

"*Listen to me.* Your life's in danger," he said. "There are people who want to kill you. For all I know, Larson might be one of those people."

I didn't believe that for a second.

"Am I in danger from you?" I said, because it was far more likely.

"Of course not, Kendra! I'm trying to protect you!"

"You've got a funny way of showing it."

He ran his fingers through his hair. "I've not handled this well, I'll grant you that. How about we start over?"

"And forget everything you've done? No. Oh, wait, sure! Just give me back my Butler watch, and we'll start over, no harm, no foul."

"Butlers have the equivalent of a secret back door that allows certain entities to eavesdrop on us all," he said. "Remember Edward Snowden? The idea of privacy's an illusion. When you wear a Butler, or you allow a Butler device in your house, every single conversation you have is recorded and stored somewhere, just waiting for the opportunity to be used against you."

"I remember specifically that Butlers have some kind of encryption so that doesn't happen," I said. "It was one of the selling points when they first came out."

"It's also a complete lie. The group I work with spies on people all the time through their Butlers, and we're the good guys. You can bet the bad guys do the same."

Good guys. Bad guys. Dr. Ridgeway was out of his mind.

"You want me to tell you about my Insight so you can save the man?"

"Yes. Absolutely. Of course."

"How do I know you don't want to kill him? How do I know *you're* not the bad guy? After all, you were just going to let Maddie get kidnapped. You didn't care about saving *her.*"

"You don't know what was happening behind the scenes."

"So tell me."

Dr. Ridgeway got up and paced back and forth in the small hospital room. It only took a few awkward circuits for him to tire of it, and then he faced me directly.

"Your father died in 9/11, yes?"

"Yes. Why?"

"If there had been a way for someone to prevent 9/11 from happening, wouldn't you have wanted that person to do whatever he could to stop it?"

"Of course."

An image rushed to mind of my dad and others taking on the hijackers, as they had in real life. Unlike in real life, however—in my wishful-thinking ending—the terrorists were all restrained. The plane dipped dangerously but then was righted by the real pilot, back in charge, or maybe even by my dad, who'd been taking flying lessons in the months before the attack. The plane landed safely. My dad came back to us, and we were all happy. All the other planes were fine, too. The World Trade Center and the Pentagon never got hit.

A fatherless girl can dream, right?

"So here's the question," Dr. Ridgeway said. "What if you could be that person?"

My heart started pounding and I had no idea why.

"What are you talking about?"

"I'm talking about the next 9/11," he said. "Kendra, *you* could be the person who stops the next 9/11. All you have to do is tell us what you know. It's in the works. It's going to happen very soon unless we find a way to stop it. The Insight you had provides clues that can save the lives of not thousands of people, but millions of people."

"I really don't think it does."

"That's where you're wrong. The soldier from your Insight must have some crucial piece of information, and the people who are going to kill him are trying to make sure he doesn't act on what he knows or tell anyone what he knows."

"What makes you think that?"

"Because every Insight is had for a reason, for a purpose. They can appear very distinct and disparate, but they're all connected, and every single one serves a purpose. That's why you need to tell me what *you* know, so we can find the solider and see what purpose he's supposed to serve. You said he had a distinctive tattoo on his left arm," he prompted. "A snake and some words. What were the words?"

Don't Tread on Me or I Will Strike.

"I don't remember," I said shakily, not used to lying.

His eyes hardened. "This is your chance to make a real difference in the world, Kendra. Don't you want to make a difference? Don't you want your life to mean something?"

"Really, all I want is to go back to my room."

His hands balled into fists. "The world as we know it is literally weeks away from changing forever, and not in a good way. This attack is huge, and we're racing against the clock to stop it, and we need literally every single person who can to step up. Kendra, you've got to step up."

No, I really didn't.

"All I'm saying is have this conversation in front of my mom and Detective Larson, and if they agree I should tell you about my Insight, then I will. But getting me alone in a room to try and intimidate me isn't going to work. I'm not going to tell you anything, no matter how long you keep me here."

"You understand the soldier may very well die because of your refusal to tell me?"

"I'll tell someone," I said. "I'll tell the police."

"The police won't know what to do with the information! Kendra, this whole thing hinges on you. Could you really live with yourself after all those millions of people are dead, knowing you could have made a difference and chose not to merely because you didn't like me?"

"Yes, I could," I said, and it was easy to say not because it was true, but because I didn't believe his story.

Besides, I knew what my mom would say: It wasn't my job to make a difference.

It was my job to stay safe.

WHEN WE GOT BACK TO MY ROOM, I NEARLY BURST INTO
tears of relief when I saw Matt was there, waiting for me. He'd been
pacing, and stopped when he saw the look on my face.

"What's wrong?" he said. "The nurse told me you needed to
have an MRI. Hi, Dr. Ridgeway."

Dr. Ridgeway ignored his greeting. Instead, he gave my wheelchair one last rough push into place near the bed and bent close so
only I could hear him.

"You'll keep our conversation private."

I ignored him. "Where's my mom?" I asked Matt. "Where's
Detective Larson?"

"You think we haven't dealt with people more difficult than
you?" Dr. Ridgeway said. "We have. I was trying to be nice, but
there are people who can get you to talk, and I'm going to bring
them in. Matt, can I speak to you for a moment in the hallway?"

"Okay," Matt said cautiously, his eyes alarmed by what Dr.
Ridgeway had said. "Is that okay if I go with him for a minute,
Kendra?"

"Where's my mom?" I said again.

"I don't know," he said. "Probably at lunch with Larson. Do you mind if I go with him for a minute?"

"Go ahead," I said. "Just don't believe a word he says, and don't ever let him be alone with me again."

His eyes narrowed. "What the hell happened?"

Dr. Ridgeway waited expectantly. "Matt?"

"I'm going to stay with Kendra," Matt said. "Anything you want to say to me, you can say to her, too."

Ha, I thought. *Take that.*

Dr. Ridgeway shook his head in disgust and left. Matt came over by me and kneeled so we were eye level.

"Hey." He covered my hand with his. "You're shaking. What happened? You always got along with him before now. Did he do something to you? Did he hurt you?" I shook my head, and his eyes lit up, relieved. "Do I have to go kick his ass?"

"Yes, please."

"Man, I leave for a couple hours and everything falls apart."

"So don't ever leave me," I said.

Our eyes met in that awkward way they had the night of the party, when there was more going on behind our words than we were willing to say but couldn't help but feel.

"I won't," he said. "I'll never leave you."

"Good." I squeezed his hand. "And will you trust me?"

"Of course."

"Okay, so trust me when I say we need to get out of here. Ridgeway's dangerous." I looked around at my little hospital room. At the plants people had brought me, cards people had sent. There was my favorite blanket from home, a suitcase full of my underwear and clothes, posters on the wall, and framed photos from my nightstand. "We can't even pack my things. We just need to go."

Matt gave me a long look. "You really think he's dangerous?"

"I think we shouldn't wait to find out."

Matt nodded and then stood. As he did, he leaned close enough to me that I could take in his clean scent, that of soap and after-shave and shampoo and deodorant that all worked together somehow and mingled into a smell that was perfectly Matt.

"What if someone stops us on the way out?" he said.

"Nobody's going to because you won't let them," I said. "You'll kick their ass."

Matt grinned. "That's right. I'll kick their ass. Are you ready?"

"I'm ready," I said.

And so we did it.

Matt and I made a run for it.

•   •   •

He wheeled me out of my room and down the long chaotic hallway in a leisurely manner, not rushing at all. During our elevator ride to the ground floor, shared with two unfamiliar hospital employees, he rambled on about how the hardware store was going to be able to sell fireworks again for the Fourth of July after not being able to for several years because of fire restrictions, and how his parents were really happy about that because it was always a nice boost to their income. Once on the ground floor, he pushed me past the main-desk information booth that appeared to be staffed with unimposing volunteers, through the automatic doors, and kept on going along the walkway that connected to the parking lot, all with a smooth confidence that surprised me.

"I'm impressed," I said. "I'm starting to think you might have a career as a sneaky dude."

"Let's hope your mom doesn't pull in before we can get out of here."

"It doesn't matter if she does. I'm not going back." I'd resolved that after one second of being outside again, breathing fresh, non-hospital air.

"I may have to steal this wheelchair," Matt said. "I don't know how you'll be able to get around otherwise."

"Bad idea," I said. "I don't think what we've done so far is technically a crime—it's just going to piss off a lot of people—but stealing from a hospital definitely is." The last thing I wanted was for Matt to get arrested trying to help me. "I can get around pretty well on crutches. They probably sell those at Walgreens, right?"

"I know—we'll stop at Goodwill on the way home," he said. "They have a section for medical supplies. I'll run in and see if they have any."

Getting into Matt's tiny, cramped Camaro was somewhat painful, but I didn't complain. At that point, I just wanted to get out of there. I couldn't wait to get home. My mom always said home should be a refuge, and ours really was. I could come home after the worst day ever and feel better the second I walked through the door. We had burlap curtains, white linen slipcovers on our living room couch and chairs, and sea-grass rugs, and the wall colors were all deep jewel tones. Although our house was a small brick ranch from the 1960s, nothing architecturally interesting, we kept it clean and uncluttered and for me, it was true: There was no place like home.

While we drove, I filled Matt in on everything that had happened since I'd last seen him: My visit from Governor Rhodes, followed by my new Butler and a video call with Jeff Meyers, followed by my so-called Insight, followed by Dr. Ridgeway's strange behavior and subsequent explanation that he'd acted the way he had because I supposedly had the power to prevent an impending terrorist attack that was going to kill millions because secret clues were hidden in my Insights. And, oh, by the way, my life was in danger, as these same bad guys wanted to kill me.

Matt listened, jaw dropped. "I don't blame you for wanting to run." He thought a minute and then added, "What sort of terrorist attack could kill millions of people? That would have to be something nuclear, right? A nuclear bomb in New York City? Or something like that?"

Now I was the one whose jaw dropped. "You don't actually believe him, do you?"

He gave me a conflicted look. "We don't have any other explanation for your Insights, and they've got to mean *something*. Everything happens for a reason, right?"

"Wrong," I said. "The universe doesn't work that way. Everything *doesn't* happen for a reason. People like to pretend it does because it's easier to deal with bad things, but what was the reason my dad had to die on 9/11? There isn't one. His death was random. Bad luck. A shitty fact of life, and we don't have to pretend it has some larger meaning in the grand scheme of things. A girl lost her dad; a wife lost her husband. That's all. Small tragedies in the shadows of a larger one."

"That's all?" Matt said. "You're so clinical about it. So business-like. Don't you believe your dad's in heaven?"

He's scattered over the fields of Pennsylvania, I thought but didn't say. People tended not to like it when I said such things.

"I believe my dad was a good and decent man. That's all I know for sure."

"And that's enough?"

"It has to be." I shrugged. "Back to the point. What could Maddie's kidnapping possibly have to do with this so-called conspiracy Dr. Ridgeway's talking about? How are they linked? They're not. That's my point. It's all random."

"You don't know that," Matt said. "Maybe they *are* linked. Maybe the guys kidnapping Maddie are the same ones planning the attack. Maybe they were going to hold her for ransom, and if her dad wouldn't pay up, they were going to drop a nuclear bomb on New York City. And maybe in real life, her dad *wouldn't* have paid up, and there you go. There's your terrorist attack—but you prevented it by stopping her from being kidnapped. But maybe the bomb is still ready to go, and maybe your new Insight has something to do with preventing that."

"And maybe it's all connected back to 9/11, and maybe *this* is why my dad had to be on that airplane all those years ago, so my mom and I would move here, and I'd be in that car with Adam at that exact moment, and we'd get into the accident, and I'd wake up having these Insights which will now allow me to heroically save the world from death and destruction." I laughed. "How's that for a full circle? Do you see how ludicrous that sounds?"

"I think it sounds pretty cool," Matt said.

"And I think it sounds like wishful thinking. Hey, what do you think's happening back at the hospital? Do you think all hell's broken loose?"

"Maybe they don't even know you're gone yet."

"With that nurse, Olivia, always hovering? They know. Where do you think my mom is? I'm surprised she hasn't called you yet looking for me."

"She's probably doing something with Larson, and maybe she's turned off her phone."

"Why would she be doing something with Larson?"

"Why wouldn't she? I think they've become friends. He was very . . . attentive to her those first couple days you were in the hospital. He brought her Starbucks every day, and he baked a coffee cake for her, and they spent a lot of time in the hospital cafeteria together."

"Sounds romantic," I said.

"It wasn't like he was hitting on her."

"Well, but he *baked* for her? That's kind of . . . something. Picking up Starbucks is one thing, but when you bake for someone, well, there's time and effort involved."

"Note to self," Matt said. "Bake for Kendra." I felt compelled to punch him in the arm. "Should I pick up if she calls?"

"Here, give me your Butler," I said. "I think it's better if I message her before she goes nuts. I'll say I forced you to help me leave, against your vehement protests. That way, you won't get in trouble with her."

He pulled into the parking lot, took off his Butler watch, and handed it to me.

"I'm fine with her being mad at me, but I don't think she will be once you tell her what's going on."

"Except I haven't decided if I'm going to tell her what's going on."

He gave me a scolding look. "Kendra, you have to. She's your mom."

"That's exactly my point," I said. "You know her. She'll completely freak out. She doesn't even let me stay out past midnight because she's so afraid of what might happen. How do you think she'd react if she heard even one-tenth of what Ridgeway said? She's more than a little sensitive on the topic of terrorist attacks, in case you haven't noticed."

"For good reason."

"I mean, don't you think I should have flown on an airplane by now?" I said. "It's not that I don't get why it would've been hard, but she should've had us both fly that first year. I'm terrified to fly now, and I wouldn't have been if we'd done it right away. How am I supposed to backpack through Europe if I can't even get on an airplane, you know? It's just . . . her fear has kept my world small, and I don't want to give her a reason to make it any smaller."

"But what if all this is true and you keep your mouth shut? You've got to at least tell Larson."

"Larson the baker? He'd tell my mother over coffee."

"He's a decent guy, Kendra. He might not if you asked him not to."

"All right," I said. "I'll think about it."

"Good, but think fast. It's too much responsibility having this information."

"All you have is a story made up by a crazy doctor."

"You took it seriously enough to run away from the hospital," he pointed out.

"I took Ridgeway's craziness seriously enough to run away from the hospital," I corrected him. "Not the story itself."

"I see."

"There is a difference."

We'd pulled into the Goodwill parking lot. Matt parked and eyed the pajamas I was wearing, with one leg cut off to accommodate my knee wrappings.

"Speaking of crazy, do you want to come in with me?"

"That's so funny," I said in a not-funny tone. "I think I'll stay right here and enjoy some alone time."

After he left, I sent a text to my mom: *Mom, it's Kendra. Couldn't stand the hospital. See you at home. Love you! XOXO!* Then I sank my eyes shut and leaned back against the headrest and thought about how she'd be both furious and relieved to receive it. The first thing she'd do would be to inform everyone around her that I was okay. Everyone, including Dr. Ridgeway.

I sent another text: *DON'T tell Dr. Ridgeway. I'll explain later.*

Two seconds later, Matt's Butler sounded with a call from her, and I was too chicken to pick up. I looked to see if Matt was coming, and it was then I saw the sleek red motorcycle at the edge of the parking lot. I couldn't see the face of the man sitting on it, because he wore a tinted helmet that shielded his face. But when he saw I'd seen him, he waved.

My heart thumped in fear.

Who was he, and why was the sight of him so terrifying?

Matt came out of Goodwill right then carrying a four-legged cane, and the motorcycle sped off.

"They didn't have crutches," Matt said when he got back to the car. "Do you think this'll work?" He peered at me. "What's wrong? You don't look so good."

"My mom called," I said, because it was the easier thing to say. "I didn't answer it."

"She'll forgive you," he said. "She always does."

"Hey, um, what do you know about my accident?" I asked once we were back on the road. "Can you walk me through what happened, as best you know?"

"Sure. You were on Mayfair Road. Adam was drunk and speeding, and a truck driver fell asleep behind the wheel and crossed the centerline and smashed into you head on."

I went over that in my head, and it wasn't right.

"Here's the thing," I said. "I'm pretty sure a motorcycle caused the accident." As soon as I said the words out loud, it all came back. "The motorcycle *did* cause the accident—I remember! He came up behind us really fast, and then he crossed the middle line and went into the oncoming traffic lane. The truck driver swerved into us because he was trying to avoid the motorcycle."

"Are you sure?" Matt glanced over. "I never heard anything like that."

"I'm positive," I said. "The motorcycle driver caused the accident. It was all his fault."

"But the truck driver admitted to causing the accident," Matt said. "Why would he take the blame if he didn't have to?"

I looked out the window and thought about it.

"I don't know," I said. "But I'm going to find out."

A SMALL AIRPLANE LANDS SMOOTHLY AT THE QUIET AIRFIELD *and pulls alongside a black sports car with a man waiting beside it. Dr. Ridgeway, the only passenger on the plane, descends the steps and approaches the man.*

"I'm sorry, Bill," he says as they shake hands. "I know I complicated things."

"It's okay. We'll take care of it."

"What are you going to do? Go in, guns blazing, take her in?"

The man's expression is grim. "We will if we have to. I'd hoped it wouldn't come to that. The whole situation with her is so tricky."

"I don't suppose you've had any luck finding the soldier?"

The man shakes his head, no. "There are too many soldiers with snake tattoos and too many soldiers who've been to both North Africa and Iraq. But we need to find him. At this late date, he's got to have critical information that could blow this thing wide open."

"So what do we do?"

"The girl will lead us to the soldier." He claps Ridgeway on the shoulder. "In any case, your part's done and you look exhausted. Go home and see that pretty wife of yours and your beautiful children and remember what we're doing all this for."

"Truth to power," Ridgeway says grimly. "I never forget, Bill."

"Nor do I."

Ridgeway gets behind the wheel of the black sports car and drives along winding roads, deep in thought. As he nears his destination, his expression lightens. When he arrives home, three young children race to the car and jump on their father after he climbs out. Laughing, he falls to the grass. The kids leap on top of him, and a bout of tickling and roughhousing ensues.

But later, as darkness falls, over cocktails on the patio with his wife, Ridgeway's dark mood reemerges as he tells her what happened. How he made Kendra sick. Ruined her Butler. Trapped her in a room and used the trauma surrounding her father's death to try and convince her to help them.

"I really messed up," he concludes miserably. He finishes his drink and then swirls the ice in his glass. "Still, she's disappointingly small-minded."

"Most people are unable to see themselves as heroes," his wife says. "They're slow to ignite their own spark of greatness. She also can't possibly understand what's truly at stake. She looks at you and all she sees is the bastard who ruined her Butler." She stands. "Another drink?"

Ridgeway hands her his glass and watches her go inside to refill it. Once she's gone, he closes his eyes and rubs his temples like he's got a headache.

A man dressed like a cat burglar in all black and wearing a knit ski mask silently emerges out of the hedges. He sneaks up behind Ridgeway, yanks back his head, and in one slick, skilled maneuver slits his throat with a long-blade knife before disappearing again into the darkness.

Ridgeway's wife stops short when she comes back outside and sees her husband slumped forward. She sets down the drinks she's carrying and tentatively goes to him.

"Jonathan?" She shakes his shoulder and then turns her hand palm-up. It's sticky with his blood. She tilts his head back and sees his wide-open eyes, his bloody neck, his lifeless body.

And then she screams.

• • •

She screamed, and then I screamed.

"Kendra!" My mom shook my shoulder. "Kendra, wake up!"

My eyes bolted open. It took me a moment to realize I was back in my own house, in my own bed.

"They killed him, Mom! They killed him!"

She smoothed back my hair. "You're having another dream about the soldier?"

"No," I said. "They killed Dr. Ridgeway!"

Her eyes widened in alarm. "This is a *new* dream?"

Insight, Mom, I thought. *It's called an Insight.* But my mom didn't know that, of course. When she'd arrived home, I'd received a colossal lecture covering everything from how I showed a complete lack of respect to her and the hospital staff by leaving to how dare I expect her to keep secrets from my doctor? She hadn't, and although I'd known it was too much to hope she would, I still accused her of choosing him over me, and we argued back and forth until I'd claimed exhaustion. And now here we were, however many hours later.

"What time is it?" I asked.

"Nearly ten," she said.

"It happens right after dark, but I don't know what part of the country he's in. There could still be time if he's on the West Coast, right? We need to call him! To tell him to get away from his house—away from his backyard—and to get somewhere safe."

"I'll call the hospital and have him paged."

"He's not there," I said. "He left after I did. He flew home, wherever that is. Do you know where he lives? Do you have his personal number?"

"I assumed he lived in Minneapolis."

"I don't think he does. He flew home on a private plane."

She lifted her Butler to her mouth. "Call Dr. Ridgeway."

Ominously, he didn't pick up.

"Call Detective Larson!" I said. "Maybe he could send the cops to his house—but hurry!"

Detective Larson answered right away. My mom quickly explained I'd had another dream and then put her Butler on speakerphone.

"Dr. Ridgeway's going to die!" I said, not bothering with a greeting. "It happens tonight! He's in his backyard and a guy comes out of the bushes, sneaks up behind him, and slits his throat! I don't know where he lives, but he took an airplane to get there. A private plane, and he drove along winding roads to get home."

"I'll track him down," said Larson. "But how do you know it's tonight?"

"Because he was talking about me to somebody, about how he messed up with me. Please, there's no time for me to explain. Send the police to get him!"

With that, I hung up and again called Dr. Ridgeway. This time, his wife answered.

"Oh, God! Mrs. Sinclair?" She gasped to catch her breath. "My husband's been murdered! He's right here, in my arms." There was some sobbing, and then, "Is Kendra still alive?"

"*Still* alive?" My mom stood frozen, gawking at me. "Yes, of course."

Sirens sounded on the other end of the line.

"The police are coming." Mrs. Ridgeway said it to herself, not us. "How did they know to come?"

"I had an Insight about Dr. Ridgeway," I said. "I saw what happened—what was going to happen—and we called the police. I'm sorry they didn't get there in time."

"I need to go," she said hurriedly. "Stay safe, Kendra. Stay safe!"

"Why would she say that?" my mom asked. "Are you in danger?"

Not ten seconds later, a multitude of cars screeched to the curb in front of our house. My mom and I looked at each other in terror as car door after car door opened and slammed. Heavy footsteps ran in multiple directions across our yard.

"Kendra," my mom whispered. "What's happening?"

There was a pounding on the door, and something Jeff Meyers said to me earlier that day popped into my head: *Toto, I've got the feeling we're not in Kansas anymore.* In that moment, I wished a twister *would* come and swoop me up and take me to a land far, far away.

But that wasn't going to happen.

I had no idea who was at the door.

All I knew: They wanted me.

EPISODE
TWO

"RIDGEWAY'S DEAD," SHE INFORMED HIM. "WE'RE MOVING on to the girl."

"Change of plans, Buttercup." He stared out the window at the ocean, where his ashes would soon be scattered. "The girl needs to live."

"But Gardiner's literally minutes from her house with his full posse," the woman said. "Kendra Sinclair could be a non-issue in minutes. And don't call me Buttercup."

"She needs to live," he said again. "I'm sure you can see why."

"Enlighten me." There was a bitchy edge to her voice, but that was nothing new. "The way I see it, without the girl they'll have nothing."

"But with Hendricks, they'd have everything."

"That's right," she said in a clipped voice. *Because of your screw-up,* he heard in the silence that followed.

"Where are you at with Hendricks?" he asked.

"He's proving surprisingly elusive."

"I'm not surprised," the man said. "He was special ops for years."

"Edgewater should know where to find him."

"True, they should, but they don't. We should never overestimate the competence of other people."

"We shouldn't underestimate it, either," she said. "We should take out Kendra Sinclair while we have the chance."

"We'll need her to lead us to Hendricks if we can't find him on our own," he said. "And in the meantime, we can use her to draw out the other side. The girl's a nothing—just a non-committed teenager who has no idea about anything—but the others are going to be desperate to find and save Hendricks, and for them to do that, they're going to have to go through the girl."

"So instead of killing her, we watch her?"

"Yes," he said. "We watch the girl. We find the others. We kill them all, and then everything proceeds as planned."

"You're not having second thoughts, are you? No pangs of conscience?"

Bitch, he thought. "Of course I don't have second thoughts. We're on a noble quest, Buttercup."

He called her that because she'd played Little Buttercup in their summer camp's rendition of H.M.S. Pinafore, while he'd played Sir Joseph. She'd been miscast and mad about it—how dare she be forced to play a woman of humble origins? He, from comparatively modest origins himself, was happy just to be at the exclusive camp. If he hadn't been the nephew of the camp director, he would've been back in California at the local YMCA camp with all the other yuck-yucks, as his dad called them. Whenever possible, Buttercup convinced him to sneak away from the play rehearsals and smoke the clove cigarettes she'd stolen from one of her counselors. Summer after summer, the two of them snuck away from camp activities and did things they shouldn't, but although there were secrets and sex between them, there had never been honest affection. She was incapable of it; not only did her blood run blue, it ran ice cold. Back then he'd always known his place with her. It wasn't until his earned wealth surpassed her inherited wealth that she'd considered him a near-equal. Only then had she invited him to join the Legacy Foundation as a shadow board member.

"If I were having second thoughts, would I have released the codes to you?" he said. "Doing that was our fail-safe. Now if something happens to me, everything can still proceed as planned."

"What happened to change your mind so suddenly? We've been asking you to release them for a long time and you've been holding out on us."

"It was always my plan to tell you now," he said.

"Not in front of Hendricks, it sure wasn't. I'll never believe that."

She was right, but he certainly wouldn't tell her he'd had a panic attack. That he'd awoken drenched in sweat with a wet weight bearing down on his lungs. He'd thought he was dying—too soon, and naturally, instead of by his own hand at the time and place of his choosing. In the light of day, his fears seemed foolish, but in the moment, he'd really thought the end was near, and it wasn't the ending he'd planned for himself.

"You best go," he said. "Call off Gardiner."

"I hope I'm not already too late," she said. "Be well, Sir Joseph."

After she clicked off the line, he turned from the window and sank into his recliner. As much as he despised her, he was thankful, too, that she'd brought him onto the Legacy Foundation board, founded in part with her family's money and established for the sole purpose of achieving radical global population reduction within the members' lifetimes.

That was its secret mission; the stated mission was to wipe out third-world disease through effective vaccination. All but one member of the public, pansy board worked solely and optimistically on the latter goal, while he and Buttercup and others worked behind the scenes on the true goal: Kill off the losers of society and keep them from reproducing. Bright side: His illness had crystallized their plan, inspired its brilliance, and forced it forward at a pace even they hadn't imagined was possible.

He pulled his cashmere blanket over him and closed his eyes. Immediately, he was taunted by the image of Hendricks and his low-class tattoo. The warning inked beneath the coiled snake now seemed worryingly prophetic: Don't Tread on Me or I Will Strike.

Not if I strike first, you bastard.

Not if I strike first.

• • •

"We can't go out there." My mom stood frozen, terrified by the heavy sounds of our house being surrounded. "Why did Dr. Ridgeway's wife ask if you were still alive?"

"I have no idea," I said, which wasn't entirely true.

"Are you in some sort of danger?"

Knock. Knock. Knock.

I saw shadows through my curtains as whoever was out there established a position outside my bedroom window.

What are you going to do, Ridgeway had asked in my Insight. *Go in, guns blazing?*

We will if we have to, the man had said.

So maybe that's what this was, I thought, the good guys coming to protect me.

Knock. Knock. Knock.

Or maybe it was the bad guys coming to kill me.

I struggled to get out of bed without causing my leg to throb any more than it already was.

"Call 9-1-1," I said.

My mom snapped out of her stupor. As she called the emergency number, another call came in. "It's Detective Larson! Detective Larson, thank God! Dr. Ridgeway's dead, and there are people pounding on our door, and we—! . . . What? Oh!" She laughed. "Thank God. I'll be right there."

She clicked off the line and exhaled in relief. "That's Detective Larson at the door."

"Him and who else?"

"He brought backup. I'll go let him in."

"I'll be right behind you."

Seeing as there were armed men outside my window, I dressed in my en suite bathroom while she answered the door, and then I joined them in the living room. To say Detective Larson looked tense would be a gross understatement.

"He wants to take you into protective custody." My mom's voice was swollen with years of pent-up fear that maybe *this* was the thing that would ruin me. She'd been waiting for it, all this time, and maybe *this* was it.

"Are you part of Ridgeway's group?" I asked Larson calmly. I was shaken up, too, but that was how we handled things: When my mom fell apart, I kept it together.

"I don't know what you mean." Larson tilted his head questioningly. "To what group are you referring?"

"Why do you want me in protective custody?"

"We got an anonymous call saying you were in imminent danger," he said. "I think it's best not to take any chances."

"Who called?" I asked.

"We don't know."

"I meant who *would* have called?"

Not Ridgeway, I knew. Not his wife. Who else was there? Who else was involved with this?

As much as I hated to think it, my last Insight and Ridgeway's death gave heaps of credibility to everything he'd said earlier in the day. Should I not have left the hospital? Should I have told him my Insight? Would he still be alive if I had?

"What's going on?" my mom wailed.

"Mom, calm down," I said. "Don't go into panic mode."

"Here, let's have a seat," Larson said gently, taking her by the arm and guiding her to her favorite armchair.

He and I remained standing.

"Can't you trace back all the calls you get on that line?" I said. "It was the 9-1-1 line, right? Doesn't it automatically bring up the caller's location?"

"This one came from a pay phone," he said. "And we have cameras on all of them, but it's going to take some time to run through the video surveillance. We'll learn who made the call soon enough, but in the meantime, we're taking the threat seriously."

"What was it exactly?" I said.

"Why would anyone threaten Kendra?" my mom said before Larson could answer. "She doesn't have any enemies. Everybody loves Kendra! But, then, Dr. Ridgeway's wife said she's in danger, too, so it's not some sort of high-school stalker situation, is it?"

"Perhaps Kendra can explain some things to us," Larson said and looked at me expectantly.

"I wish I knew."

"But you do know something, don't you? Something that caused you to leave the hospital today in such a hurry?" He studied me with the suspicious eyes of a cop. "Well?"

"Why did you lie about my accident?" I said.

That caught him off guard. "I didn't."

"But you did," I said. "I remembered what happened, and it's not like you said. The truck driver wasn't asleep when he crossed the centerline—his eyes were wide open and we looked at each other. We actually looked at each other! And it wasn't his fault, either. The man on the motorcycle—*that's* who's to blame. He should be charged with murder. He was driving on the wrong side of the road and basically played chicken with the truck. The truck only swerved into us to avoid hitting him."

"That doesn't agree with anyone else's recollection," Larson said.

"Then everyone else lied."

"I'd be happy to show you the report."

"I don't care what the report says. I care about the truth."

"Why is Kendra in danger?" my mom interjected. "Who'd want to hurt her?"

"Ask your daughter," Larson said. "She knows more than she's saying."

"Maybe someone was trying to kill me the night of the accident," I said, and my mom gasped. "Did you ever think about that? Maybe the motorcyclist was trying to kill me."

"From your description, it sounds like he was trying to kill himself, if anything," said Larson. "Kendra, you're remembering wrong, which happens a lot in times of trauma. Think about it. In particular, why would the truck driver lie? It's a given that he lost his job by admitting he was at fault."

"Maybe he was asleep and woke up at the last second, and that's when you saw him, when he realized it was too late to prevent the accident," my mom suggested. "From his perspective, he'd been asleep and that's what caused the accident; from yours, he appeared wide-awake. When you fall asleep behind the wheel, you don't sleep for long periods of time. You doze off, then quickly rouse yourself."

"But he came around the curve perfectly," I argued. "He stayed exactly in his lane and never swerved once. He was awake. I'm positive, because I was hyper-aware of what was happening. And, like I said, we made eye contact."

"Do *you* think someone's trying to kill you, Kendra?" Larson said.

"I don't know." I sank onto the couch. "I don't know what to believe."

I wondered if I should tell them more about my latest Insight or about my bizarre conversation with Dr. Ridgeway earlier in the day, but I decided against it. My mom was pale and every muscle was tensed, and I thought back to all the white-knuckled moments she put herself through over the years, convinced the worst was going to happen to me because, after all, it had happened to my dad. She couldn't handle bad news.

Larson could, but with him it was a matter of trust. I used to trust everyone until they gave me a reason not to, but now that seemed like a dangerous way to live.

"I guess maybe I *should* see that police report," I said.

"Shall we go to the police station right now?" he offered.

"I'm too tired to do anything tonight. I can't think anymore," I said, and it was true.

"Why don't you come to the station in the morning, then?" Larson said. "I'll keep my men here overnight, and we'll pick up with this discussion in the morning."

"So the men with guns stay?" I said.

He smiled. "The men with guns stay."

My mom got up and walked Larson to the door. They both went outside, closing the door behind them, and when I peeked through the curtains, I saw them whispering together.

I didn't like it.

I didn't like it one bit.

THE NEXT MORNING WAS MY FIRST ONE HOME FROM THE
hospital, and even though I had so much on my mind, I luxuri-
ated in a long, hot shower, glad to be using my own shampoo and
conditioner and soap. While I hardly felt like myself anymore since
the accident and the Insights began, it was nice at least to smell like
me again.

I found an emerald-green sundress in my closet that I'd bought
the week before my accident and had forgotten about. I put it on,
not letting myself think too much about how much fun I'd had at
the mall with Nora that day, going from store to store trying on
things way beyond what we could afford, and seeing a movie, and
getting frozen yogurt afterwards. She'd bought an oversized ring,
while in addition to the dress I'd bought a new lipstick, which was
my favorite thing to buy when I hardly had any money but wanted
something new.

I put on that lipstick, Black Honey by Clinique, did the rest
of my makeup, then braided my hair. That took all the energy I
had and then some, so I lay back down on the bed to rest for a few
minutes, but as soon as I did, I started having flashbacks of Dr.

Ridgeway getting his throat slit, and then the solider getting his brains shot out, and so I got right back up.

After I had waffles with my mom, she drove me the short distance to the Brookview Police Department, parked, and walked me inside. The front lobby was surprisingly nice, with furniture and lighting that made it feel like a waiting room at a dentist's office rather than a police station. There were no America's Most Wanted posters to remind us where we were; instead, I paged through the latest issue of *People* until Detective Larson came to greet us.

"You look nice," he told me. "Until last night, I think I've only ever seen you in a hospital gown." To my mom, he said, "I'd like to speak to Kendra alone today, if that's alright."

My mom looked at me for my reaction, and I shrugged that it was fine with me. It was what I preferred, actually, but I wondered if this was what they'd been whispering about the previous night, plotting behind my back.

"Okay, then," she said. "I have errands to run, anyway. My oil change light's been on for weeks." She kissed me. "Call when you're done. I'll come back and pick you up."

I agreed, and after she left, Detective Larson and I went through a heavy locked door to the main part of the station, which looked more like I'd imagined a police station would, with its linoleum floors, mismatched desks configured haphazardly, and ugly fluorescent overhead lighting. Larson had his own office, though, and while his furniture was still old, at least the office was quiet and lacked the locker-room feel of the main area, which he referred to as the bullpen. He pointed to a chair that faced his desk and offered me a cinnamon roll from a plate. I poked one. It was warm, and even though I'd recently had breakfast, I couldn't resist.

"This looks so good." I pulled it apart. "Is it homemade?"

He nodded. "I bake when I can't sleep."

I took a bite. "Mmmmm. Why can't you sleep?"

"I've got a lot on my mind. There's a girl I'm trying to keep alive."

I licked my fingers. "And a girl's mom you're falling for."

His eyes popped with surprise but not exactly denial, and when I looked pointedly at his wedding ring, he held up his hand so I could get a better look, or to show he wasn't hiding anything.

"I'm a widower," he said, gesturing to a framed photo of a nice-looking-but-not-beautiful woman. "My wife died six months ago. Cancer, and probably the main reason I can't sleep. And I'm not falling for your mom. I like her, yes. I've enjoyed getting to know her a bit over the course of my investigation, but I'm not in a place where I'd be falling for anyone right now. It's way too soon."

I felt like a real jerk.

"I'm sorry for your loss," I said. "I take it you know about my dad?" He nodded, and with that I felt our relationship shift to that deeper place shared only by those who'd lost someone they loved.

"Your mom told me there were some hard times for her after your dad passed, where you more or less became the parent, taking care of her."

"It wasn't so bad," I said, although it had been. "She was just a little . . . fragile." I thought back to those times I'd euphemistically called "episodes" that had happened since my dad died, when she'd disappear into her room, pulling the shades and lying in bed for hours at a time when she should have been making dinner, helping me with homework, or going to work. It didn't happen anymore, hadn't for years, but the potential was always there, lurking in the background, ready to be triggered by situations such as this.

"I thought she handled your accident very well," he said.

"She did, actually."

"She's probably stronger than you give her credit for."

"She probably is," I agreed.

"I got the sense last night you were reluctant to speak in front of her."

"Well, things got very weird with Dr. Ridgeway yesterday, and some of what he said would definitely freak her out."

He leaned forward, interested. "What did he say?"

"Weren't you going to show me the police report of the accident?" I said, reaching for my second cinnamon bun.

He slid it over to me across his desk. "Don't get your sticky fingers all over it."

"Funny." I pretended to do just that.

"And don't think I'm unaware this is now about the third time you've avoided answering my questions about Ridgeway. Information sharing's got to go both ways, Kendra. Ridgeway's death is a murder investigation, and my counterparts in New Hampshire are more than a little curious as to what prompted me to call in a well-check on him, soon after which he was found with his neck slit open. If you don't talk to me, you're going to end up talking to them. You probably will, anyway."

"Everyone wants a piece of me," I said quietly, digging into the report, growing increasingly angry as I did.

The report described the weather, the road conditions, the traffic patterns from that night, and all those details were how I remembered them, but the statements from the motorcyclist and truck driver were flat-out lies. The motorcyclist said he'd been driving a couple hundred yards behind us on Mayfair Road, had seen the truck swerve into the convertible, and had stopped to help. After realizing Adam died on impact, he'd turned his attention to me. I hadn't been breathing, but he revived me through chest compressions, and after that I was in and out of consciousness until the paramedics arrived.

The couple that had been following closely behind us corroborated everything the motorcyclist said.

The truck driver made no mention of the motorcycle driving on the wrong side of the road. Instead, he said he'd been driving for twenty hours that day and had been trying not to nod off for at least the last hour before the accident.

"This isn't right." I looked across the desk at Larson. "I'm absolutely positive the truck driver was awake."

"I tried calling him before you got here," he said. "But the number he gave has been disconnected, and the trucking company said they haven't been able to get in touch with him, either."

I stopped chewing. "You mean he disappeared?"

"It seems so."

"And you don't think that's weird?"

"I'm concerned," he allowed.

"What about the motorcycle driver, Martin Putnam?" I asked, referencing his name from the police report. "I know he's in town, because I saw him yesterday in the Goodwill parking lot."

"I don't think so. He doesn't even live in the state," Larson said. "He was just passing through. In any case, I left a message for him, and I expect I'll hear back later today."

"It was him," I said definitely. "I recognized the motorcycle. He even waved at me."

Larson frowned. "Waved at you?"

"He followed me," I said. "He must have followed me from the hospital."

"*Why*, Kendra? Why would he?" His frustration with me finally came through. "I'm not a genius, but I'm not an idiot, either, and I can help you if you'll let me. If there's one thing I know beyond a doubt, it's that you need help."

"Thanks for the vote of confidence," I said, although I knew he was right.

He stopped talking, and I stopped talking, and a stubborn silence ensued until I finally caved.

"So let me ask you a question, and don't read anything into it, okay?" I said.

"Ask away."

"Do you get a list every day of, like, terrorist chatter?" His eyebrows raised in surprise. "Like, if there was a big terrorist attack being planned, would you know about it?"

Larson cocked his head. "Did you have one of your dreams about a terrorist attack?"

"Not exactly," I said. "And they're called Insights, not dreams."

"What the hell's an Insight, and how do you know what they're called?"

Before I could reply, a uniformed officer burst into his office.

"We have a possible 187 out on Cagill Farms Road," he said to Larson, glancing at me. "Figured you'd want to be there from the start."

Larson studied me. "Kendra, should I stay?"

"What's a 187?"

"Homicide."

"You should go."

"We'll talk later?"

"Sure," I said, glad for the reprieve.

Larson got to his feet, and it was clear our conversation was over for the time being. "Can you wait for your mom in the lobby?"

"You don't trust me in your office?"

He grinned. "I'm afraid you're going to steal all my pastries."

"Funny." I got up, and he walked me to the lobby and then turned to go. "Detective Larson?"

He paused and turned back to look at me.

"Did you ever find out who made that call last night saying I was in danger?"

"I did," he said. "You should ask your friend Matt."

• • •

Once I was in the lobby of the police station, I called my mom on the old-school cell phone she'd given me, but it went to voicemail. Home was less than a mile, and my physical therapist had told me to walk as much as possible, so I sent a text to my mom to let her know I was going to walk, and then I set out into the sticky summer day, glad I'd braided my hair because otherwise it would have frizzed unmercifully in the humidity.

Brookview was a middle-class suburb without too much crime. An occasional house got robbed while empty during the day, and occasionally cars got broken into at the mall, but there weren't really any street people or bad-bad parts of town. Having said that, the part I had to walk by to get home between the police station and the river was probably the most run-down area. I'd biked through it plenty of times, but when you're on a bike, it's easy to overlook things you notice when you're walking.

One thing I'd never noticed was a boxing gym tucked away in an alley off Grover Street. It was easy to miss, as there was only a little sign hanging from the wall, and I might have missed it that day except for what was parked further in the alley—a flashy red motorcycle with a familiar helmet locked to it. My heart pounded, because it was *the* motorcycle—the one I'd seen yesterday in the Goodwill parking lot.

Fast, before I could talk myself out of it, I walked to the door of the boxing gym and stepped inside, pausing to let my eyes adjust to the cave-like, boy-sweat atmosphere. I scanned the room, unsure what to do next—ask the manager for help, or simply call out, *Hey, who's the asshole-murderer who owns the red motorcycle?*

It turns out I didn't have to do either, because my eyes landed on someone familiar, and in that instant I knew exactly who'd driven the motorcycle that night.

I knew exactly who'd killed Adam.

It was Dark & Mysterious Dude from the party: Daemon Godwin, who'd stared at me all night with that freakish intensity.

"YOU!" I screamed across the room at him.

He'd been punching a bag when I walked in, but he stopped at the sight of me. He didn't look surprised or guilty or happy or nervous. He merely wiped away the perspiration glistening from his forehead and unlaced his boxing gloves like he had all the time in the world. As I started toward him, it registered that literally everyone in the gym was watching me. I could feel their curious eyes on me, hoping there would be drama.

I did not disappoint.

"That's your motorcycle out front?" I asked him when I got close, even though I already knew it was.

His dark brown eyes were unreadable. "It is."

"Do you remember me? Do you know who I am?"

"Of course," he said calmly. "You're the girl who lived."

"THE GIRL WHO LIVED?" I YELLED, RECOGNIZING THE HARRY
Potter rip-off line. "You mean I'm the girl whose boyfriend you killed!"

Daemon's look was casual. "I guess that, too."

I took my cane and raised it and smacked him with it as hard as I could. He barely flinched, so I did it again. He just stood there and took it and didn't try to defend himself or make me stop, and I knew from how he was built like a Marine and obviously was a boxer I wasn't making a dent in him, even when I switched to using my fists. Still, he let me try, until finally when he'd had enough, he took me by the waist and hoisted me over his shoulder like I was a sack of rice.

Zap.

There was that lightening strike again. I hadn't thought about it since the night of the party, but now I remembered how the same thing happened the last time he touched me.

"Hey, ow!" I banged my fists on his back. "Put me down, you jerk!"

Feeling like a toddler throwing a tantrum, I swung wildly. The others laughed. Daemon carried me to the manager's office as I humiliated myself further by screaming the whole time for him to put me down. Once we were inside the tiny, cramped office, he closed and locked the door and then set me on the floor.

"Okay," he said. "You can keep hitting me now if you want to."

As if I needed his permission!

"You killed Adam!" Smack. "You nearly killed me!" Smack. "I can hardly walk, thanks to you!"

And on and on. He took in what I said and offered nothing in return, so I hit him and hit him and hit him until I was crying so hard and my hands hurt so bad that I had to stop. Why couldn't I hurt him? Why didn't he care that he'd ruined my life?

Why didn't he care?

I sank into a wobbly office chair and forced myself to take deep breaths and count to ten. He leaned calmly against the desk and waited.

"Martin Putnam?" I said finally, referencing the name he'd used in the police report. "You told me your name was Daemon Godwin."

"It's Daemon," he said.

"You lied to the police?"

"Sure."

"So what's your real name?"

"For our purposes, it's Daemon."

"Why?" I finally said, staring for a long time into his cryptic brown eyes. "Why'd you do it?"

"Do what? Save your life?"

"The accident was your fault, and you know it. You forced that truck driver into our lane. You killed Adam and could've killed me, which you've got to live with for the rest of your life."

"That I do," he said, as if I'd asked whether he had a dollar in his pocket.

My skin prickled. "You're okay with that?"

"There are worse things in the world to have to live with."

"Why are you doing this?" I hated how my voice shook. "Did you randomly pick me out of a crowd and decide to ruin my life? Explain, because I just don't get it."

"I did not pick you out of a crowd, Kendra. There was nothing random about it."

I looked at him standing there, all deceptively good looking and chiseled, and realized I'd met my first true psychopath. My body broke out in chills. How stupid was I to be there, alone? No one knew where I was, and I'd been aware going in that he'd purposely caused the accident. He'd also admitted we'd been targets, and it was obvious now he'd been stalking us—more precisely, stalking me. I didn't want to be that stupid girl from every horror movie who has the audience screaming at her to *not be alone in a locked room with the bad guy*, so quickly, I stood.

"Hold on a minute," I said.

I couldn't leave, because I still needed answers, but I'd never forgive myself if something happened to me after I'd realized my stupidity and not corrected it, so while Daemon stayed where he was, leaning against the desk with a slightly amused look on his too-handsome face, I unlocked the door to the manager's office, stepped outside, and sent a quick text to Matt.

FYI, dude from party. At boxing gym in alley off Grover. Name = Daemon. Fake name. Crazy dude.

I knew the message wouldn't make sense to him, but that wasn't the point. The point was if I disappeared, Matt would show the police my message and they'd have a place to start looking for me, and at the very least, Daemon wouldn't be able to get away with my murder like he seemingly was with Adam's. Once the message was sent, I went back into the office holding my phone, making it obvious I'd contacted someone in the outside world.

"Darn," Daemon said. "Now I won't be able to kidnap you like I planned."

"Very funny."

"Who says I was joking?"

My phone buzzed with a return text from Matt. *Huh? You okay? Need me to come get you?*

I sent back, *I'll call you, 30 min.* Then I faced Daemon. "How did you convince the truck driver to lie for you?"

I expected him to deny he had, but yet again he surprised me.

"Simple," he said. "We were working together."

"You were *what*?"

"We worked together," he repeated. "I told you, Kendra: Nothing about that night was random. From now on in your life, there's no such thing as coincidence. Every single thing happens for a reason."

I barely heard that last part because I was so stunned by what he'd said about the truck driver. My knees threatened to give out, so I grabbed onto the chair inside the doorway.

"Have a seat," he said.

"Don't tell me what to do."

Still, my injured leg was throbbing and I felt disoriented, so I sat in the chair. Daemon pulled the manager's chair over and sat so close our knees touched.

"Give me your hands," he said and held his out for me to take.

"Uh, NO. You're not touching me."

"You want an explanation for what's going on, don't you? Press your thumbs into my palms like this," he demonstrated, "and you'll have your explanation."

"I'm not touching you." The very idea made me shudder.

"Show and tell, Kendra, that's all I'm trying to do, but I suppose I can tell you before I show you if that makes you more comfortable. You know those weird-ass dreams you're having that turn out to be not really dreams?"

"You mean my Insights?" I said.

"Where did you learn that term? Ah, from Ridgeway, of course," he said, answering his own question. "In any case, I have them, too."

"I'm sorry," I said, because what he'd said was so bizarre it didn't quite register. "You have what, too? And how do you know who Dr. Ridgeway is?"

"Ridgeway and I work—worked—on the same team."

I felt my jaw drop. "You know he's—?"

Daemon nodded. "I was the one he was going to bring in to talk to you yesterday when he was unable to convince you to tell him about your Insight."

"That wouldn't have gone well."

"You leaving the hospital didn't go well, either. It left a good man dead."

"Oh, so that's my fault?"

"You think it's not?"

"It's definitely not!" I said, guilt-ridden. "I left because I thought he was crazy. I still think he was."

"But less so now, right?" he said. "Now you know there are

actually people out there trying to kill us, and quite competent ones at that."

"You say you have Insights?"

"I do," he said. "You and I are alike in that way."

"We're not alike." *He has Insights. He has Insights. He has Insights.* No matter how many times I said it to myself, the impact of his words refused to sink in. I wanted my situation to be isolated. Unique. *Not* part of a global conspiracy. "We're not alike at all."

"We're more alike than you know. Can I show you something?"

He again held out his hands, and I again rejected them.

"No. Keep talking. Explain about the night of the party."

He couldn't stand talking, I could tell. Couldn't stand feeling. Couldn't stand having to deal with my emotions. Well, too bad.

"You want to know? Fine." He shrugged. "I had an Insight about you, and that's why I showed up at the party. That's why I told you not to leave with your boyfriend—because I knew what was going to happen."

"You knew?" My words came out in a whisper. "You knew about the accident?" He nodded. "Of course you knew. You *caused* it. You just admitted you planned it with the truck driver."

He shook his head, no. "That wasn't my Insight. I caused the accident you had in order to prevent the one from my Insight, which would have been even worse. You know that railroad crossing you were coming up on? About a mile away?" I nodded. "Well, in my Insight, you and your boyfriend were driving down Mayfair Road. He was driving like a jerk—even without me there—and you were railing on him for being drunk and he was refusing to pull over, and you were begging him to let you out and he wouldn't. 'I love you but I hate you' . . . sound familiar?"

I nodded, because that had been our special, used-too-often phrase when we argued, and while we hadn't said it to each other that night, the fact that Daemon knew the phrase was significant. Plus, what he described was a pretty likely account of what might have happened next. I remembered how intimately Daemon had looked at me at the party, as if he knew me all the way down into my soul. It was because he'd seen the worst happening to me. He'd seen it happen in his Insight, and he knew it would be happening for real later that night.

"I don't get it," I said. "Why didn't you warn me?"

"I did," he said. "I said don't go home with your boyfriend."

"Yeah, but that just sounded creepy."

"And I slashed your boyfriend's tire."

"Anyone can change a tire."

"You wouldn't have believed me," he said. "You wouldn't have listened."

"I might have."

"And I would have told you if I hadn't gotten kicked out of the party once your boyfriend showed up."

"That's why you were trying to take his car keys."

He nodded. "In my Insight, you were coming up on a railroad crossing. Cars were backed up on the other side of the tracks, and your boyfriend—"

"His name was Adam."

"He was going to stop right on the tracks, and then someone was going to pull up behind him so he couldn't get off in time. A train was coming, and it was going to crush your convertible like a flimsy aluminum can, with both of you in it. *That's* why I caused the accident you had."

The lump in my throat was huge, nearly unbearable.

"Am I supposed to be grateful?"

"No, Kendra," he said, a bit impatiently. "You're supposed to be dead."

MY PHONE BUZZED WITH A RETURN TEXT FROM MATT.

Kendra, you okay?

No, Matt, I thought. *As a matter of fact, I'm not okay.* I ignored the text and returned my attention to Daemon, who now seemed slightly less evil and vastly more complicated.

"I have questions," I said.

"And I have answers, but they should wait because there's a man about to die, and I need to save him."

"Who?" I said, wanting to wail. "Who's going to die now?"

"The man from your Insight. The soldier. You had the Insight yesterday—that means the clock's ticking. You had your Insight about Ridgeway last night and he's already dead. Now do you see why we don't have a second to waste?"

"Do Insights always come true that fast?"

"Not always, but everything's coming to a head now. We're rushing toward the finish line, the too-late-to-go-back line. It's all about to go horribly wrong if we aren't able to put a stop to things. We're living on borrowed time."

He again extended his hands, and I again shrank back.

"I don't want you touching me."

The exasperation on his face was plain as he pushed back from his chair and began to pace the small room.

"I can certainly get you to talk, Kendra, so this little game you're playing, while maybe it's cute to you, is a waste of time to me."

"What, are you going to torture me to get me to talk?" I tried to laugh with bravado but didn't quite manage it. My laugh came out scared and nervous, which made sense because it was how I felt.

"It wouldn't take torture," he said as if he were an expert in the subject. "Although if it did . . . well, let's put it this way: We're all insignificant in the overall scheme of things, and the people I work with would all willingly sacrifice the one to save the many. You're in this thing until the end whether you want to be or not, Kendra. It's your fate, and you can choose to live with it, or you can choose to die with it, but you can't walk away from it."

"Nice little speech," I said. "Only, I *can* walk away from it. Watch me."

I got up and brushed by him in my limping attempt to leave, and faster than I could even register it was happening, Daemon grabbed me and shoved me against the wall, pinning me there and in the process zapping me yet again.

"Ow! Why does that happen whenever you touch me?" I tried to wriggle my way out from his hold, but my strength was about a tenth of his and therefore completely ineffective as a weapon against him. "It's like getting struck by lightning."

The sensation started to fade, and he waited until I stopped wriggling.

"It's a code," he said. "A cosmic handshake, if you will. It happens because we both have Insights. It's how we recognize each other."

"But at the party, my Insights hadn't started yet, and I felt the same thing."

He nodded, remembering. "That's when I knew there was a chance you'd live."

My anger flared again. "And why you didn't care if Adam died."

"It's not that I didn't care," he said. "It was beside the point."

"Let me go. Please."

He did, but he also took my hands and held onto them firmly. "Okay? Can we do this?" His voice dropped. "You have to be brave. You have to be willing to see things other people can't and to know things other people don't. Can you do that? Can you be brave?"

I'd much rather curl up into a ball on my bed and clench my eyes shut and never leave my room again, but I knew it wasn't an option, so I nodded, and he nodded back, telling me I was doing the right thing. Then he pressed both his thumbs into my palms, and instantly my entire body relaxed, but then my eyes sank closed and I was thrown into the worst Insight yet.

•   •   •

The hospital room was built for one, but six beds have been shoved into it, all filled with patients. Swollen, painful-looking boils cover their faces and bodies. All are pale, with cracked lips and sunken cheeks.

Three are unconscious, and in fact might be dead, because they show no signs of labored breathing like the other three do. There's no pus or blood oozing from the lumps on their bodies like on the other three.

There are no curtains to provide privacy. No doctors. No nurses. No IVs hooked up to hydrate them. No monitors to track their vital signs. No electricity.

Two of the conscious patients groan constantly from the pain.

The other whimpers.

"Kendra," she mouths, barely able to speak through her weakness.

Her face is to the side. She's staring vacantly out the window.

"Kendra," she says again, and again, and again.

Nobody hears her. Nobody helps her. Nobody comforts her.

"Kendra," she says again and reaches toward the window, grasping for something that's not there.

My mother is in an abandoned hospital dying a horrible death, and she's calling for me, and I'm not there for her.

•   •   •

As suddenly as it began, it was over. I opened my eyes and saw Daemon had dropped my hands.

"What was *that?*" I said, as my entire body shook from the horror of what I'd just seen.

"That was your mother, dying."

Well, duh, I thought.

"I mean, what *was* it?"

"You read one of my Insights. One that's going to happen unless we figure out a way to stop it."

"We?"

"The choice for you couldn't be simpler: If you walk away—if you refuse to help—your mom dies."

"What could I possibly do to stop something like that? What even *was* it? What *caused* it? Why were so many people shoved into one hospital room, and why wasn't anyone helping them? It was like they were abandoned there."

"That's exactly what happens, because the medical system is

overrun by the disease that's going around. There aren't enough caregivers; half won't even come to work anymore because they're so afraid of getting sick themselves."

"But what is it? What's the disease?"

"That's what we don't know. We do know it's manmade. The disease—a biological weapon—somehow gets released, but we don't know how. We don't know what the disease is, how it gets released, how it spreads, or how to cure it, which is why we're trying so desperately to prevent the release of it in the first place. We need to stop it before it starts, because once it does, it's going to be out of control. It's going to be game over for life as we know it. We're talking millions of deaths here. Billions, actually."

I looked around the cramped, windowless office. I wanted desperately to get up and run away, only, of course, I couldn't run at the moment because of my injury, which Daemon had caused, allegedly—probably—to save my life. And I couldn't run away metaphorically because of my mom.

"When did you start having the Insight about my mom?"

"A few days ago."

"Are you part of the same group as Dr. Ridgeway?" Daemon nodded. "Did he know about it?"

"Yes," Daemon said. "I think that's probably why he handled your situation so poorly; he'd learned about my Insight immediately before you had yours of the solider. He really liked you guys, you and your mom. He was a bit emotional. A bit on edge. Feeling the urgency. He didn't handle himself as well as he usually did." He put his hand on my knee. "Hey, stop trembling."

I looked down at my body. I hadn't realized I was. It was more like twitching than trembling, though. Nervous twitching.

"Is there any way to stop it?" I said. "For it not to happen? For my mom not to die?"

"Of course," he said. "That's the whole point I'm trying to make. If you do your part, your mom will live."

"What's my part?"

"For now, it's just keeping yourself alive."

I swallowed hard. "How do I do that?"

"You come with me," he said.

I felt my heartbeat pulsing all the way into my brain like sometimes happened when I was sick. I hoped I wasn't about to faint.

"Where?" I said.

"We have something we call the Underground Railroad, which is a network of hideouts throughout the country. I'm going to take you right now and get you somewhere safe. In exchange, you'll need to share your Insights with us the instant you have them."

"Why am I in danger?"

"Because they know about you. Ridgeway's death confirms it."

"But I don't know anything! I don't know what any of this means!"

"But we do. Every Insight is like a piece of a puzzle we're trying to put together, and so while every Insight by itself might not make it obvious how it ties into the larger conspiracy, the more pieces we put together, the closer we get to figuring it out."

"I don't know why you haven't figured it out yet! You all don't seem very good at what you do!"

"That's because people like you keep dying." We both fell silent, until he asked, "Did he suffer?"

"Did who suffer?"

"Jonathan Ridgeway. I heard you had an Insight about his death. Did he suffer?"

"No." I shuddered, remembering how quietly the man snuck from the bushes, how efficiently he did his job. "Not at all. It happened so fast he didn't have time to be afraid."

Daemon nodded and looked relieved.

"The problem is I won't go anywhere without my mom."

"That's not a problem," he said. "We'll take her, too."

●　●　●

I had about a million more questions for Daemon before agreeing to go with him, but Matt burst into the office all red-faced and vicious, and I didn't get the chance.

"GET AWAY FROM HER!" he yelled at Daemon.

He moved as if to attack him, but Daemon quickly immobilized Matt, twisting his left arm harshly behind his back. Matt was a wrestler and typically hard to restrain, but he'd more than met his match with Daemon.

"Let him go!" I said. "He's my friend—stop it!" Instead, Daemon pulled his arm higher, and Matt winced. "I said stop!"

With the door to the office wide open, Daemon's boxing buddies gathered outside, curious to see what was happening and eager to jump into the brawl if the opportunity arose. I kicked the door shut. Unfortunately, I did it with my bad leg, which caused shooting pain.

"Daemon! Let him go." Finally, Daemon did, and I quickly placed myself between them, facing Matt. "Matt, I'm fine. Really, I am."

"You didn't answer my texts."

"I'm sorry. I should have. I was just . . ." How to explain? I stepped aside. "Matt, meet Daemon. Daemon, meet Matt."

Unsurprisingly, they didn't shake hands. Each stared at the other for a good long minute in what felt to me like a pissing contest.

"You were right about the accident," Matt said, his wary eyes not breaking from Daemon's. "He ran you off the road, didn't he? After stalking you at the party."

"He did, but it's not what you think. It's very strange and complicated, but I promise it's not what you think."

"Kendra, we need to go."

"She's not going anywhere with you," Matt snapped.

"We'll see about that." Daemon raised his eyebrows at me. "You ready?"

"I can't go with you."

"You don't have a choice."

"Like hell she doesn't!" Matt grabbed my arm and started pulling me to the door. "We're going straight to the cops."

"Wait, wait, wait!" I had to grip the doorway to keep Matt from pulling me through it. "Matt, listen. I need to talk to Daemon alone for a minute."

"Hell, no," he said.

"Just for one second." He stopped tugging at me and opened his mouth to say something, but fumbled with what to say. "Just one minute. Wait outside here, okay? I'm not going anywhere. I need to finish this conversation, and then you and I will leave together. All right? Okay? One minute."

I put my hand on his shoulder and guided him through the

door, which the others found amusing. I closed the office door and faced Daemon.

"I can't go with you right now," I said. "I need to talk with my mom before I agree to do anything."

Daemon's expression darkened. "You know who else wouldn't go with us because he wanted to talk to his family? Jonathan Ridgeway, and look what happened to him. You're not safe out there, Kendra. We're watching over you, we're doing what we can, but you're not entirely safe. You're not very well protected, and we shouldn't be spending our time looking out for you when we can put you somewhere safe. We have better things to do. You waste our time. That's all you've done for us so far, and we don't have time to waste. People die when you waste time arguing or questioning or running away from the hospital like a scared little girl."

"I am a scared little girl," I snapped.

"So grow up. We need you, and we need you alive. You play an integral role in how this all unfolds."

"What's my role?" I demanded. "Tell me or I walk out the door."

"You're there at the end," he said. "You defeat the bad guy. We win because of you."

I didn't intend to laugh, but I couldn't help it. Of all the crazy things I'd heard so far, that was the craziest.

"I'm not kidding," Daemon said, and his face indeed lacked humor. "Kendra, you're the hero of this whole damn thing."

    MATT POUNDED ON THE OFFICE DOOR.

"I called the cops!" he yelled. "Larson's on his way, and he's bringing a bunch of backup!"

"Damn it," Daemon said. "Your friend's an idiot."

"He's trying to protect me."

"He's going to get you killed. Be ready. We'll come for you later."

Daemon burst out of the office, shoved Matt aside, and ran for the door. Matt went after him but came back moments later, having been unable to catch him.

"He disappeared," he said. "His motorcycle's still out front, but he completely disappeared."

"It's Brookview," I said. "Downtown Brookview. How could he have disappeared?"

But he had. Larson arrived within minutes and sent patrol cars in search of Daemon, but they couldn't find him. I ended up in the alley, which was blockaded by patrol cars, with Matt and Detective Larson at my side like they'd been attached with Super Glue.

"You were supposed to wait for your mom." Larson's blue eyes were steely. Now that he knew I was okay, his concern had turned to badly repressed anger. "What do you think you're doing walking around town when there's very good evidence you're in danger?"

I shrugged. "It was a nice day. I wanted to walk."

"I'll take you home now."

"No thanks. Matt will give me a ride."

"No, Kendra. *I'm* taking you home."

Livid, I left the two of them and wandered over to Daemon's motorcycle. It was one of those made-for-speed kinds where the driver leaned far forward. *He saved me,* I thought, running my hand along the length of the seat. *He killed Adam, but he—no, that's not right. He didn't kill Adam; he just didn't save him.*

After briefly conferring with Matt, Larson came over.

"Kendra—"

"I'm an adult," I interrupted. "I'm an adult, and you're not my father, and unless I'm under arrest, you can't tell me what to do."

"What'd I do to make you so angry with me?"

"Nothing," I said. "You did nothing. I had to find Daemon. I had to get him to tell me what's going on. You did nothing! You're supposed to be the detective, aren't you? You should have known there was something going on with Dr. Ridgeway. You should have investigated him. You shouldn't have let him take me for an MRI when I didn't want to go. You basically let him kidnap me! You did nothing except stand by and watch my life fall apart. I can do that on my own, thank you very much."

"Matt says this guy stalked you at the party you were at before the accident. Is that true?"

"I don't want to talk about it."

"Then I *will* arrest you."

I laughed. "For what?"

"I'll come up with something."

"No, you won't," I said. "You'll do nothing like always."

With that, I called back to Matt. "You ready to go? I'm done here."

Matt headed over. "I'm ready if it's all right with Detective Larson."

"It's fine with Detective Larson."

Larson ignored me and spoke to Matt. "Be in touch and let me know when you've gotten her safely home."

"Yes, sir," Matt said.

"I knew he'd let me go," I said as we walked to Matt's car. "I knew he wouldn't do anything. He never does anything."

"He sent a SWAT team over to your house last night to protect you, and he got four patrol cars here within minutes of me calling him. What else are you expecting him to do? And he and I already talked about me taking you home while you were over by the motorcycle. I said I'd take you straight home and stay with you until your mom got home, if she wasn't there already. Larson said that was fine, as long as I stayed in touch. He's doing plenty from what I can see."

"Good to know whose side you're on."

"I didn't know there were sides."

"There are," I said, getting into his car and slamming the door. "Trust me, there are."

"Well, then I'm on your side." Matt got in, too, and waited until I looked at him. "I'm always on your side."

·   ·   ·

Matt didn't take me straight home. He fell silent as we inched our way out of the alley in his Camaro, the cops backing up their patrol cars to let us through.

"Thanks for coming to get me," I said once we were on the road. "I'm really sorry I didn't text you back." Not acknowledging what I'd said, he kept his eyes on the road and firmly off me, which was not typical Matt-like behavior. "You're mad at me, aren't you?"

"I'm worried," he said. "That *was* the guy who killed Adam, was it not?"

"Yeah, it was."

"What were you doing with him, huddled in a private little room with the door closed?"

I drew back, startled by the insinuation. "Excuse me?"

"Why didn't you call the cops the minute you saw him?"

"Because a lot's happened since you brought me home from the hospital yesterday."

He slid a glance my way. "Such as?"

I sighed. The thought of telling him exhausted me. "I'll tell you later, okay?"

"No, it's not okay."

I thought he was merely being argumentative, but when we got to the street where he was supposed to turn, he kept going.

"Uh, Matt?"

"We're making a detour."

I groaned. "I really just want to go home."

"We can't always get what we want, Kendra."

"But doesn't Larson want me going right home, too?"

"Since when do you care what Larson wants?"

He drove beyond my neighborhood, past the town limits, and as Brookview got farther away—as Matt drove up the highway in a direction I hadn't gone since *that night*—I didn't need to ask where we were going. I knew. He was taking me to the cemetery. He was taking me to Adam's grave.

"Matt, I don't want to," I said. "I'm not ready."

He slowed when the cemetery came up on the side of Highway 41, and he slowed further as he drove past the chapel and into the cemetery proper. He pulled the car to a stop near an area of new graves, turned off the ignition, got out, came around to my side, opened my door, and held out his hand.

"Come on," he said, firmly but gently.

Reluctantly, I let him help me out of the car. Arranged on a new mound were framed pictures of Adam, as well as notes, candles, and flowers—a mini-shrine to the golden-boy athlete. Until that moment, I'd been somewhat successful in pushing Adam out of my mind, but there, in the cemetery, there was no denying it. I felt it in every bone and in every ounce of blood: He'd been alive, and now he was dead.

"Like all the candles?" Matt asked, still holding my hand. "People from school did a couple vigils out here the first week or so after the funeral. I went to a couple."

"You didn't tell me."

"I was working through some things."

"Thank you." I squeezed his hand. "I know you didn't like him much."

We sat for awhile in the grass without talking, and the sounds of the cemetery became clear to me: A lawn mower, chirping birds in the old oak trees, an American flag flapping in the breeze. It felt ordinary and ancient, peaceful and calm—I guess the way a cemetery *should* feel. It smelled like fresh-mown grass and wet dirt and lilac trees. It smelled like life, not death.

"Why'd you bring me here?" I asked.

Matt's gaze lingered. "Do you miss Adam?"

"Obviously, things weren't great between us at the end, but I remember how he was when we first dated," I said. "He used to be happy, and I think he would have been again if he could have moved away to college and gotten on with his life without his parents messing things up for him. You know, swimming at the U of A, doing his own thing, but he'll never get to. I guess it's not so much that I miss him as I feel really bad—awful—he's never going to get that chance. He died unhappy, and that totally sucks."

I looked at the pictures people had left. There was one of me and Adam at winter formal, and seeing it made my heart smile and ache simultaneously. We'd only been dating a few months at that point, and Adam had color-coordinated the cummerbund on his tuxedo to match my red dress. Our relationship was fairly new and still so full of hope that Adam had even been willing to dance with me for more than just the slow songs. Unfortunately, that willingness hadn't lasted very long.

"I didn't like him," Matt said.

"I know."

"But I didn't want him to die."

"Of course," I said. "I know that."

He looked at me earnestly. "Kendra, I've got something to say, and I brought you here because I want you to understand how serious I am when I say it."

I looked away from him and pulled a few blades of grass from the ground, letting them fall from my hand after I'd yanked them free. "Okay?"

"Adam wouldn't want you hanging out with the guy who killed him."

"I wasn't *hanging out* with him!" I pulled more blades of grass and this time threw them at Matt. "I was *confronting* him."

"When I walked in, the room had this . . . I don't know . . . vibe. It was charged. Emotionally charged."

"That's because we were talking about some extremely serious things. And yeah, they were emotional things."

He looked hurt. "Like what?"

"I don't even know where to start."

"How about the beginning?"

"I think you're better off not knowing."

"No." He took my hand. "Listen, I can't stop thinking that I never should've let you leave the party that night. I never should've let you go."

"You couldn't have made me stay."

"Yeah, I could've."

"How?"

His blue eyes were dark that day, matching the navy in his T-shirt. "Maybe if I'd kissed you."

I felt my face redden. "I . . . I wouldn't have let you. I was with Adam, remember?"

"But would you have *wanted* to let me?"

I was tempted to say yes, and it would have been the truth, but I couldn't say it—not then, not there. "It's colossally bad timing to be having this conversation." I swept my free hand in the direction of Adam's grave while Matt held tight to the other one.

"I know," he agreed. "But I've been wanting to have this conversation with you for a long time now, even before the night of the party. I just . . . I worry we're going to miss our chance. You know how that happens sometimes? When two people have been friends for so long they can't make the leap to boyfriend and girlfriend?"

I nodded. "Yeah, I know how that works sometimes."

"Well, I don't want it to happen to us."

"I don't want it to happen to us, either, and I wish you'd made me stay that night, too. I can't even begin to tell you how much I wish you'd made me stay."

But you didn't, I thought, pulling my hand back. *And now look at things.*

WE LEFT THE CEMETERY SOON AFTER. I MANAGED TO AVOID telling him what had happened with Daemon by promising to tell him later once I'd had a chance to process it myself, and while he said it was okay, I could tell he was none too happy when he dropped me off at my house. I couldn't blame him for being mad at me—if I was him, I'd be mad at me, too.

My mom was there when I got home, but she'd gotten called back to work for that night. She'd been off since my accident, and the restaurant had been really nice to her, letting her take as much time as she needed, but that day the catering manager quit unexpectedly, and there was a wedding for two hundred people scheduled for that night. My mom was a chef, not a catering manager, but she'd done catering before so they begged her to come in and help.

I assured her I'd be fine at home alone. I tried to assure myself, too.

I had a sandwich for dinner, put on my pajamas, and cuddled in bed with Huckleberry, like old times. He and I liked to binge-watch TV shows on my Butler together, not that he actually watched. He just liked to be with me. As I flipped through the channels looking for something to watch, Jeff Meyers was on one of the news stations, so I paused to see why.

Each time he released a new product, he did the same sort of press conference. It was in an auditorium somewhere in California, and he wore his trademark jeans and white oxford shirt with the sleeves rolled up. His shirt was tucked in precisely, and his height and good posture gave him a strong stage presence. Reporters watched from their seats, and you could see they were as excited to be there as he was—especially after he made his big announcement: He was turning fifty, and he'd decided that instead of getting gifts himself, he wanted to give a gift to the American people—free Butler watches for everyone!

At first, I was stunned. They cost five hundred dollars apiece, and he was giving them away? And not the old model, either, but the new one he'd given me. It took a couple minutes, but then I realized the brilliance of the plan. Butler Systems got a cut of every single purchase made on them, not to mention whatever profit they made on the monthly service fees. With the watch giveaway, the first three months of service would be free, but after that, we'd be back to paying. If he raised the service fee by even one dollar per month, he'd stand to make several hundred *million* dollars more each and every month. Pure profit. And we'd happily pay, because the watches were so awesome and we'd gotten them for free.

I watched the rest of the news segment. Meyers introduced Brian McDouglas, his second-in-command, and then left the stage as Brian answered reporters' questions and explained how the giveaway would work. Butler Systems would roll out the giveaway the very next day, starting in the Midwest and expanding both east and west from there. Within a week, people across the entire country would have new watches. Trucks would be set up in the parking lots of all the major stores like Target and Walmart, as well as at grocery stores and shopping malls. People could drive or walk through the line, receive a watch from workers who'd hand them out from the back of the truck, and get help setting it up if needed from stations established nearby.

He broke out the order people would go: He explained that everyone must bring ID and arrive at a predetermined time, based on the first letter of their last name. I was sure it would be a nightmare of a process, but Brian said they'd modeled it, and if everyone went to the giveaway location nearest their houses at the right time, it should all flow fairly smoothly. There would be lines, but nothing worse than the ones on Black Friday. If you didn't go on the day they were in your neighborhood, you could still get a watch inside the respective stores.

I spent the next hour flipping channels, watching everything I could about the giveaway. All of social media was on fire, too, with hashtags like #jeffmeyersisawesome and #jeffmeyersforpresident and #cantwaitformynewbutler.

I finally tired of it and decided to watch *Lost In America*, the reality show I'd been watching before I went to the hospital. Producers gave contestants a certain amount of money and a destination to reach. The goal was to get there before a team of private detectives caught them; basically, it was a high-tech game of hide-and-seek. It was super fun to see what mistakes the contestants made and to say, *If it were me . . .*

It was also amazing how easily they were tracked down. I didn't realize it until I started watching the show, but it had become nearly impossible to get lost on purpose. I was into the show's second season, and only one set of contestants had made it to their destination. There were few places to hide from all the technology in our lives. In fact, the first thing contestants always did was to remove their Butlers; not to do so would have been game-show suicide. Even so, they were often captured on surveillance video and identified by facial recognition software.

The episode I watched that night was about a boyfriend-girlfriend couple in college trying to make it to Billings, Montana, starting from Pittsburgh, Pennsylvania. They were given a Ford Focus (obviously product placement), a thousand dollars cash, and a credit card with a thousand-dollar limit.

In a move I thought was pretty smart, they went to Walmart and made a deal with another customer to charge his items in exchange for him charging some of theirs, to hide their purchases from the detectives. What the detectives would see when they reviewed the transaction was a bunch of diapers, DVDs, gardening supplies, socks, heavy coats, and random groceries. What they wouldn't see was how the team got backpacks, sleeping bags, and bicycles. They also bought two jerry cans for gasoline storage. With the remaining balance on the credit card, they bought ammunition so they could resell it somewhere when they needed more cash. *Very smart*, I thought.

After that, they went to a gas station and filled the jerry cans with enough gas to get them probably halfway to their destination. Then they drove to the student union of their college and looked on the ride-share bulletin board. They found a listing where someone had a car, was driving to Denver, wanted to share gas, and had room for their bikes. From a borrowed Butler phone, they arranged with the guy to leave the next day and then spent the night in the university library, which was open twenty-four hours. *All very smart*, I thought, with the possible exception of leaving their car parked in the university parking lot, because I was pretty sure all universities had cameras these days that could read license plates.

But that's not what got them caught.

They got caught because once they were on the road, the girl asked the driver to send a Butler message to her mom to tell her she was okay, and the detectives, who'd somehow accessed her mom's communication records, tracked down the location of the Butler that had made the contact—heading west on Interstate 80 toward Denver. The detectives flew ahead, set up surveillance at a rest stop, and waited for them to drive by. When they did, the detectives followed and caught them the next time they took a bathroom break at a McDonald's off the highway.

Note to self, I thought: *If you really want to disappear, you have to cut all ties with the people you leave behind.*

The second episode had just begun when Huckleberry jolted up and started barking like crazy. He jumped off my bed and raced from my room. I followed and found him practically body-slamming into the patio door that led from the kitchen to the backyard. I unlatched it for him, and he raced outside. Within seconds, he fell eerily silent.

"Huck?" I called.

No answer. I stepped onto the patio and glanced around the yard, but it was pitch black because the moon was hiding behind a cloud. I flicked on the outside light, but it didn't go on. I looked closer and saw the bulb was missing. I knew the chill I felt wasn't from the hot summer night; it was from my instinctive, prickling fear.

"Huckleberry!" I called. "Come here, boy!"

Nothing.

"Huck? Did you find a dead bird or something?" I forced my voice to be light, even though my yard suddenly felt like a black hole that would swallow me up if I went too far into it, like it already might have swallowed up my dog. I took a step deeper into the yard, and another, and another, until I was around the corner where the backyard turned into the side yard, and once there, I saw the reason for Huck's silence.

A man was squatting in front of my dog, head bent, offering him food from his hand.

My heart lurched. "Who's there?"

The figure looked up. My heart lurched again when I saw it was Daemon.

"Dog treats." He stood, wiping his hands on his jeans. "A burglar's best friend."

"Are you here to burgle me?"

He stepped toward me. "You know I'm not."

We locked eyes, and I cursed the closeness I already felt with him after only one conversation.

"I found your guy," he said as Huckleberry looked up at him eagerly, wagging his tail, hoping for more treats.

"Huckleberry, come here." I scooped him up. "What guy?"

"The guy from your Insight. The soldier."

It took a moment to process. "How is that possible?"

"Because when you were reading my Insight this morning, I was reading yours. You need to come with me and meet him. He's got a story you'll want to hear."

"I can't." The idea of meeting someone I'd seen blown to bits in my dreams was way too strange. I wondered if that's why Daemon always looked at me with such intensity—after all, he'd seen me die. It must have been a constant shock for him to see me alive.

"I'll have you back before your mom gets home," Daemon said. "She'll never even know you were gone."

"She'll be home any minute."

"Nice try. She won't be home before midnight."

"And you know that how?"

"Really? We need to have this conversation? You should assume anything you say or do is being monitored, both by us and by the other side." He pressed a couple buttons on his watch, held it up, and showed me a perfect view of my bedroom. "Butlers have a glitch in them—an on-purpose glitch—that regular people don't know about. If activated, it can stream a feed to a Command Center far, far away. So as you were watching your reality show, I was watching you. Or I would've been if I hadn't been busy with Russell Hendricks."

So much for being alone, ever.

"Russell Hendricks?" I said.

"Your soldier."

"So he's alive? Really?"

"He's alive, but I want you to see for yourself, so let's go." He gestured toward the blackest part of my backyard. "My motorcycle's parked a couple streets over."

"I'm *not* getting on your motorcycle."

"Listen, we don't have time to go back and forth on this. You need to meet him."

"How did you find him? My Insight didn't have enough information to track him down."

"I was able to see things in your Insight you're not able to yet. Once you get a little more skilled, you can learn to maneuver around inside them and see things from different perspectives. You can even go back in time and see what led up to the moment of the Insight. It's a pretty useful skill once you figure out how to do it."

"How do you do it?"

"I'll show you, but we don't have time right now. I really need to get this guy underground."

"What did he say when you found him?"

"Put it this way: He wasn't at all surprised people would be trying to kill him. He knew right away what it was about."

"And?"

"And he'll tell you, but you need to hurry. His wife and kid are already safe, but this guy's not until I get him off-grid. Every minute we delay is a minute closer they are to finding him."

You may not go with him, said the common sense side of me. *You may not ride off on a motorcycle with a stranger—especially this particular stranger. You may not, Kendra. You may not!*

But the image of the soldier's death had been haunting me for days. I had to know; I had to see for myself he was still alive. I had to see if Daemon could really do what he said he'd done. If he could, it was a game changer.

"I'll put the dog inside," I said.

"You might want to put some clothes on, too." I looked down, suddenly embarrassed by the thin pajamas I wore. "And shoes, too, unless you want to ride barefoot on the motorcycle, which I don't recommend."

He waited outside while I took Huckleberry inside and got dressed in my bathroom where there were no Butlers. As I did, I thought about my mom. She had strictly forbidden me from riding motorcycles, and I very seldom disobeyed her, but this felt like another world I was entering into—one where none of the old rules applied.

I came back out and locked the patio door behind me. "I need to be home way before midnight."

"No time to waste, then, Cinderella. This way." Daemon led me through a bunch of backyards that just so happened to follow the identical path I always took when going to Nora's house.

"How do you know this route?" I asked.

"It's the path you took to your friend's house the night of the party, isn't it?"

"Yeah, but you're not supposed to know that."

"Must I say it again?" He gave me a mocking smile. "We know everything."

"Yeah, well, that's creepy."

"I agree," he said. "But it might just save your life one day."

His motorcycle was parked a few houses up from Nora's, and when we got to it, he handed me a helmet. I struggled with getting it on right, and after he helped push it down, I felt like an alien with a too-big head. He lent me an arm for balance as I climbed onto the back of the seat, and then he got on after me.

"Hang on," he instructed.

Well, duh, I thought. I was thankful to be wearing jeans, even though I knew that if we crashed, scraped knees would be the least of my problems. My mom's doctor friend had told me once the shorthand lingo for motorcyclists in ER rooms was motor donors, since so many motorcycle victims died from their injuries that— bright side—their various organs were often harvested for people who needed transplants.

I wrapped my arms around Daemon as if my life depended on him, which it did.

It was not a fact I found reassuring.

THE MOTORCYCLE RIDE WAS QUICK. WE DIDN'T HAVE FAR TO go, and about all I can say is it was a lot like Daemon himself: A dangerous thrill that was oddly compelling, even as you knew it was bad for you—even as you knew you should stay away.

I felt like the world was big and we were small. Like we could ride all night and zoom from one side of the country to the other. Best of all, I felt like we were invisible. For our short ride, I forgot about the danger and relished the rest of it.

Daemon drove to downtown Brookview. He went through the same alley as the boxing gym but a couple blocks further and pulled into an open garage. I climbed off the motorcycle, took off my helmet, and looked around. The old garage had rotten wood and slanted in places it shouldn't, with a manual garage door Daemon brought down as soon as he got off his bike.

"You okay?" he asked.

"I'm fine," I said, although I realized I'd done it again: Gone off with a stranger to a place where no one would know to look for me. This time, I didn't even have a cell phone. I was the dumb girl from every horror movie I'd ever seen.

"This way," he said.

The side door led from the garage to a small backyard belonging to a little brick house with painted trim that had seen far better days. But instead of going into the house like I expected, we went down a flight of cracked concrete steps to a basement entrance with a solid steel door.

"Is this where you live?" I asked.

Daemon shook his head. "It's where I put Russell for the time being."

"Russell," I said, just to hear his name out loud again and help associate it to the face from my Insight. "Where does he go from here?"

"Like you, he'll go for a ride on the Underground Railroad."

"Underground Railroad," I said. "That's so Harriett Tubman of you."

"Isn't it?"

"I'm not going tonight, though," I said. "I'm not going without my mom."

"So you keep saying."

The damp basement had low, black metal beams that barely held the house at bay. It smelled of cobwebs, and I had the icky sensation that rats or bats might come at me any second. The only light was moonlight from an open crank window encased by security bars. Standing in the moonlight was the thick-necked soldier from my Insight with his military-grade haircut, alive and in person. His hair was as blond as Daemon's was dark.

"Hi, Kendra. I'm Russell Hendricks. It's great to meet you." He stood with the posture of an off-duty soldier but spoke as if I were a well-liked sister.

"It's great to meet *you*." I couldn't stop staring at him. My

Insight had been so real—realer than real—and it was hard to reconcile the image I still had of him, brains blown out, with the
perfectly whole and living man before me.

"I hear I owe you my life." He came over and took my hands in
his. His were the sort that could have crushed mine with one little
squeeze, and he was definitely the kind of muscled guy you'd want
on your side in a fight, even more so than Daemon, whose build
was certainly sturdy but not the size of a super-hero. "Thank you.
I'm your loyal soldier for life."

Without meaning to, I giggled. I'd never had a loyal soldier
for life before. "Uh, well, really, it was Daemon. He's the one who
found you."

"Enough with the love fest, people. We don't have much time."
Daemon came close, and Russell let go of my hands. "Russell, I
want you to tell Kendra what you told me, all except for the parts
I told you not to mention."

"I want to know everything," I said. "I *deserve* to know
everything."

"I know you think you do, and maybe you're right, but there
are certain things you can't know yet," Daemon said. "And I know
it's going to piss you off, but that's too bad. Let's not waste time
arguing about it. Russell, the sooner you talk, the sooner I can
deliver you to your wife and kid."

Russell gave me an apologetic look. "My hands are tied. If I
don't stick to the script, he could keep me from my wife and baby,
and he's said as much."

"Yeah, he's a real nice guy that way. It's fine," I said, although it
was anything but. "Can we turn on a light or something? It's creepy
down here."

"It's better not to," Daemon said.

"Not even one lone dangling light bulb like in the movies?" I said, because it was that sort of basement.

Russell noticed my unease. "Here, why don't you have a seat?" He pointed to one of two folding metal chairs. "Daemon told me about your accident. I'm glad you're okay."

"It wasn't an accident," I said. "Daemon ran me and my boyfriend off the road on purpose, and he killed my boyfriend."

"I love how she neglects to mention I was trying to save her life, which I did," Daemon said.

"How'd you do that?" Russell asked.

"Short story: I had an Insight about her like she had about you."

"Is that why she has Insights?" Russell asked. "Because she was supposed to die but didn't?"

"That's right," said Daemon. "She beat her destiny, but it comes at a price."

"Will I have Insights now, too?"

Daemon reached and touched his shoulder. Neither flinched. "No. Not everybody does, but don't worry. We'll find other ways for you to be useful. For now, clue Kendra in on the parts I told you to."

"Okay." Russell sat in the chair opposite me, flipping it around to sit on it backwards in a way men sometimes do but women never do. "Up until very recently, I worked for a private security firm, Edgewater. Have you heard of it?"

I shook my head, no.

"It's mostly made up of ex-military—I'm former Delta—and we protect oil fields, expensive equipment and property, that sort of thing. Another one of the functions we perform is providing security for high-end clients. That's what I've been doing, ever since I got shot up in North Africa. Now, my most recent client's got lots of weird habits, which is common with the super-rich. He's quite paranoid, and he does *not* want to engage with the riff-raff. That would be you and me and basically ninety-nine-point-nine percent of the population. He doesn't even want to breathe the same air, and I mean that literally. He's got oxygen purifiers running at all his properties, filtering out particles that people like us don't think twice about."

"Who's your client?" I asked.

"He's not going to tell you," Daemon said. He'd been pacing around the basement in what felt to me like a random maze pattern. Every so often, he'd stop abruptly and turn a different way, whether there was something blocking his path or not. "It's outside the scope of what you need to know right now. Russell, continue."

"My client's dying, anyway, even with all his obsession about health," Russell said. "He's got a fatal illness, and although he's not quite in his final stages, he's struggling and definitely on the decline. The other night, he had a medical emergency while I was on duty. He hit his panic button, and that's when things got weird."

"Weird how?" I said.

"Well, for one thing, he's got his private master suite and nobody's allowed in—even if his family enters, we're supposed to treat them like intruders, and, trust me, we don't treat intruders well. At the same time, we need to be able to get to him within seconds if needed, so we stay overnight in a little room right behind his suite that has an access door, but we're only allowed to go in if specifically summoned or if we're doing our drills, such as what to do if there's a kidnapping attempt or other need to flee, and—"

"Tell Kendra what you'd do in that situation," Daemon said. "If you needed to flee."

"He's got an underground tunnel that runs from right below his bedroom to outside his property a good few acres away. The tunnel's tall enough to stand up straight, and it's encased in concrete. There's food and water stored there in case we need to hunker down for a period of time. We do a practice run extricating him every other week. We've got it down to clockwork."

"How do you access it from the bedroom?" Daemon said.

"Through a closet that's right next to his vault. It's got stairs leading to the tunnel."

"Vault?" I said.

"His whole suite's basically a panic room. And his vault is like a steel-encased office—a panic room within a panic room. I'm telling you, the guy's obsessed with privacy."

"What's in the vault?" I asked, fascinated.

"No one knows," Russell said. "To the best of my knowledge, no one except him has ever been inside it or even seen the door open."

"Is he married?" I wanted to know.

"He is, but they maintain separate lives. Definitely separate bedrooms. His wife lives in the background. She's nice."

"He's not?"

"Not so much. He's all right, but—" He shrugged. "No, to be honest, I hate him. He's a complete narcissist. I mean, if you had this great fear of being kidnapped and went to the trouble and expense of building a full-size tunnel underneath your property and had your security team practice with *you* every other week, don't you think you'd make provisions for your family? He doesn't. They're not part of the drills. There's a procedure for us to go get them and take them to safety, but they're more of an afterthought. We don't actually practice it with them like we do with him, which to me says something."

"It says he's a complete jerk," I said.

"Exactly," he agreed. "In any case, we're supposed to be able to get to his room within seconds. He's got a panic button, and we—security—sleep in that little room directly behind his suite that I described. We have a key, but that night, he had both doors to the room triple-bolted, so I was unable to get in. I actually had to climb through the ductwork overhead and drop into his room through the ceiling." He laughed. "You should have seen his eyes bulge when I dropped down. Thankfully, I fell onto his bed—which he wasn't in. He was collapsed on the floor in front of his vault, yanking at this gold chain around his neck. Shows how important that vault is. If you were having problems breathing, wouldn't you have gone for your oxygen tank instead?"

Daemon pivoted and faced Russell. "You didn't mention the gold chain before. Describe it, and why was he pulling on it?"

Russell shrugged. "There's not much to mention. It's a standard gold chain. Went down to about here." He touched his sternum. "It had a pendant on it, which was bullet-shaped, but it looked like it was also a capsule, like you could twist it open."

"Was he trying to open it?" Daemon wanted to know. "Had you ever seen it before?"

Russell thought back. "No and no. He was trying to yank it off like it was choking him or something, but, of course, it wasn't. I think he was having trouble breathing and wasn't thinking straight. He *definitely* wasn't thinking straight, because we have oxygen and a defibrillator and a protocol for every possible situation that might come up, and he's a stickler for following protocol, but that night, he refused to follow his own protocol, which, in this case, would have been for me to administer oxygen and call his personal physician and instruct our security people to be on call to transport him to the hospital if necessary."

"You're all medically trained?" Daemon asked.

"Of course. We've all had basic EMT training plus whatever we each individually obtained in the military, which in my case is pretty extensive."

"Who's his personal doc, by the way?" Daemon asked.

"A guy named Benjamin Hardy, but he insisted on calling Karnow, his lawyer."

It was a familiar name to Daemon. "Phillip Karnow?"

Russell nodded. "A real prick. I got him on the line and introduced myself. Told him my client wasn't feeling well and insisted I call him rather than his doctor or an ambulance, at which point, Karnow instructed me to put my client on the phone and leave the room. I refused, because my client was clearly in distress—definitely having trouble breathing, and clutching my wrist like he needed me there and wanted me there. I was trying to administer oxygen, and I wasn't going to leave. The bastard said I was signing my own death warrant." He smiled wryly. "Turns out, he was right about that."

"Go on," Daemon said.

"So I'm on the phone with Karnow, and I handed my client the phone. It was a short conversation. I don't know what Karnow said, but I believe—and this is only a guess—my client provided him with the code to get into the vault and then a second code. I thought possibly it's a computer password, if there's a computer inside the vault, which there very well might be. I'm sure he's got a full office setup in there."

"Tell Kendra the codes."

"The first one was eight, three, six . . . something," Russell said. "I can't recall the last digit."

Daemon looked at me. "Tell me back the code Russell just told you."

"Oh!" I'd been so fascinated by Russell's story that I hadn't paid strict attention to the details. "Um. Eight. Three. Something. Something. Why do I need to know it?"

"Eight. Three. Six. Something. Try again."

"Eight. Three. Six. Something," I said. "But, again, why do I need to know this?"

"Russell, what was the second code?"

"*One hundred years from now,* all one word. Spelled out, first letter capitalized, if that matters, which it probably does, since he made a point of telling Karnow that."

"Kendra, repeat that code."

"A hundred years from now, all one word."

"*One* hundred years from now," Daemon corrected.

"One hundred years from now."

"All one word, capital 'O,' *one hundred* spelled out in letters, not the number."

"Yeah, I got it."

He raised an eyebrow. "Just repeat both codes."

I exhaled strongly to show my frustration. "Eight. Three. Six.

Something. *Onehundredyearsfromnow,* all spelled out in letters, no numbers, and no spaces between the words."

"Excellent," Daemon said. "Russell, what happened after your client gave the codes?"

"I could tell he immediately felt better. The oxygen helped, of course, and he got his color back, but I think it was more from relief at having shared the codes than anything. Something had him spooked, and he was afraid of dying without telling Karnow his codes. He's got something in that vault that can't die with him. Anyway, I helped him back to bed and then got back on the phone with Karnow, who instructed me to stay with him the rest of the night. He said I was to forget the episode ever happened. I wasn't to file an incident report with Edgewater, which is standard protocol when anything out of the ordinary happens. If someone sneezes weird, we write up an incident report."

"Did you do what he said?" I asked.

"I did not," Russell said. "I don't work for him. And I don't work for my client, either. I work for Edgewater—*worked* for Edgewater—and Edgewater policy is to write up an incident report for situations like this. And so I did."

"You're a good soldier," Daemon said without admiration. "Okay, Kendra, you've heard all you need to hear. Let's get you home."

"But there's obviously more to the story," I said. "What happened after that?"

"We ended up here," Daemon said. "That's the short version."

"But—"

"But nothing. Russell needs to get underground."

Russell stood and extended a hand to help me up. "I can't thank you enough. I've got a new little baby, and—" He stopped, cleared his throat, and squeezed my hand. "If I can ever repay the favor, I absolutely will. You can count on me."

"Let's hope you don't have to."

"It would be my honor."

·   ·   ·

Daemon took me back then, the same way we came, and thankfully I got back home before my mom. I made sure to be in bed by the time she arrived so I wouldn't have to lie to her about what I'd done and where I'd gone that night.

Sleeping well was a thing of the past for me, so I tossed and turned all night. I kept trying to visualize the man Russell had talked about. Was he old? Young? Short? Tall? He was sick, I knew that much. And a jerk, I knew that, too. I also tried to imagine what the Underground Railroad was like. I doubted it was really underground, but how extensive was it? Would my mom and I be safe there, from both the bad guys and the virus?

On and on, my mind churned through what I'd learned so far. It felt like I'd just fallen asleep when my mom woke me early the next morning.

"Detective Larson's here," she said, and I groaned. "He wants to talk with you. He seems upset, and he said it's urgent."

"Ugh." I pushed off my covers. "All right. Tell him I'll be out as soon as I'm dressed."

"You should probably hurry."

Quickly, I used the bathroom, brushed my teeth, and threw on some clothes. As I did, my mind raced trying to figure out why he was here. I headed to the living room and stopped short when I saw the look on his face.

"What's wrong?" I said.

His eyes locked on mine. "We should talk. Outside."

That set off a warning bell. As we all headed to the back patio, my mom lingered behind to get coffee for herself and Detective Larson. The instant he and I were outside and Larson had slid closed the patio door behind us, he gripped my arm.

"Kendra, listen—this is urgent. What do you know about a man named Russell Hendricks?"

My knees nearly gave out, and Larson gripped my arm harder at the same time I tried to pull away. He watched me carefully.

"Nothing," I said shakily, knowing it hadn't come out as nonchalantly as I'd intended. "Who's Russell Hendricks?"

"You really don't know?"

"Can you let go of my arm, please?"

He did, and I headed toward the patio table, both to buy myself time to think and so he couldn't see my shock. *How could he possibly know about Russell Hendricks?*

"Maybe this will help." Larson pulled up a photo on his Butler and walked over to show it to me. "Does this man look familiar?"

I had no answer for him. Of course the man looked familiar. It was Russell, whom I'd been with less than twelve hours earlier. But I wasn't about to tell him that.

"Why would he?"

"Is this the soldier from your dream?"

"How did you get this picture?"

Before he could answer, we heard a rush of cars pull to the curb in front of my house. They came fast and stopped hard. A multitude of car doors opened and closed. It was very much like the other night when Larson and his men had come to protect us. Only this time, it wasn't Larson and his men.

"Follow my lead," Larson said. "Be very careful in what you say."

"What's happening? Who is it?"

There were yells.

Heavy footsteps ran toward us.

"Detective Larson?"

His look was grim. "These are not people to mess with."

My mom came to the doorway, holding a mug of coffee in each hand.

Then they were in the backyard—men, men, and more men—surrounding us from every side. They were dressed in black SWAT attire, and they all had guns.

It was the men from my Insight, the same men who would have killed Russell Hendricks if Daemon hadn't rescued him.

They came after me instead.

MY MOM DROPPED THE MUGS OF COFFEE. I FROZE IN MY chair and stared at the incongruous sight. The sky was blue; our lawn was green; our daffodils and irises and peonies were a plethora of summer colors—and then there was the black. Men in black, with black guns. They trampled our lawn and kicked through our flower garden in their rush to surround us.

Within seconds, fifteen men encircled us from a distance of twenty yards. Down the block, a lawnmower hummed gratingly while there, in my yard, fifteen rifles were simultaneously cocked and aimed—at me.

Detective Larson gestured downward to his badge, which he always wore face out on his belt, and shouted, "I'm Detective Robert Larson with the Brookview Police Department. Identify yourselves!"

The men kept their rifles aimed on us as another man came around the corner of the yard and strode directly to Larson. He was the taller and older of the two, with black-grey hair and eyes so brown they might as well have been black. He held out his hand, and after a split-second surprised reaction, Larson accepted his handshake.

"I'm Commander Louis Gardiner with the ITB, North American Division," the man said. "You're Detective Larson with Brookview PD?"

"I am," Larson confirmed.

"I spoke with your CO earlier today. I'm going to have to ask you to surrender your weapon." My heart caved as Larson obediently did as he asked. Gardiner then turned his attention to me. "This is the girl?"

"This is Kendra Sinclair, yes." Larson cleared his throat. "I was in the process of questioning her about Russell Hendricks. The chief asked me to after he spoke with you."

Gardiner eyed me. "Where's Hendricks?"

I withered in my seat. My heart pounded too hard; I couldn't reply. These were the men who would have killed Russell—would they kill me?

"I don't know," I whispered.

"Where's Hendricks?" Gardiner said again.

My mom finally kicked into gear. She stepped over the broken coffee mugs, rushed over, and planted herself between Gardiner and me. "You do *not* talk to my daughter! I do *not* give you permission!"

"With all due respect, ma'am, I don't need your permission." Right away, Gardiner must have realized that wasn't a winning approach with a protective mother, because he changed his tone to a friendlier one. "Listen, I'm sorry for the guns-drawn greeting. We had to make sure you were safe and the scene was safe. Kendra's in quite a bit of danger, and we're trying to protect her."

"From?"

"From a monster on the loose."

"No monsters here," she said. "Not until you came, anyway. Tell your men to lower their weapons—this instant."

Gardiner motioned the order. His men complied, and then he tried again. "Now, Kendra," he said, looking at me over my mom's shoulder. "Where is he? And don't bother lying, because—"

"Don't you dare call my daughter a liar!"

Impatience set in on Gardiner's face. "Ma'am, step aside."

"I will not."

Gardiner next addressed Larson. "We can do this the easy way or the hard way. I was hoping to do it the easy way."

"Get off my property," my mom said.

"Now, Susan—" Larson began.

"I have no time for this." Gardiner grabbed my mom's arm, spun her around, and snapped flexible black handcuffs on her. Instinctively, I leapt to protect her, but Gardiner shoved me back so hard I tumbled to the ground. Larson stood and watched uselessly from the side. He was doing it again: Nothing.

"Take her away," Gardiner said of my mom, and two men came and got her.

"You can let me go," she said, looking skittish and afraid. "I promise I won't cause a scene."

"Too late." Gardiner looked at me. "Your mother is going to wait in the car. Maybe that will inspire you to be more cooperative."

As the men dragged her away, she yelled she wanted a lawyer, but it was obvious that wasn't going to happen. As they went around the corner of the house, I saw my next-door neighbor's curtain quickly pulled back from its peeking position, and I was glad to know Mr. Swanson was witnessing what was happening.

Larson helped me to my feet.

"Why aren't you doing anything?" I hissed. "Why are you letting this happen?"

"Follow my lead," he said.

"What lead? You're just standing there!"

I brushed myself off and glared at Gardiner. As he looked me up and down, I felt his eyes judging me, taking in my bare feet, uncombed hair, and flimsy spaghetti-strapped sundress.

"You have about thirty seconds to tell me where Russell Hendricks is," he said. "Make it ten."

"First off, I don't even know *who* Russell Hendricks is," I said.

"You don't mind if we search your house, do you?"

"Of course I mind."

He gestured for four of his men to search our house. Huckleberry had been barking frantically since the men arrived, and his barking escalated as the men went inside. Then I heard a wounded squeal. I started inside, but Gardiner grabbed me.

"I'm *getting* my dog. One of your stupid men obviously kicked him, and I'm not saying a word to you until I know he's okay."

As I was saying that, one of the men inside the house slid open the patio door to allow Huckleberry outside. He slinked through it and raced over to me. I was relieved to see he wasn't limping. When he got to me, he growled and barked at Gardiner, who still had me by the arm.

"Come here, puppy." Gardiner let me go, and I scooped up Huckleberry. "Are you okay? Did those bad men hurt you? They're mean, aren't they? Yes, they are. Such horrible people."

"Enough cooing at your dog," he said. "What will it take for you to understand how serious I am?"

I knew how serious he was; I just didn't know what to do about it. Weren't Daemon's people supposed to be watching me? Shouldn't they be coming to my rescue right about now? I had the distinct feeling I was going to have to save myself. But how? By half-truths? Outright lies? Deceit and manipulation? Any and all of the above, I decided.

"I don't know where Russell Hendricks is," I said. "I didn't even know *who* he was until Detective Larson showed me his picture about three seconds before you showed up. And, yeah, he's the man from my dream, but I have no idea where he is."

"I think you do," Gardiner said. "Where did you go last night?"

I reeled at his words. They really *were* watching me. "Nowhere."

"You left your home last night for over an hour. Where did you go? Back to the boxing gym?"

They knew about the boxing gym?

"If you know I left my house, then why don't you know where I went?"

"Just answer my question."

"You answer mine."

But I didn't need him to. I knew from what Daemon told me the previous night they had the ability to spy on us through our Butlers. Dr. Ridgeway destroyed my watch, but we still had a Butler hanging on our living room wall.

"I've never heard of the ITB," I said. "What is it?"

"The International Terrorism Bureau."

"Is that part of Homeland Security?"

"We're a separate entity," he said. "More global in nature."

"I don't understand why you're here."

"Governor Rhodes reported your remarkable ability to Homeland Security, who passed the information up to us, and we've been watching you ever since."

Thanks a lot, Governor Rhodes, I thought. "Why would he do that?"

"Because it's his responsibility to protect the homeland."

"I'm not a threat to the homeland," I scoffed. "Are you kidding me?"

"You must understand there are people who would seek to exploit your talent for their own nefarious reasons, such as the man you met with yesterday upon leaving the police station. Goes by the name of Martin Putnam, and Daemon Godwin, and numerous other aliases."

"I don't know what you're talking about," I said, not very convincingly. I squeezed my dog closer, trying to calm my frantic heart.

"Why are you so reluctant to talk?" Gardiner towered over me, trying to intimidate me. "I have your mother in my custody. I have guns pointed at you. When people point guns at you, you should talk. Do you really want to be on my bad side? Take a minute to think about that."

He moved away, out of my line of hearing, and spoke into his military-grade walkie-talkie. Clearly, he was consulting someone, trying to decide what to do with me. In the meantime, the guns stayed aimed at me.

"You should tell him what you know," Larson whispered.

"Are you one of them?" I asked. "Is this you playing good cop to his bad cop?"

"No!" His face reddened. "How could you think that? I'm on your side, Kendra."

"Then step up," I said. "Help me get out of this."

"The best way to do that is by telling him what you know."

"I'm not going to tell him anything."

"I think that's a mistake. You want to be on the right side of whatever's going on."

"Gardiner and his people are the ones who murdered Russell Hendricks in my Insight," I said. "They didn't arrest him. They didn't read him his rights or question him. He opened his front door, and they executed him. There's no way Gardiner's on the right side."

"My only concern is for your safety."

"So you keep saying."

Gardiner finished up his discussion, returned his walkie-talkie to his waistband holster, and came back over.

"Here's the deal," he said. "I contacted Governor Rhodes and explained our predicament and asked him what he thought I should do." My stomach sank because I felt like I was about to learn something very bad about Governor Rhodes, but Gardiner surprised me. "He said I should let your mother go and leave the two of you alone."

"Excellent!" I said. "You shouldn't have—"

"However, I'm not going to do that," Gardiner continued. "I *am* going to leave, but I'm going to take your mother with me, and once you deliver Russell Hendricks to me, I'll deliver your mom back to you."

"You can't—! You can't do that! That's kidnapping!"

He smiled. "I prefer to call it leverage."

"Please! Let her go!" I handed off Huckleberry to Detective Larson. "Listen, I don't know where Russell is, but I'll find out and tell you. I can do that. I can find out for you."

Ignoring me, Gardiner gestured for his men to circle back to the cars. At the same time, the men who'd searched my house came out empty-handed. Gardiner gestured for them to head out, too, leaving just him, me, Larson, and my dog.

"Go put the dog in the house," Gardiner ordered Larson, who complied without hesitation. Once Larson was out of earshot, Gardiner leaned close and gave me a threatening look.

"I don't know what you think you know, but let me tell you—"

He jolted backward and then pressed his hand against his shoulder. Blood oozed out through his fingers.

"Get down!" Larson yelled, and I threw myself to the ground.

Gardiner, however, turned and ran toward the cars up front, still pressing his hand to his shoulder to hold in the blood.

"Let's go, let's go, let's go!" he yelled as he ran.

I scrambled to my feet and raced after him. "Wait! Stop! My mom!"

I got to the front yard in time to see him dive into the back seat of the front car, which then sped off. The second car contained my mom, and it raced off, too.

I chased them down the street, but there was no way I could catch up.

Gardiner might have been shot, but he still had my mom.

He must have known: I'd do anything to get her back.

LESS THAN AN HOUR LATER, DETECTIVE LARSON PULLED UP to the rotunda of the State Capitol, turned off his police cruiser, and faced me.

"Are you *sure* you don't want me to come in?" he said, not for the first time.

"I'm sure. You've done enough." *Not.* He'd let Gardiner and his men onto our property and then stood by and did nothing while they terrorized us. He'd let them take my mom. He hadn't even been able to find the person who'd shot Gardiner.

"I'll wait here, then, and drive you back."

"I don't need you to," I said. "I'll figure it out myself."

"Kendra, how? Seriously, I—"

I got out and slammed the car door. Maybe I should have been grateful that he'd quickly gotten in touch with the head of Governor Rhodes's security detail and explained my urgent need to see the governor, but I was too mad to thank him for that or for the ride. As I walked away, he lowered the passenger window.

"I'll be right here!" he called.

I kept walking, and for the first time ever upon stepping into the Capitol rotunda, I didn't stop to marvel at the gorgeous marble, soaring ceilings, or the curved dome. I was on a mission.

I zigzagged my way through the numerous families with little kids running around pointing up to the super-high, curved ceiling and getting basically nothing out of their visit except the joy of hearing their voices echo back to them; fancy-dressed people criss-crossing the rotunda on their way to or from something important; and foreign tourists taking bunches of pictures. Someone asked if I'd take a picture of their group, but I waved them off and made my way over to the security checkpoint, where my name was on a list and a pretty college-age woman was waiting for me.

"Hi," she said and shook my hand. "I'm Elizabeth Alberts. I'm an intern for the governor this summer. I can take you back."

"Thanks."

She was probably only about three years older than me, but she oozed confidence, dressed professionally, and was totally the type of person I'd hoped to morph into. Her heels clicked with importance on the marble floor as she led me to see Governor Rhodes. When we got to his office, she knocked, opened the door slightly, and popped her head inside.

"Governor, your guest is here."

"Thanks, Elizabeth."

She smiled at me and then left as Governor Rhodes came to the door.

"Kendra, hi!" His smile was warm. "It sounds like you had quite the crazy morning. Come on in. There's someone here I know you want to see."

He opened the door further, and my heart leapt when I saw my mom standing behind him, waiting to hug me.

"Mom! Oh, my God!" I hugged her fiercely. "I didn't know what to do when they took you!"

"You did exactly the right thing." She held me and smoothed my hair until I stepped back. "I can almost pinpoint the exact second Detective Larson contacted the governor, because the line of cars I was in was headed in one direction, and just that like, we changed direction and headed here."

"You know Gardiner got shot, right? Is he going to be okay?"

"I couldn't care less," she said. "In fact, I hope he suffers tremendously."

"Have a seat, you two." Governor Rhodes gestured in the direction of his seating area, where a man was sitting in one corner of the black leather couch. "Kendra, this is my chief of staff, Craig Murphy."

You could just look at some people and see they were smart. Craig Murphy was like that. Physically, he was short, bald, and super-skinny, but in an on-purpose sort of way. He reminded me of my friend Ellen's dad, who ran ultra-marathons and ate only fruit, nuts, and vegetables. The intelligence came through in his eyes. They burned with knowledge, even through the glasses he wore. I liked him instinctively.

He got to his feet and shook my hand. "Very good to meet you. I've been getting to know your mother a little bit, and she's quite proud of you."

"She's not really objective when it comes to me."

He smiled. "Most moms aren't."

We both sat on the couch, leaving the middle cushion vacant between us. My mom and Governor Rhodes sat in the nearby armchairs.

"First, I want to apologize," said Governor Rhodes. "I feel responsible for what happened."

You should, I thought. *You are responsible.*

"Why did you tell Homeland Security about my Insights? That wasn't very helpful."

He frowned. "Insights?"

"Turns out that's what my dream-like things are called."

"Says who?" my mom asked.

Both the governor and Craig Murphy studied me closely, eager to hear my response.

I sighed. "It's a long story."

"But perhaps one we should hear," said Governor Rhodes. "And I called Homeland Security at my wife's suggestion after getting briefed by your chief of police over there in Brookview shortly after Dr. Ridgeway's murder. His murder was so strange, and the kidnapping of Maddie Meyers . . . your situation just seemed . . ." He spread his hands. "My wife suggested it was perhaps bigger than your local police force was capable of handling. I *certainly* did not expect it would result in what happened today."

"He didn't listen to you," I said. "Can't he be fired for that? He didn't do what you told him."

"To whom are you referring?" asked Governor Rhodes.

"Gardiner. Commander Gardiner. When he called to ask you what he should do about my mom, he did the exact opposite of what you told him."

"I don't know who this Commander Gardiner is," Rhodes said slowly. "I certainly haven't spoken to him."

"You did," I said. "I saw him call you."

"I was in a meeting all morning. Craig can vouch for me; he was with me the whole time. The first I heard about any of this was when my security detail told me Detective Larson had called. After hearing from him, we immediately called our contacts over at the ITB, and—"

"No, but I *saw* him make the call."

"Maybe you saw him make a call, but you didn't see him call me, because I wasn't available. Craig and I were in the same meeting for the last four hours, and it was not a meeting where any of us could be disturbed. It dealt with a very serious matter and we had a certain protocol to follow."

Craig nodded, confirming the governor's account.

"So Gardiner lied?" I said.

"It seems he did," said Rhodes.

"Of course he lied," my mom said. "He's a horrible man. Kendra, who told you your dreams were called Insights?"

"Dr. Ridgeway," I said, deciding to come clean. I wanted nothing more than to get everything off my chest; I couldn't stand living alone with what I knew. Plus, Governor Rhodes rescued my mom, so he was on my permanent good side. "Dr. Ridgeway pulled me aside in the hospital and told me this ridiculous story about how he was trying to save the world from some sort of terrorist attack that's going to make everybody sick and kill off half the world's population. He said he was working with a secret group to try and prevent it."

My mom gasped. "Why didn't you tell me?"

"Because I thought he was crazy. That's why I left the hospital like I did, to get away from him, only it turns out maybe he was telling the truth."

"What makes you think that?" asked Craig Murphy. "It sounds like he suffered from delusions."

"Because of everything that's happened since."

"I'd better take notes." He looked to the governor for approval and got it in the form of a nod, so he opened his leather portfolio and readied his pen. "Let's start with why Commander Gardiner came to your house."

"He came to my house because he's an asshole."

"Kendra." My mom didn't like me to use bad language, especially around other people. "Who was that man he kept asking about?"

"Russell Hendricks," I said.

"Who's that?" Craig asked.

"The man from my second Insight."

"Wasn't Dr. Ridgeway's murder your second Insight?" said Rhodes.

"That was her third," my mom said. "She had a second one in the hospital, right after you left. Right after we talked to Jeff Meyers."

"Did you tell him how Dr. Ridgeway destroyed my new Butler watch? I'm still mad about it, even though he was right about that, too. Gardiner knew stuff he couldn't have known unless he was spying on me inside our house, and the only way to do that is through our Butler."

"Spying on you?" My mom's eyes darkened. "Why?"

"Let's stick with your second Insight for a moment," said Craig. "Can you tell us about it?"

"It was about this guy—who turned out to be Russell Hendricks—basically getting assassinated by the same people who were at my house today. Or at least I think it was the same people. A bunch of SWAT-team types in all black." I went on to explain my Insight in more detail, ending with, "They shot about a million bullets when he opened the door to see what was going on."

"Do you know Hendricks?" Craig asked. "Have you met him personally?"

"Well, I—"

"I'd like to hear more about this secret group Ridgeway referred to," said Rhodes. "What else did he say about it?"

"I still want to know why you think Gardiner was spying on you," my mom said. "And why *would* he spy on you?"

"I know he was spying on me because he knew I went out last night."

"But you didn't go out," she said.

"Uh, well, yes, I did."

Her jaw dropped. "Do you know how much danger you put yourself in? My God, Kendra! After the phone call Detective Larson got saying you're in danger? Who were you with? Matt?"

"No, not Matt."

"Nora?"

"Nora's not back yet."

"Then who, Kendra?"

"It'd be great if you could refrain from freaking out," I said.

"And it'd be great if you could refrain from sneaking out!"

"I don't think these guys need to hear us fight, do you?"

"If I may," said Governor Rhodes. "Can I suggest you start from the beginning? I'll admit I'm utterly confused."

My mom crossed her arms. "So am I."

"I guess it starts with the accident," I said. "The guy who caused my accident had actually had an Insight about me."

Governor Rhodes frowned. "The truck driver?"

"No, Daemon. Daemon Godwin. He was on a motorcycle and was the one who actually forced the truck driver to veer from his lane to hit us."

"How do you know he had an Insight about you?" Craig asked.

"He told me."

"Last night?" he said. "Is that who you met with last night?"

"What was the Insight?" my mom asked.

I sighed at the flurry of questions that skipped back and forth in time.

"Your story is amazing and at the same time preposterous," said Rhodes. "You're suggesting there's a group of people with the same sort of special powers you have, and they see themselves as . . . what? Help me understand. Some sort of vigilante group?"

"They think there's going to be a biological attack that's going to spread this awful, horrible disease throughout the world, and they're desperate to prevent it. You know . . . bio-warfare? I have no idea if they're right or not, but I think they might be."

"Why do you think that?" Rhodes said.

I looked at my mom and couldn't bring myself to say it out loud: *Because I read Daemon's Insight and she's supposed to die from it.* Instead, I shrugged.

"I just do."

"This is very interesting in light of the meeting I was at this morning." Governor Rhodes looked at his chief of staff. "Craig, do you think there's a possible connection?"

Craig bit his lip, thought, and then said, "I have no idea what to make of any of this. I'm still trying to figure out where Hendricks fits in. Did you meet Hendricks, Kendra? I feel like I need clarity on this point. Did you meet the man from your Insight?"

"The meeting I was at this morning concerned a disturbing new outbreak of a mysterious but very deadly disease," said the governor.

"Sir, that's classified," Craig said quickly.

"*What?* It's happening?"

"Kendra won't tell anyone. Will you, Kendra?"

"It's happening," I whispered, stunned. "Daemon's right, it's happening. Mom, we have to get out of here. We've got to go somewhere safe and isolate ourselves and stay there until this is all over with. It's the only way. Daemon can help us with that. He can put us on the Underground Railroad."

Craig perked up. "Underground Railroad? What the heck's that?"

"There's no need to panic," Rhodes said. "Panicking is the worst thing you can do."

"No, but my mom, you see . . ." All eyes were on me, waiting for me to continue. "Daemon had an Insight about my mom." I swallowed hard. "In the Insight, she died from the disease."

My mom paled and shrank into herself.

"We don't know that's what this is," Governor Rhodes said in a calming tone, reaching to squeeze her hand. "Okay? It might not be related at all, and I'm sure it probably isn't. There was an outbreak at a prison in Alabama. Eight prisoners became extremely ill, and two guards as well, but they were isolated and we don't believe the disease has spread beyond them. None of the medical staff caring for them has become ill, and that's significant. It means this thing might not have legs. They're doing tests right now to see exactly what it was and investigating why it appeared in this one particular prison ward in Alabama and nowhere else."

"What were the symptoms?" I asked, my right knee twitching uncontrollably as I thought, *Please don't say it, please don't say it.*

"The disease comes on much like a bout of the flu. Chills, fever, lack of appetite and energy. Within hours, though, it gets much worse. They begin to have respiratory problems, and the illness turns hemorrhagic in nature."

"What does that mean?" I asked shakily. "Hemorrhagic?"

"It means the person begins to bleed," he said, and I gasped because I knew what was coming next. "They have internal bleeding, and in about half the cases, they were bleeding from their eyes or ears."

"Did they have boils and welts with pus coming from them?"

Governor Rhodes exchanged a look with Craig. "Yes, and they suffered kidney failure and liver failure, and suffered from delirium. All but two died."

"Two out of how many?"

"Ten," he said. "Eight prisoners and two guards. All but two died."

"An eighty percent death rate." My mom pressed her hand against her heart. "Good Lord, that's not very promising. I'd better get my will and life insurance in order."

"I can assure you we're on top of it. We have protocol for every situation you could possibly imagine. The CDC is on alert and ready to jump into high gear if circumstances call for it. And the good news is that no one who's been in contact with the ten who became ill has become sick themselves, so the hope is it's not very virulent. We have no idea how this one cluster of individuals got this very rare type of disease you wouldn't typically see in the United States—"

"Where would you see it?" my mom asked.

"It's unclear," he said. "Africa, maybe. It may be a cross between two completely separate diseases, but until tests come back, it's a mystery."

"What if there's an incubation period and all these medical workers who aren't sick now get sick later . . . and what if, in the meantime, they're infecting all their other patients and their families?" my mom said. "Is the medical staff quarantined?"

"They are," Rhodes assured her and then stood. "I'm sorry to cut this meeting short, but in light of what Kendra told me, I'm going to reconvene this morning's meeting. If this is indeed a biological terrorist attack, then we need to understand what we're dealing with."

"Kendra, just to clarify—did you or didn't you speak with Russell Hendricks last night?" Craig said. "Did you meet him face-to-face?"

"I did," I said.

I answered instantly, unthinkingly, realizing only afterwards how persistently he'd been trying all along to figure out that exact thing. No matter where the conversation went, it's what he'd always come back to. My stomach sank; I wasn't sure why—maybe because of the tiny flicker of satisfaction I saw in his eyes when I told him, yes, I'd met and spoken with the man considered so dangerous by the bad guys they'd do anything to silence him.

"Uh, what people will you be meeting with?" I asked Rhodes. My voice felt far away, hollow, laced with fear, but at least it didn't quiver.

"I chair a group called the Committee of Ten, which is a coalition of ten governors from around the country," he said. "We were established by executive order after 9/11 as an additional line of defense in case something catastrophic rendered the usual constitutional line of succession impossible."

"Meaning?"

"If, say, a nuclear bomb dropped on Washington, D.C., while Congress was in session and obliterated not only the president and vice president, but every politician and member of the cabinet, then under executive order, this committee is charged with maintaining a rule of order until such time as a new federal government could be properly elected. Not that it would ever happen. It's simply a worst-case-scenario planning exercise the government loves to do."

"So you're like a backup to the normal government?" I said, avoiding Craig's eyes, although I could feel him watching me closely.

"The normal federal government, yes," said Rhodes. "As governors, we already govern our individual states. And in a significant crisis, we would be available to step in and govern the entire country through the crisis until the proper line of succession could be reestablished through elections."

"When you say we, you mean the committee?"

"That's right."

"So if this disease spreads and killed the president and vice president and all those other people . . . who'd be in charge?"

"I'm sure it won't come to that," Rhodes said.

"But if it did, who'd be in charge? The whole committee? Or . . . who, specifically?"

"Well, as chair of the committee, that would be me."

My eyes sank closed. How could I have been so stupid?

"We shouldn't keep you." My mom stood and then extended a hand to help me up, too. "Thank you so much for everything you've done. I'll see you, I guess, in a couple days?"

"That's right," he said, heading out a side door. "Craig will get with my wife and arrange that."

"Arrange what?" I said, feeling panic rise in my throat.

"Governor Rhodes has asked me to cater a fundraiser for him on Thursday night," she said. "His regular caterer flaked at the last minute, and as we were waiting for you to arrive we got to talking about my work as a chef. Just making small talk, you know? He inquired as to whether my restaurant might like to pick up the catering job, and I said I was sure we would. He said he'd make it happen, on the condition I'm the chef for the evening. Isn't that nice? And such a lovely coincidence?"

"Lovely," I said, but it was no such thing. Daemon had told me the first time I met him there was no such thing as coincidence anymore in my life, and now—in this awful moment—I let go of whatever lingering doubts I'd still clung to.

What had taken me too long to understand was that in real life, you can't always tell the bad guys. Unlike in the movies, they don't always have evil laughs and wear black hats and point guns at you. In real life, they can be nice and friendly and even visit you in the hospital.

In that awful moment, I finally understood: Governor Rhodes was one of the bad guys.

FROM HIS CHAIR, THE MAN CRANED HIS NECK AND STARED at the 80-inch touch-screen computer closest to him as he absorbed the news his old friend Buttercup had just conveyed.

The Prince Philip quote took up the top fifth of the screen, below which was a heat map showing how his plan was unfolding, exactly on schedule, exactly as it should. There were little dots of red and little dots of green, and they blinked to life a millimeter at a time.

It was a thing of true beauty.

"You're sure?" he asked, his voice tight, his neck strained.

When he'd installed the three 80-inch computers in his vault, he'd been a healthy man and stood more often than he sat, walking around feverishly between the three screens, dissecting and combining disparate information and theories, expanding and minimizing charts and graphs and key words and then having them scroll at an almost-too-fast-to-read, over-stimulating pace until something—some new thought, some new idea—made him press his palm into one of the screens and have it all STOP.

That's how brilliance was born.

"Of course I'm sure." Her nippy tone came at him in surround sound, reverberating off every wall in his vault. It made him cringe. "She met with Russell Hendricks."

Instead of responding, he read the Prince Philip quote again. It was from 1988, before the World Wide Web was even invented. The old chap had gone on to live and live and live and do absolutely nothing remarkable with the remainder of his life, but the quote had inspired a generation of population reductionists, of which he was one.

Today, though, the idea seemed hopelessly quaint. One didn't need to be reborn as a virus in order to reduce the population. Today, technology could achieve the same goal.

"You know what this means, right?" she said. "It means they know who you are."

Good, he thought, and it was partly true. He wanted the world to know, but only after they'd reached the point of no return and they weren't quite there.

"I can deal with anything they throw at me," he said. "What's happening on your end? Can we speed up things?"

"The prison outbreak's over," she said. "It went exactly as expected. We wish it would have spread a little more, but it was still severe enough to kick the CDC folks into action. The prison guards' families should start showing symptoms later today, and then we've got the D.C. outbreak tomorrow at Walter Reed. Twenty patients, minimum. The entire wing the president visited."

"He was there today?"

"Yes, for over an hour. Held their hands, kissed foreheads, the usual. Put on a nice show for the cameras."

The man smiled. "What media was there? CNN? Fox? Please say both."

"Both, and *The New York Times* as well," she said. "The fear mongering will be in full swing by Saturday."

"And the vaccine?"

"About to be fast-tracked."

"Fantastic," he said, but his throat was starting to constrict. He looked at the middle of his three giant computer screens, which showed the porcelain-pretty face of Kendra Sinclair. "And the girl . . .?"

"She'll die. Very soon."

"You'll see to it personally?"

"I'll kill her with my own hands if I have to. Are you alright?" she asked. "You're breathing funny."

"I'm fine," he said, but he wasn't. His heart raced and his breathing felt like it was shutting down, the same way it had a few nights back. This time he knew: It was just a panic attack, and he wasn't about to tell her that.

He looked at the third screen, the one he'd been avoiding. The top part of it, too, had a quote that inspired him, said by his idol, the late, great Steve Jobs: *I think death is the most wonderful invention of life. It purges the system of these old models that are obsolete.*

That's exactly what his fatal diagnosis had done—inspired the plan they were now enacting.

"I'll take care of the one girl." Buttercup's voice was uncharacteristically soft. "You'll take care of the other?"

The man looked below the Steve Jobs' quote at the bottom part of the screen. On it was the face of another girl with Insights.

Another girl who knew too much: His daughter, Maddie Meyers.

"I'll take care of her," he said, and he would—because this plan could only be defeated if those two girls ever crossed paths.

Jeff Meyers was not about to let that happen.

EPISODE
THREE

AFTER THE INCREDIBLY STRANGE AND HORRIBLE DAY WE'D had with Commander Gardiner and his men showing up in our backyard, their kidnapping of my mom, and her later rescue by Governor Rhodes—who I was now convinced was evil—I was ready for the day to end. My mom had to work that night, but the only way she'd go was if someone came over to be with me. She gave me the choice of Matt or Larson, and of course I chose Matt.

He showed up freshly showered with the ends of his hair still wet and curling in cute ways, smelling of aftershave and Ivory soap, leaning forward on the doorstep, nearly standing on his tippy-toes, eager to come in.

"You look happy," I said.

"That's because I'm excited to see you," he said. "You've been blowing me off ever since the cemetery, and don't think I don't know why. We're going to have a talk tonight, you and I."

I liked playful Matt, always had, but he was especially refreshing then when everything felt so bleak. I pulled him inside my house and hugged him in the foyer, relishing how safe I felt with his arms around me.

"I'm not afraid of you," I said.

"I'm not afraid of you, either."

We separated when my mom came into the living room. "Matt, hi! Good to see you. It feels like it's been a long time. After all our time together at the hospital, it feels a little strange not to see you every hour of every day."

"I know," Matt said. "A part of me kind of misses it."

"Not me," she said. "Listen, I need you to keep a good eye on Kendra tonight. She's gotten in the habit of sneaking out when I'm gone."

"Once," I said, noticing Matt's changed, now-worried expression. "I went out once!"

"Once is more than enough." She gave me her best version of the evil eye. "I should be home by midnight or one. That's not too late, is it, Matt? You're welcome to spend the night, of course."

"Of course?" I said. "Since when is it okay for a boy to spend the night?"

She shrugged. "He spent the night with you in the hospital several times. Besides, when said boy is Matt, I think I can handle it. I'm just saying . . ."

My mouth dropped open—was she really suggesting what I thought she was suggesting?

She gathered her keys and purse, waved goodbye, and headed down the hallway to the door to our attached garage, then stopped and turned around. "Matt, would you be able to help out at a catering job at the Capitol tomorrow night? I'll pay you, of course. We're short-staffed, and I've got to make this come off well. It's my first catering event for the governor, and I'm hoping it turns into a regular thing, maybe even a job working directly for him."

"Sure," Matt said, looking at me. "You're going, too, right?"

"Of course she is," my mom said. "Can you be here tomorrow at, say, four o'clock? We'll need time to get down there and finish setting up. The event's at six, but it's only drinks and appetizers, so it'll be easy. I'll have a shirt for you to wear, and you can wear khakis for pants, okay?"

"Works for me," Matt said.

After she left, I headed to the kitchen, knowing Matt would follow. I rummaged through the refrigerator and grabbed salsa, guacamole, and two Coronas.

"She's driving me to drink," I said. "You want one?"

"Sure." He took the beer bottles from me, set them on the counter, and then found the bottle opener in our junk drawer. I busied myself pouring the salsa and guacamole into serving bowls and filling a larger bowl with tortilla chips.

When I turned around, Matt handed me my beer. "So am I spending the night?" I laughed awkwardly. "Where'd you go last night, Kendra?"

Not here, I thought. I stepped close to him, close enough to kiss, and wrapped my finger around a still-damp lock of hair. His breathing slowed as if he didn't want to do anything to alter the course of the moment, and that made me smile.

"Interesting how my mom wants to push us together, isn't it?" I said.

"Not as interesting as where you went last night, or the fact that you're trying to distract me now so you don't have to tell me."

"It's not you I don't want to tell."

I'd unplugged our living room Butler the minute we got home from our visit from Governor Rhodes, but there was still one of his security men parked in front of our house (he'd insisted, and my mom had happily agreed), and I felt like every move I made and every word I said was being watched and listened to.

I took a swig of my beer and tried again. "You still owe me a dance."

He raised his eyebrows. "And you still owe me an explanation."

"Can you *believe* you're blowing me off right now?" I teased. "Don't you think you might regret it?"

"That's a very good point." He took my beer from me, set both bottles on the counter, and then pulled me close. "All right, let's have that dance."

We barely swayed. I wanted to melt into him and cry, hard.

"You make me feel safe," I whispered.

"You are safe. I'm never going to let anyone hurt you ever again."

He kissed me then, and kissing Matt, I felt like myself again, like the world was a mostly good place and moments of perfection were definitely possible, like I had a future that could be better than my past. I felt . . . hopeful.

Our kisses grew more passionate, and it seemed like we were making up for all the years we could have been more than just friends. *This is Matt!*, I kept thinking, getting lost in the moment— so lost that after awhile in my mind, it wasn't Matt I was kissing.

It was Daemon, and where Matt had been gentle, the Daemon of my imagination was rough. Where Matt cradled my face in his hands, Daemon backed me into the wall and trapped me. Where Matt's skin was freshly shaven, Daemon's was scratchy. I hated how controlled Daemon always was, and so I touched him and kissed him in ways I knew would make him lose control, because him being out of control was even more dangerous, and that danger had sucked me in, made me want more, made me think all sorts of dirty thoughts I'd never once thought with Adam.

He pulled back suddenly, and I was shocked to see it was Matt again, breathing heavy, wanting more but wanting to make sure that's what I wanted, too. And it wasn't, not right then—and not with Matt.

"Whoops. I forgot myself for a minute there." That wasn't true. I hadn't forgotten myself; it was him I'd forgotten. I laughed awkwardly. "Sorry. Uh . . . drink! I'm thirsty. Are you thirsty? Want a drink?"

"You're cute when you're embarrassed, but don't be embarrassed." Matt picked up our beer bottles, gave me mine, and then held his up for a toast. "Cheers, to . . . whatever that was. The start of us, maybe."

We both drank, watching each other, me still very confused and disturbed at how in a moment of passion with Matt my mind went straight to Daemon. I did *not* want Daemon, so why had I fantasized about him? Daemon had a sort of smoldering sexuality about him, the kind every girl at a party would notice, but he'd never directed it at me. In fact, it often felt like he kept a deliberate distance. He was watchful of me in the extreme, but he wasn't lustful.

Still, how would he feel to see me kiss Matt like that?

"I need some air," I said.

I went to the patio door, slid it open, and stepped outside. The night was thickly hot, coated with humidity—but even so, I shivered because I imagined Daemon out there, watching me from some lonely perch in the darkness, him and his smoldering sexuality.

Then Matt was there, wrapping his arms around me from behind. I leaned back into him and again felt safe.

"You okay?" He kissed the back of my head. "You don't regret what we did, do you?"

"No regrets," I said.

"Then why do you seem so sad?"

I swallowed hard, unable to lie, unable to tell the truth.

"Are you thinking of him?" he asked, his tone understanding.

"Who, Daemon?" I wasn't thinking clearly or I never would have said it. Matt stiffened, then stepped back and turned me so I had to face him.

"I meant Adam," he said. "You *do* have feelings for that guy, don't you? I knew it."

"I *don't* have feelings for him. I swear, I don't even *like* him, much less have feelings for him! In fact, I think he's disgusting!"

Hear that? I imagined him out there laughing at me. *I find you disgusting!*

"You're lying." Matt crossed his arms. "The least you could do is admit the truth. You owe me that much, Kendra. You owe me the truth."

"I am telling you the truth, and I *will* tell you the truth, which is that there's so much going on you need to know, way beyond what happened that day at the boxing gym, which I know I still haven't told you about. But I will. I want you to know everything. You're the one I want to be with, Matt."

"Was he the reason you snuck out last night?"

"Not in the way you think."

"Girls always like the bad boys, don't they?" There was huge betrayal in his eyes. "They always like the ones who aren't good for them. And I'm just a—" He stepped away, dismissed me—us—with a derisive wave. "I can't compete with that. With him. I'll never be anyone other than who I am."

"Matt, I don't want you to compete."

"Did you kiss him like you just kissed me?"

"I've never kissed anybody like I just kissed you." He smiled unwillingly, and I stepped closer. I put my palm on his chest, over his heart. "You're my guy. You're the one I should've been with all along."

He gave me a long look. "But am I the one you want to be with now?"

"Absolutely," I said, and it was true. Matt had my heart. I just needed to get Daemon out of my mind.

"Then tell me everything."

It was a request and a dare and a demand. I knew if I refused, we'd have no chance for a future.

"I will," I said. "But not here."

"Then where?"

"Wherever Daemon is," I said. "Because for any question you have, he's got the answer."

Whether or not he'd tell Matt was another issue, but my mom often said the questions a person asks are as important as the answers.

The time had come to test that theory.

LEAVING HIS CAR PARKED IN MY DRIVEWAY TO SERVE AS A
sort of decoy, I led Matt on my usual route through backyards to
Nora's house.

The night was crisp and silent, the quarter-moon dim and
lonely in the cloudless sky. I knew the four-minute route to
Nora's backyard by heart; I probably could have closed my eyes
and counted steps and angles and gotten there blind. Her family
always left their side garage door unlocked, and numerous bikes
usually leaned against the wall right next to it. I took Nora's old
beach cruiser while Matt took her dad's ten-speed bike. We stayed
on side streets and took the long way around the park because the
police tended to patrol there, and running into cops was not part
of my plan.

I knew of only two places Daemon might be, the boxing gym
and the house where he'd taken me the previous night to meet
Russell. We biked to the gym; unsurprisingly, it was closed. We
biked on to the house, and upon peeking through the garage door
window I was disappointed to see no sign of Daemon's motorcycle.

"This is where I was last night, but I don't think anyone's here,"
I said. "Let's peek inside the house."

"Whose house is this?" Matt asked.

"I have no idea."

We left our bikes in the alley, went through the gate to the backyard, and climbed the cement steps to the back door. Looking through the kitchen window, it was obvious the house was vacant, as there was no furniture in the room and the refrigerator was unplugged and its door hung open, empty.

We then checked the basement, but the door was locked. Looking through the grimy window, there was no sign anyone had been there recently, even though we'd used it the previous night. *Find me,* I wrote with my fingertip on the smudged-glass window.

"Now what?" Matt asked.

"Someone should've come for me," I said. "After the day I had, you'd think someone would've come. They're supposed to want to protect me."

We sat on the steps, and I told Matt everything. I would have preferred for him to hear it from Daemon, but that wasn't going to happen so I explained the best I could. Matt listened, but hardly said a word.

"What are you thinking?" I asked after I was done.

"That these guys are not looking out for your best interest."

"Do you believe it, though? Do you think it could be true?"

"My dad's into all those conspiracy theories," he said. "He'd believe it in a heartbeat."

"Yeah, but do you?"

He thought for a long time. "The thing is, if we go back to the very beginning and look only at that first Insight you had of Maddie Meyers—that was an impossible thing you did, to predict or foresee that kidnapping. It was completely, utterly impossible—and yet it happened. I was there; I saw it with my own eyes. And if that impossible thing can be true, then doesn't it stand to reason that all the other impossible things potentially can be true, too?"

"They do all kind of build on each other. Like, I'll think, *Oh, this can't possibly be true,* but if it is, it explains certain things which then lead to other certain things. There's a definite pattern at work. I can feel it."

"It's like destiny in action," Matt said.

"But destiny can be changed," I said. "That's the whole point of what's going on, right? Which version of destiny is going to win?"

"I hope it's the version that keeps the world intact, life as we know it."

"I hope so, too." I stood and reached for his hand to pull him up. "But we can't just hope. We have to take action. Let's go back to the boxing gym and snoop around."

We biked back there through the alley. It was not a well-kept building, and the ground around it was littered with broken bottles. The small rectangular windows on the side of the building were too high to look through from the ground, but Matt hoisted me onto the garbage dumpster, and by leaning forward, I was able to see through one. A fat grey cat lounged on a weightlifting bench. Its spooky gold eyes latched onto mine and freaked me out, but other than that, the gym was empty of life. I noticed a lit-up exit sign toward the back of the gym that hung over a doorway leading . . . somewhere. I leaned precariously closer to see from a better angle. The doorway led to a hallway, and the hallway had stairs leading up, which was odd because it was a one-story, high-ceilinged build-ing. Then it struck me: The roof!

It could be the perfect place for Daemon to camp out. It seemed to me that a person could probably stand up straight in the middle and remain invisible to those below. High up, out of sight, he'd be safe at night both from people and from the bloodsucking Minnesota mosquitoes.

Matt helped me down, and we went around to the back of the boxing gym. Long weeds in the narrow space leading to the rear door were stamped down, creating a makeshift footpath.

I pointed them out to Matt. "Footprints."

"Someone's using that door," he whispered back.

Tentatively, we made our way to it. I thought for sure it would be locked, but there was duct tape on the latch so it would remain unlocked. Score!

I stepped inside first, with Matt right behind me. We paused to let our eyes adjust. The grey cat jumped off the weight bench and came toward us, stopping about five feet away. His freaky-gold eyes glowed. I made a low hissing sound, but he stood his ground like he was the guardian of the place. I turned my back on the cat.

Matt and I climbed the metal stairs, every step delivering a little shock of pain to my injured leg. At the top landing, there was another door leading to a set of seven outdoor stairs. Finally we were on the roof, which had been converted into a completely cool rooftop hideaway. There was a tent, a lawn chair, and a kitchen table and chairs I suspected had been pilfered from the vacant house. Best of all, fifteen feet away from me, lying in a string-net hammock, was a sleeping Daemon, looking even more handsome than I remembered. So he *hadn't* been hiding in a tree in my yard seeing me make a fool out of myself with Matt.

"Stay here," I whispered to Matt. I crossed the space between where we were and where Daemon was, pulled up a nearby milk crate, sat on it, and touched his arm.

Zap.

He bolted awake.

"What the—?" He gripped my arms and held on as if for dear life. "Am I awake? Is this real? Are you really here?"

"I'm really here," I said. "Were you having an Insight?"

He nodded. "Tell me again this is real."

"This is real," I said. "What was your Insight?"

"It's nothing," he said, but his eyes latched onto mine and they were full of terror. "I heard *you* had quite a day."

"Was your Insight about me?"

He sat up sideways in the hammock so his feet were solidly on the ground, but then he buried his head in his hands. I'd never seen him less than confident—less than cocky, actually—and his fear unsettled me.

"Tell me what's going on, Daemon."

He looked up. "I can't tell you, Kendra. Not yet." He noticed Matt. "What's he doing here?"

"I told him everything."

Matt came over and held out his hand for Daemon to shake, but Daemon ignored it.

"I wish you hadn't told him," Daemon said, not taking his eyes off Matt.

"And I wish you hadn't let men point guns at me today, but you did," I said. "Is Russell safe?"

"Russell's safe." He stood and faced Matt. "People on the

periphery usually end up dead. That's why I wish Kendra hadn't told you anything."

"Don't worry about me."

Matt again extended his hand, and this time Daemon shook it.

"I have a question," Matt said. "Why do you have Insights? I know what happened to Kendra to make her have them, but what happened to you?"

I bit my lip, fully expecting Daemon to tell Matt to mind his own business, but to my surprise, he answered.

"My parents and I were headed back from dinner at a restaurant." He cleared his throat, and from the look in his eyes I could tell he was back at that dinner. "It was Thanksgiving. We always went out for Thanksgiving—my parents weren't cooks, they were scientists—and on the way home, we were run off the road. The car went down a steep embankment." He cleared his throat again. "I lived, and now I have Insights."

In the silence that followed, an owl hooted from a distance. The air smelled of coming rain. The sadness that had pierced Daemon's normal stoniness made me want to put my arms around him, but I fought the urge because I knew Matt wouldn't like it.

"Your parents didn't survive?" I said.

"They were pronounced dead at the scene. I was unconscious for several days, after which I began to have Insights."

"Like me," I said.

"Is that where you got the idea of running people off the road?" Matt said.

"Matt," I scolded.

He shrugged. "It's a fair question."

"You were run off the road, or was it an accident?" I said.

"We were run off the road."

"Do you know who did it?" I said. "Was it the same as me? Did someone have an Insight about you and was trying to save you?"

Daemon laughed. "No. You're going to love this part. You know what my parents did for a living? I told you they were scientists, and I'd grown up thinking they were developing vaccines for third-world countries and such—pretty cool, right?—but I found out after the accident they'd been trying to weaponize a rare hemorrhagic disease. You know, the kind that gives people bleeding boils and kills more than half of its victims. Sound familiar?"

A hot anger overtook me. "You're saying *your parents* created the disease that's supposed to kill my mom?"

"That's what I'm saying, yes."

I wanted to push him, to shove him right off the roof, but as I stepped toward him, Matt took my arm to hold me in place.

"So someone ran your parents off the road to stop them from developing this disease?"

"Yes."

"And now you're working for those very same people?"

"I am."

"Man, what tangled webs we weave," Matt said. "What a crazy, mixed-up world this is."

"Tell me about it," Daemon said.

I shook off Matt's hand and strode to the far end of the roof, as far from Daemon as I could get.

"Hey, get away from the edge," he called. "Someone could see you."

I ignored him.

"Kendra, come back over here," Matt said.

I ignored him, too.

I felt someone come up behind me and stand close, but I couldn't tell which of them it was and didn't turn around to find out. It was only when I felt the quick shock of Daemon's touch when he pulled me away from the edge that I knew it was him. I fought him for a second, but he had his arms around me tight, trapping me in something resembling a bear hug.

"Listen, your mom's not going to die," he said softly. "We're not going to let that happen, right? You and I are going to stop it."

He loosened his hold on me so I could turn and face him.

"How does it end, Daemon?"

"We win."

Then why do you look so sad?

"What was the Insight you were having when I got here?" I tried to take his hands to find out, but he wouldn't let me. "You were having an Insight about how it ends, weren't you?"

"Maybe," Daemon said, and I knew it was as close to an admission as I'd get.

"Do I die in the end? Is that why you were so freaked out to see me?"

"Don't worry," he said. "You live."

"What about you?" Matt called.

Daemon stepped away from me then and went back over by Matt. "I'm there at the end, too," Daemon said.

"But do you live?" I said, even though I already knew the answer. I'd been wrong about how he'd grabbed me when I woke him up. He hadn't grabbed me as if my life depended on it, but as if *his life* depended on it.

"Don't worry about that," he said. "It doesn't matter. Poetic justice, I suppose. All that matters is stopping the attack."

But it did matter. Of course it mattered. I'd seen how terrified he was when he woke up, and even if it didn't matter to him, it mattered to me.

"We'll change the outcome," I said. "Our destinies aren't set in stone—that's the whole point of the Insights, right? You changed my destiny when you caused my car accident, and I'll change yours, Daemon. I promise I will."

"When the time comes, don't worry about saving me," he said. "You just worry about saving the world."

IT'S AN OUTDOOR EVENT, A BEAUTIFUL DAY, IN DOWNTOWN
St. Paul.

The crowd's large, close to a thousand, made up mostly of men. They stand, facing a stage. Seated on the stage to the side of the podium are a few men, as well as a little girl and her parents. The girl, about eight, wears a sparkly green tutu and holds a baton. She can't stop smiling. Behind the podium is a fat man in a white shirt and red suspenders. He's not the main attraction, and the crowd's only half-listening, but he likes being center stage and speaks enthusiastically over the crowd's collective chatter.

Close to the front of the crowd is a man who stands out. Like others on this blue-skied day, he wears sunglasses and a baseball cap. Unlike the others, who are T-shirt-and-shorts casual, he wears jeans and a windbreaker and gives off a jittery vibe. He's noticeably taller than those around him.

On stage, the fat man wraps up his speech. The crowd cheers at something he says—at his introduction to the next speaker . . . the governor of the great state of Minnesota . . . Governor William Rhodes!

There he is, Governor Rhodes, with his sparkling white teeth and rich man's smooth skin, looking every inch the triumphant politician.

He waves to the crowd as he ascends the stairs to the stage from the side. His bodyguard stands at the base of the stairs, his mirrored-glassed eyes scanning the crowd. Governor Rhodes pauses to take in the crowd and to let them take him in, too. He's in his glory.

The man in the windbreaker firms his cap low on his forehead and reaches into his jacket pocket. Out comes a mean-looking pistol. It's big, thick, powerful.

He raises it above the shoulders of the people in front of him, and in one clear shot, he fires a single bullet.

The governor, hit in the temple, crumples instantly.

He's down.

He's dead.

Governor Rhodes is dead.

•   •   •

What, exactly, am I supposed to do with that?

Over and over that night, I had that Insight—each time experiencing it fresh, as if for the first time. I couldn't stop myself from falling back into it. Neither could I stop myself from jerking awake at the exact instant Governor Rhodes died.

Who was going to kill him? Daemon's people?

I couldn't let that happen . . . could I?

I'd talk with Daemon about it later, I decided. Before Matt and I came back home the previous night, Daemon told me why I wasn't yet safe on the Underground Railroad: There was something they needed me to do first—namely, they needed me to help Daemon break into Governor Rhodes's office so he could plant a bug and see what the governor was up to.

Matt protested, and I did, too, but Daemon refused to let me out of it. So it was that later that day I found myself putting on khaki pants and a black shirt to go help my mom cater the governor's fundraising event. The doorbell sounded as I was halfway through braiding my hair. I braided the other half as I went to answer the door, finding Matt outside.

"Hey," he said, not looking like he'd slept any better than I had. "I'm thinking I should—"

I planted a kiss on him to stop him from saying anything else. He got wrapped up in the kiss and didn't understand the reason behind it. Our Butler was unplugged, but I still didn't think we should talk freely in my house.

"Listen," he said. "I can do this as well as—"

I kissed him again, and this time I bit his bottom lip and then pulled back and gave him a warning look. Thankfully my mom pulled into the driveway right then and honked the horn of the restaurant's cargo van.

I finished getting ready and soon enough the three of us were heading toward the Capitol, sharing the cramped front seat. While Matt and I held hands, my mom talked continuously about how she hoped this job would be a new beginning for us. Blissfully unaware of both my suspicions of Governor Rhodes and the Insight I'd had the night before of him being assassinated, she hoped to impress him so much that night he'd hire her to be on staff at the Capitol. I didn't have the heart to tell her it probably wasn't going to happen.

Once we arrived, she drove the catering van up to the service entrance. Fifteen employees had reported directly to the Capitol, and they were waiting for my mom by the entrance. I started to follow her as she got out to greet everyone, but Matt held me back.

"I don't think you should go," he said. "It's too dangerous for you to be connected with him. Let me do it. I'll make sure he gets in okay."

My responsibility was actually very simple. Daemon said he'd be disguised as a server, and all I needed to do was make sure he got inside. From there, I was to ignore him completely, no matter what happened.

"He insisted on me," I said.

"Well, be careful."

"I will," I said. "You, too."

We got out and went around to the back of the van to help unload. When I saw the other employees were gathered around waiting for their catering shirts, I jumped into action.

"Here, I'll hand them out." I pushed to the front of the group. Matt came, too, and held the box while I distributed them. I gave the women theirs with no second thought, but as each guy got his, I looked close. With about half of them, it was obvious immediately they weren't Daemon because they were too short, which was one thing Daemon couldn't change about himself. He could feasibly make himself a little bit taller, but definitely not shorter. The other thing hard to change was his build. His forearms were sinewy and his biceps well developed, so I began looking at the guys' arms, which led me to eliminate everyone except one of three guys who was around Daemon's height and the only one not in short sleeves.

But whereas Daemon had near-black, really short hair, this guy's hair was a messy, curly, surfer-bleached blond. He also wore tortoiseshell glasses, which, granted, might not have been prescription glasses, but the other thing I saw when I got closer was that his eyes were blue, not brown like Daemon's. Plus, he was unguarded, laughing freely with the others—and laughing freely was something I'd *never* seen Daemon do. It was the baggy, long-sleeved, button-up shirt worn in the stifling day that made me suspicious.

"Here you go," I said, handing him his uniform, expecting him to wink at me or give me some sort of sign, but he didn't. "You look familiar. Have we met before?"

"I don't think so." His blue eyes weren't even curious and his voice sounded nothing like Daemon's.

Okay, so not him, I thought. Was he not there?

After everyone had a uniform, my mom called for us all to gather around her. When she asked who had bartending experience, one woman and the guy I'd suspected was Daemon raised their hands, so my mom assigned them as bartenders. Since it wasn't a sit-down dinner, there wouldn't be a need for us to wait tables. We were to set up appetizer buffets and then take turns manning the buffet tables and walking around with food and drink trays.

The others changed into their uniforms in the hallway of the service entrance, women first and then men. The men unloaded the van while the women changed, but since I was already in my uniform, I climbed into the van and handed down trays for people to take inside. The surfer-blond guy lingered in line until it was only the two of us.

"Everything cool?" he said under his breath as he took a large bowl of salad from me.

"Ha," I said. "I knew it was you. Listen, I had an Insight about

Rhodes being assassinated." His blue not-Daemon eyes widened. "Do you have time to read it?"

"Not now," he said and left.

I kept distributing items from the back of the van, waiting for him to come back, but he never did. Soon enough, the party started and I was kept busy offering appetizers to all the well-dressed rich people roaming around. When Governor Rhodes and his wife arrived, it was like those scenes in movies where the king and queen arrive at the ball, arm in arm. The chattering all shushed and there was a spatter of clapping as guests parted to make way for them to pass into the center of the room. Governor Rhodes wore a dark grey suit and royal blue tie, while his wife wore a silver strapless dress. She was super-skinny and glamorous, and her skin was so white it was almost translucent. Her salon-blond hair was thin, straight, chin-length, and cut into a razor-sharp bob. The consummate politician's wife, she never stopped smiling.

He's down. He's dead.

Governor Rhodes is dead.

That's all I could see when I looked at him, a bullet to the temple, and when he made eye contact with me through the crowd, I could tell he saw something was wrong, because his expression changed from one of a politician's pressing-the-flesh to one of hidden concern. He said something quietly to his wife, and they made their way over.

"Kendra, I'd like to introduce you to my wife, Lacy. Lacy, this is Kendra, the girl I've told you about."

His wife smiled with polite interest. "I'd shake your hand, but it looks like they're full at the moment with those gorgeous appetizers. I hear your mom's the grandmaster chef for the night? How lucky we are to have found her."

"Kendra, is something wrong?" Governor Rhodes asked. "Should we steal a minute away together to talk?"

Being alone with him was the last thing I wanted.

"Nothing's wrong except I'm afraid I'm going to drop this tray! I've never been a waitress before, and I don't want to mess things up." My arms indeed felt shaky, but I knew it was from nerves and not arm fatigue. "Want some herring? It's mustard-and-dill based, and everyone says it's really good."

"I love herring." He took a cracker with herring from my tray and popped the whole thing into his mouth. He ate it in about two bites and then took another and did the same thing.

"Would you like one?" I asked his wife.

"No, thank you." She leaned close and whispered, "My diet's a bit restricted."

"Your mother has a gift with food," said Governor Rhodes as he scanned the crowd. "There she is. Babe, let's go say hello. I'd like to introduce you."

"Nice to meet you, Kendra," said Lacy. "My husband has such wonderful things to say about you."

They linked arms and made their way toward my mom, stopping every few feet to talk with someone else. I made my way over to Matt, who was bearing a cheese tray.

"Nothing seems to be happening yet," I said, glancing at Daemon, who was busy behind the bar.

Famous last words. Just then, a man climbed onto a small platform that had been set up along one wall of the room. He asked everyone to gather around, but I made my way over to my mom near the back.

"It's going well, isn't it?" she whispered, radiant.

"Everyone loves the herring."

The man on stage talked about what a great cause they were supporting, something to do with sick children, and how much money they'd collected that night. I only half-listened because out of the corner of my eye I saw Daemon come out from behind the bar pushing a cart with an ice bin on it, as if going to refill it. I didn't watch him directly but was keenly aware of him nonetheless, and as he turned the corner from the doorway leaving the banquet hall, I saw a white keycard slip out from the bottom of his pant leg—which was bad because I knew he needed it to get into Governor Rhodes's office.

I handed the appetizer tray to my mom and whispered, "I need to use the bathroom."

"Use the employee one," she whispered back.

"This one's closer."

Forcing myself not to rush, I headed for the same door Daemon went through, bending to pick up the keycard as inconspicuously as possible. I made a pretense of going into the ladies' room, although all I did was rush in, slip the keycard up my sleeve, and rush back out, heading towards Rhodes's office. I turned a few corners and finally found Daemon in front of Rhodes's door, pressing his hands all over himself, feeling for the swipe card he'd dropped.

"Pssst." I held out the card. He sprinted down the hall and grabbed it from me. "You're welcome."

"Now get out of here," he hissed.

I turned back and began retracing my steps, but as I rounded the first corner, I slammed into a beefy security guard whose body was so solid I literally bounced off him and whose face was one big scowl.

"Sorry, excuse me," I said and tried to go around him.

He grabbed me by my braids and yanked me back. "What are you doing here?"

"Looking for the bathroom."

He slammed me into the wall and held me there by grabbing my shirt collar. "I'll ask you again: What are you doing back here?"

"I'm part of the event tonight—I'm one of the caterers—and I was just looking for the bathroom."

"Nice try." He held me in place with one arm and with his other raised his Butler watch to his mouth. "Henderson, come in. I've got a trespasser."

"I'm not a *trespasser*. I'm a—"

"HEY! ASSHOLE!" It was Matt, at the far end of the hallway. "GET AWAY FROM HER!"

As he came at us, the security guard pulled a gun from his holster and aimed it at Matt. Matt stopped in his tracks.

"Smart boy," sneered the guard.

"Let her go, or I'll kill you," Matt said, and while I appreciated the sentiment, it seemed highly unrealistic.

The guard grinned. "You threatened an officer of the law with deadly force."

Matt laughed snarkily and came closer. "You're just a rent-a-cop."

"Unfortunately for you, I'm a federal agent, assigned to protect a sitting governor, and you're about to be in a lot of pain."

With that—unprovoked—he fired his gun, but instead of a gunshot sound, there was a threatening sizzle. Matt cried out in pain and crumpled to the ground.

"Matt!" I pulled free of the guard, ran to Matt, and dropped to my knees. "Matt, are you okay?" Obviously, he wasn't. He had no muscle control and was shaking like he'd been electrocuted. I looked at the guard incredulously. "Why would you do that?"

"He was a little too cocky for his own good. Don't worry, he'll survive. It's only a Taser gun. Just fifty thousand volts."

"People have *died* from Taser guns." Matt stopped writhing. His eyes were vacant but wide with shock, and he wasn't moving at all. "Call someone! He needs help! Can't you see he's not okay?"

As the guard calmly reported into his Butler that he had a code-red situation and needed medical attention for a suspect shot with a Taser gun, I took Matt's hand. When I felt a faint squeeze, tears came to my eyes.

"Can you move?" I asked. He lifted his right arm weakly, and I breathed a sign of relief. "You're going to be okay," I reassured him, hoping it was true.

With my help, he was able to sit up. As soon as he did, the guard bent to handcuff him.

"Leave him alone!" I yelled. "Keep your hands off him!"

The guard grabbed my braid again, hauled me up, and threw me aside. I crashed into the wall but charged back at him, at which point he put his hands around my throat and choked me until I was lightheaded and unable to breathe. I fought to maintain consciousness.

"Stop that!" called Lacy Rhodes, hurrying down the hallway.

The guard gave one last squeeze and pushed me away. I gasped for breath, thankful she showed up and wondering what would have happened if she hadn't.

"What's going on?" she asked the guard.

"She was sticking her nose where it wasn't supposed to be," he said.

"He Tasered my friend for no good reason—look at him!"

"What were you two doing back here?"

"I was just going to the bathroom, and Matt came looking for me!"

Two more security guards had arrived and hauled Matt up off the ground.

"Be careful!" I yelled. "Mrs. Rhodes, please help!"

Her look was unexpectedly icy. "You and I should talk. We'll go to my husband's office and have a word."

"No!" I said because Daemon was in there, or near there, or trying to get away from there. "I have to go back and help my mom, and I need to stay with Matt."

"Arrest this kid," she told the guards, and then turned to me. "Let's go."

She started down the hallway toward her husband's office, her high heels clicking rhythmically on the marble floor. When I hesitated, the guard who'd Tasered Matt and assaulted me grabbed my arm, pressed into my flesh, and half-walked, half-dragged me down the hall. I thought my artery was going to explode.

"Let's talk right here!" I cried, because as best I knew Daemon was still in there and about to be caught red-handed. "I really have to get back to my mom. She's counting on me."

Lacy Rhodes spun around. "You *were* going to my husband's office, weren't you? I'm merely taking you where you wanted to go."

"No," I said. "I promise I wasn't."

"I'll take it from here," she told the guard. "You wait outside and make sure no one disturbs us."

He unlocked the door to the governor's office, flicked on the wall-switch lights, and then took up his position outside the doorway. I followed her inside the office, holding my breath, not knowing what to expect, and was ultimately relieved Daemon was nowhere in sight. I'd imagined him rushing us, trying to force his way out, and I hadn't been optimistic that would end well, not with the heartless guard so quick on the trigger. Was Daemon still inside, hiding somewhere, listening?

Lacy Rhodes closed the office door and faced me.

"I honestly wasn't doing anything wrong, Mrs. Rhodes," I said. "I was just walking down the hallway. I don't know why that guard went all crazy on me."

"He's paid to protect the governor and he saw you as a threat."

"But I'm not a threat," I said. "I promise I'm not."

"Oh, believe me, I know you're not." It wasn't only her words but the way she smiled—condescendingly, all-knowingly—that took my unease to a whole new level. "Have a seat."

Reluctantly, I sat in a chair near the small conference table. She remained standing.

"You look worried," she said. "Are you afraid of me, Kendra?"

At the moment, I most definitely was.

"Should I be?"

"My husband's intern reported her swipe card was stolen," she said. "What were you hoping to achieve by breaking into my husband's office?"

"I wasn't breaking in."

"So you say."

"And I don't have his swipe card. You can search me. I promise I don't have it."

She smiled. "You were looking for something, right? You were going to take something. You're a taker, Kendra. A taker of things that don't belong to you."

"Uh, no—"

"I worry about you," she said. "I've worried since the day my husband told me about you. I've been praying for you." She pulled a chair close and sat next to me. "Can we say a prayer together, Kendra? And then you can be on your way."

"Um, I really don't—"

Before I could refuse, she grabbed my hands with both of hers.

"Ow!" I felt that familiar painful jolt as she pressed her thumbs into my palms. "Please don't! Let go!"

I tried to pull away, but Lacy Rhodes clenched her eyes closed and pressed her thumbs harder into my palms.

I could not *believe* what was happening.

Mrs. Rhodes was stealing my Insight . . . and giving me hers.

● TEN PEOPLE IN FULL-BODY BIOHAZARD SUITS WALK AS A
group through the baggage-claim area of the Denver International Airport, identifiable not only because of a sign, but by the colorful, horrid apocalyptic mural that depicts dead children in caskets and forest fires and militaristic figures wearing gas masks. They walk past the mural and around the corner and eventually come to a halt within a large box that has been painted on the airport floor, along with the words STOP HERE. IF YOU PROCEED BEYOND THIS MARKED STAGING AREA, PREPARE TO BE SHOT.

About twenty feet away in a similar box that does not contain such a warning is a waiting Commander Gardiner, flanked by six soldiers with guns. They are dressed in paramilitary uniforms but do not wear biohazard suits.

"Take off your facemasks," he orders, adding, "You're safe here. We'll quarantine you for a bit, and then you'll be able to join us."

First one and then another and then the rest take off their biohazard facemasks. The first to do so is Daemon, and the last to do so is Robert Rodriguez, the current vice president of the United States.

Gardiner startles when he recognizes the vice president and immediately salutes, his men following suit. Rodriguez stares at Gardiner for a pointed moment before returning the salute and instructing him to be at ease.

"Sir," Gardiner says. "Forgive me, sir, but no one has seen you in weeks. I was told you were dead."

"Well, I'm not."

They each size up the other—the vice president defiant and wary, Commander Gardiner clearly conflicted.

"Is Governor Rhodes here?" Rodriguez asks, emphasizing the word governor. "It seems we should talk."

"Sir, you're the rightful Commander in Chief." Gardiner says it as if he can't quite believe it, as if it's still sinking in that the vice president is alive and therefore legally, if not in practice, in command.

"Yes, I am."

"I've sworn to protect and defend you against all enemies, foreign and domestic." Gardiner nods with determination. "And I will, so help me God."

"Let's tell Governor Rhodes that, shall we?"

• • •

When Lacy Rhodes opened her eyes and dropped my hands, I stared at her with my mouth agape. That wasn't how things were supposed to end! Not that I knew what the ending *was*, but Daemon had flat-out said—or implied?—he wasn't going to live, so how was he alive in that Insight?

And where was I?

It looked like the outbreak *had* occurred, and Daemon's side was conceding defeat . . . or was it?

Was Daemon working with people who went as high up as the vice president?

Did I live, or did I die?

"What's wrong, Kendra?" she asked with faux innocence. "You look upset."

"So do you."

"Did you happen to mention his impending assassination to my husband?"

"His what?"

"Ohhh," she laughed. "Don't bother."

"I don't know what you saw, and I don't know what you're talking about." I stood. "I'd like to leave now."

"But where would you go? What would you do? It doesn't seem wise on my part to let you leave, does it?"

She's going to kill me, I thought, my skin prickling with the realization. *How will she do it? How will she do it and not get caught?*

It couldn't be something physically violent, like stabbing or choking or shooting me. It had to be somehow that could be explained away—a fall down a flight of stairs, maybe? From her perspective, now was actually a really bad time for her to do it, simply because her absence from the party would be noted, as would mine, and my mom wouldn't physically leave the Capitol without me. What she needed was a good reason to postpone killing me; I needed to give her one. I also needed to let Daemon know what was happening, if he was hiding somewhere in the room.

"How long have you been having Insights?" I asked her.

"A long time."

"What happened to you?"

"A boating accident when I was younger. I nearly drowned." She laughed. "Too bad I didn't, you're probably thinking."

"I don't know how you can stand it."

She seemed surprised. "Having Insights? Why, I find them very useful. Extremely useful, in fact. Don't you? They're a gift, if you choose to see them as such."

"All they've done is ruin my life."

"Well, they've made me who I am." She studied me. "But then, you're not very ambitious, are you?"

I bristled. "Being a governor's wife is ambitious?"

"I'm far more than simply a governor's wife," she scoffed. "I have a PhD in biomedicine. I used to run a clinical lab at Johns Hopkins studying heredity and intelligence, and I'm presently on the board of trustees at the Mayo Clinic and chair of the Legacy Foundation. I assure you I'm more than just a governor's wife."

"So why was the vice president wearing a biohazard suit in your Insight?" I asked, for Daemon's benefit as well as my own.

"Excuse me?"

"Why was the—" I stopped myself as I noticed her confusion and remembered that having an Insight was not the same as reading an Insight. Different people saw different aspects of a particular event.

"Go on," she prompted.

"I'll tell you what," I said, thinking fast. "You're right; I'm not very ambitious. The only thing I care about is keeping my mom safe. Did your husband tell you about the Insight of my mom dying from the outbreak?"

"I'm aware of Daemon Godwin's Insight, yes."

"Well, I guess what I'm saying is if I have to pick a side, I'm going to pick the one that keeps my mom safe. It's pretty obvious from reading your Insight that Daemon's people aren't going to be able to stop the outbreak, and like I said—I want to be on the winning side. And I want to stay alive. So I have a proposal for you."

She looked intrigued. "What's your proposal?"

"If you keep me and my mom safe from the outbreak, then I'll share all my Insights with you. I have a new one every couple days, and, I don't know . . . don't you think they might be useful to you?"

She smiled. "Yes, I believe they would."

Which was how I made my deal with the devil.

A FEW MINUTES LATER, I WALKED OUT OF GOVERNOR Rhodes's office—alive. I had no intention of sticking to the deal I'd just struck, but I hadn't seen any other way to get out of there.

My first concern was Matt. Arriving back at the ballroom, I found the fundraising event wrapping up. My mom beckoned me from across the room.

"We need to get out of here," I said.

"Where have you been? Matt got taken away in handcuffs, and you were nowhere to be found! Nobody would tell me what's going on!"

"Did you ask Governor Rhodes?"

"I couldn't find him. Kendra, what did Matt do? I don't have to tell you this isn't going to reflect well on me. I was really hoping—"

That should be the least of her worries.

"Trust me, Mom, you don't want to work for these people. Do you know where they took him?"

"To the police station, I imagine. What did he do, Kendra?"

"He defended me, that's all. Listen, Mom, I've got to go. Can I borrow the catering van?"

"No! You're not insured, and—"

"Seriously, I've got to go. Whether or not I'm insured doesn't matter. I need the van."

"You can't have it." My mom looked around. "I'm not done here. I'm nowhere near done. I've got at least a couple hours of cleanup ahead of me."

"Mom, this is more important. It's life or—"

"Maybe you could call Detective Larson and see if he can help."

Governor Rhodes was on his way over, looking at me with concern. He held up a hand indicating I should wait for him. That wasn't going to happen.

"I need to go," I told my mom hurriedly. "Listen, stay away from the governor and his wife, okay? I'll explain later, but they're not nice people. Make sure you get out of here as soon as you can. In fact, you should come with me right now. Let's quietly walk out of here right now."

"That's not going to happen, Kendra. It's ridiculous you'd even ask."

"They're part of this, Mom! They're on the wrong side."

She finally got it and gripped my arms, her eyes darkened with concern. "You go, then. Right now. I'll say you went out to the catering van, but you go out there and keep walking. You get yourself somewhere safe."

"What about you?"

"Don't worry about me," she said. "Don't ever, ever worry about me. You just keep yourself safe. You hear?"

I nodded and told her I loved her and fled before she saw the tears in my eyes.

The moment felt like goodbye.

• • •

Forty minutes later, Detective Larson and I arrived at the precinct where Matt was being held. I'd called him after making my keep-on-walking escape from the Capitol, and he came right away in his classic red Ford Mustang.

"I had no idea you drove such a cool car," I said when he pulled up and I got in.

"They're charging Matt with a felony offense," he said. "Assaulting a federal officer. He's got to stay in jail overnight."

"Can we see him?"

"Not until his arraignment."

"Can you pull some strings so we can?"

"We'll see, but I doubt it."

Why did that not surprise me?

In fairness, he tried hard with the officer behind the desk, but all we ended up with was the time of Matt's arraignment. We went for a late-night breakfast at Denny's, camped out in a corner booth, and because I really thought I might be dead or disappeared in the extreme near future, I told Larson everything—finally.

"This is like something out of a movie, Kendra," he said when I was done, understandably stunned.

"Do you believe me?"

"Why wouldn't I?"

"I didn't believe Dr. Ridgeway when he first started telling me things. I thought he was absolutely bonkers."

"But I've been on the periphery of your situation the entire time, and it's abundantly clear more is going on than meets the eye.

The question is what can be done. Who's safe to tell? How do we stop it? How do we keep you and your mom alive?"

Those were all very good questions. Unfortunately, I had no answers.

"Do you know anyone really high up in the government?" I asked. "Someone you trust with your life?"

"I'd have to think on that. There are people I know, but only in a professional capacity. I never fought in a war with them, you know? I don't have those sorts of bonds with anyone. Let's check on your mother."

He called her Butler phone, but she didn't answer. We debated driving back to the Capitol to see if the van was still there, which meant she was still there, but ultimately Larson refused because he felt it was unsafe for me. Neither would he leave me at the restaurant and go himself.

When we couldn't drink another sip of coffee and couldn't stand being in Denny's any longer, we drove to the police precinct where Matt was being held and spent hours sitting on a hard wooden bench waiting for him to be brought out of his jail cell and taken to court for his arraignment. Hours later they finally brought him out, pale and in handcuffs, looking exhausted and scared-but-trying-to-hide-it. I jumped up and tried to hug him but was blocked by the officers escorting him.

Detective Larson and I followed the patrol car to the courthouse. We had to go in a different entrance, and once we went through security, we got settled in the courtroom where Matt's hearing was to be held, sitting toward the back. I'd never been to court before, but it was pretty much like I'd expected, with a bailiff standing by the door and wooden benches and a little gate between the court area and the spectator area, and the judge's bench up high and the court stenographer's down low. It was more crowded than I expected, but Detective Larson explained suspects were brought in as a group for their initial appearance since they had to be formally charged within a short period of time after their arrest. Most of the people waiting, he said, were their families and friends. I looked around but didn't see Matt's parents anywhere.

By that point, I was stupid-tired and began to doze off while waiting for Matt to be brought in. I dreamt there was a swarm of bees chasing me and woke to realize it was actually the collective buzz of numerous Butler alerts going off at once.

"What's happening?" I asked Larson.

"Stay here."

He hustled over and conferred with the bailiff, who'd blocked the main doorway and locked it from the inside.

"Ladies and gentlemen," the bailiff called. "We're under code-red lockdown! There's an active shooter on the loose. Turn off the sound on your phones and move away from the doorways—and stay calm. We'll get you out of here as soon as it's safe."

Blocking the main door, he kept one hand on his holster as if to warn us not to try and leave.

No one outright screamed, but you could sense the panic as everyone scurried to get out of the potential path of the shooter's gun. Fear crackled in the air, and it had an actual bitter smell to it. There had been so many mass shootings in the last few years around the country—one at a movie theater, one at a church, one at a shopping mall, one at an elementary school, one at a college campus. We all knew the worst-case scenarios.

Meanwhile, Larson rushed to the judge's chambers and

delivered the judge to the jury box, which had its back to an exterior, windowless wall. He gestured for me to come sit in the jury box, too, and I quickly did so. While all this was happening, a few other law enforcement people took up similar positions by the other courtroom door. Some people crouched on the courtroom's far side, using the wooden benches as makeshift blockades. Two people hid under the judge's podium. We all just sat, or crouched, or cowered, waiting to see what would happen.

All around me, Butlers were beeping with breaking news alerts. I overheard snippets of conversations from around the room.

Mass shooting in downtown St. Paul . . .

Political rally . . .

Six dead . . .

One shooter subdued, tackled by Governor Rhodes . . . oh my God—he's a hero!

I flinched when I heard that one, but it got even worse.

A second shooter on the loose. Dark hair, brown eyes, twenty-one years old.

Name: Daemon Godwin, although that may be an alias.

Larson and I stared at each other. We both knew something was wrong. Daemon wasn't the shooter.

At least he hadn't been in my Insight.

In my Insight, he wasn't even there.

•   •   •

We were stuck in the courtroom for hours as the manhunt for Daemon continued.

Within the first half hour, the SWAT team came through and searched the room. After declaring it clear, one SWAT officer was stationed outside each door while on the inside the bailiff and law enforcement officers kept guard.

At that point, people's fear lessened. A woman let me watch the news on her Butler with her, and because a news station caught the actual shooting on camera, I was able to see it over and over, but no matter how many times I watched, it never made sense.

It was the exact same rally as my Insight. It was in the same spot, which I learned was Winthrop Square, directly across the street from the courtroom where I was now hiding with fifty strangers. The crowd was the same as in my Insight—about five hundred, mostly men, and I learned it had been a labor-union rally. There was the same fat man in red suspenders, giving the same introduction as in my Insight. There was the same little girl with a green tutu and a baton, sitting on stage with her parents. But there was no man in a windbreaker with a baseball cap tucked low on his head.

The shooter from my Insight was not today's shooter.

Today's shooter was a shorter man, and he used a rifle instead of a handgun. He was off to the side of the stage at the far back of the crowd. He carried himself like a soldier, like Russell Hendricks and all the other military and ex-military people I knew—straight posture, shoulders back, all-business demeanor. As the red-suspenders guy spoke, the shooter stood perfectly still, but as Governor Rhodes headed toward the stage, he pulled a rifle from his duffel bag and methodically fired.

Bam, bam, bam, bam.

The girl in the tutu, both her parents, the man in the red suspenders—all shot, all killed.

There was screaming. Panic. Chaos. Everyone ran away from

the shooter, except for two people: Governor Rhodes, who jumped from the stage and ran straight at him, tackling him expertly; and Daemon, who'd been at the outer edge of the crowd. He also ran toward the shooter.

It was weird, how the video camera caught the whole thing.

It was weird, how the shooter was able to hit everyone else so easily but didn't even seem to aim at Governor Rhodes, the only target who made sense.

It was weird, how the police and media kept saying Daemon was trying to attack Governor Rhodes, when to me it looked like he and Governor Rhodes had the same aim—to bring down the shooter.

A man in the crowd tackled Daemon. He fell but then scrambled out of the man's grasp and ran away, clutching the knife he'd been holding. He definitely looked scary and a little crazed, and maybe because he ran off, or maybe because people see what they want to see, I saw something different than what everybody else saw, but what I saw was Daemon trying to be a good guy.

Footage of the shooting was shown over and over, cementing in everyone's mind not only that a dangerous assassin was on the loose, but—almost equally bad—that Governor Rhodes was a hero.

I realized what they'd done: Lacy Rhodes had read—stolen— my Insight and then they'd twisted it so when the outbreak happened and the president and all the others died, leaving a vacuum of power that a desperate country would need to fill, they'd be relieved to learn that the "heroic" Governor Rhodes was waiting in the wings to take charge.

It would be a government overthrow, and nobody—except for me—would even know it.

Unless I told them.

Unless I could make them see.

Unless I could stop it.

IN ALL THOSE HOURS WE WERE THERE, MY MOM NEVER GOT in touch with me, which was increasingly alarming.

After we were finally allowed to leave, Detective Larson drove me home. I held out hope she'd be there, maybe so exhausted from the catering job she'd fallen into an incredibly sound sleep and hadn't heard me calling the numerous times we'd called. Or maybe she'd turned off her Butler, which she seldom did, or maybe the battery had died, which sometimes happened, but not for the entire time I'd been gone. Despite my mind working through those possible scenarios, I knew in my heart something was horribly wrong.

When we got there, our car was in the garage, but that didn't mean anything since my mom had used the catering van, and I knew from Huckleberry's desperately eager greeting he'd been alone for a long time. Larson made me wait inside the doorway while he searched the house. After finding nothing, he had me look around, and it didn't seem to me she'd been back since the fundraiser.

"They took her," I said, sure of it then. "Lacy Rhodes went back on our deal."

The deal had allowed for me and my mom to have gone home the previous night, packed some things today, and report to the governor's residence sometime today, together and at a time of our choosing. In retrospect, it didn't surprise me she'd gone back on her word; I'd certainly intended to go back on mine.

"What do we do now?" I asked Larson, who looked as exhausted as I felt.

"Why don't you pack a bag? At least that way, you're ready to join your mom once the Rhodes camp gets in contact with you."

He winked so I'd know he was saying it for the benefit of whoever was listening.

"Okay," I said. "I'm going to take my dog over to Mr. Swanson's house, though, because I forgot to ask Mrs. Rhodes if I could bring him, and I can't leave him here all by himself."

Mr. Swanson had been our next-door neighbor as long as we'd lived there. He watched Huckleberry when we went on trips and while I was in the hospital.

"Want me to go with you?" Larson asked.

"Why don't you stay here and call the governor's security people to make arrangements for me to go to the residence?" I said. "I'm not going to go until I talk to my mom, though, no matter what. If I don't know she's already there and safe, I'm not going."

I packed up Huckleberry's food, water dish, and the blanket he liked to sleep on, and headed next door. Mr. Swanson stuck his head out his door before I was halfway there. He was in his early seventies and reminded me of a leprechaun because he was short and Irish and his blue eyes usually twinkled with mischief. But not that day.

"The police have been in and out of your house all morning," he said. "Your dog's been going crazy. What's going on?"

"What police?"

"Brookview PD."

That didn't sound right, as Larson had told me nothing about it and would have known. "You're sure? Was my mom with them?"

"Yes, I'm sure, and no, she wasn't. You don't know where your mother is?"

I shook my head.

"You'd better come in."

Mr. Swanson was like a grandfather to me. An odd one, for sure, with lots of what my mom called *interesting* ideas, but one thing about him: He loved us like family. He joined us for holidays and often invited us for dinner, made with lots of vegetables fresh from his garden.

Huck ran to the living room, jumped on the couch, and rolled around. It was his coming-to-Mr.-Swanson's-house longstanding habit. I remained just inside the door.

"How much trouble are you in, Kendra?" Mr. Swanson asked.

I let out a big breath. The enormity of the question overwhelmed me.

"I'm in a ton of trouble," I said. "Will you watch Huckleberry for me?"

"Of course I will," he said. "Where are you going?"

"That's the thing," I said. "I have another favor to ask. I need to disappear, and I was hoping maybe I could use your cabin up north."

I knew from previous discussions it was "off the grid," because Mr. Swanson was one of those survivalist types who stored a year's worth of food and water and had a "bug-out" location to go to when things fell apart in the city.

"I can take you there right now," he said. "We'll get in my van, bring your dog with us, and leave right now."

I shook my head. "Then Detective Larson will know where I am. I don't think anyone should know, not even him."

"What about your mom?"

"I think they're keeping her to use against me."

He peered at me. "Who's *they*?"

I hesitated, not because I didn't trust him but because I didn't have one spare minute to get into it.

"Can I tell you later?"

"Of course. But you can't let them use your mom against you. She's an adult and can take care of herself. She'd want you to go."

I knew he was right.

I also knew I couldn't leave without her.

The problem was I couldn't get to her; I had to wait for them to come to me.

I LEFT HUCKLEBERRY WITH MR. SWANSON, AND WHEN I GOT back to my house, I learned that Larson had been unable to get through to the governor's security people. Deciding I'd be a sitting duck if we stayed at my house, I packed a backpack and we went to his house—not that I thought that was much safer. He lived three miles away, in the newer part of Brookview where the houses were bigger but the yards smaller.

Not having slept for going on thirty-six hours, I fell asleep in the car on the way over, and once we arrived, I stumbled to the guest bedroom, where I fell into a deep, Insight-ridden sleep.

• • •

It's dusk, the darkest part of day. The sun is gone but the stars aren't out yet.

There's a red-haired teenage girl, very pretty, dressed in a light-blue prom-type dress. She's standing in a clearing in the woods. Nearby there's another girl, same age, wearing jeans and a messy T-shirt. She sets up a tripod and secures a camera to it while the other girl waits to be photographed, swirling around occasionally to make her dress spin. She has a crown of flowers in her hair, and she adjusts it frequently.

Suddenly, she freezes and a look of horror crosses her face. Her eyes are wide with terror, and her mouth opens in a silent wail. I follow her gaze, and I see them.

I see what they do to her friend.

Three men have surrounded the teenage photographer. Her camera has crashed to the ground. She, herself, is on the ground, facedown in the gravel. Two scraggly, scruffy, horrible-looking men with knives grab at her. Her eyes plead to her friend to help or to hide. But her friend is paralyzed by her fear, and a third man grabs the girl with the flowers in her hair and points a gun at her head.

The two men take turns raping the girl on the ground. They choke her until she nearly, but not quite, passes out. One takes his knife and slices an artery in her neck. She lies on the ground bleeding to death, eyes open.

Then they go after her friend, but the gunman fires a bullet into her temple before they get to her, before they can rape her like they did the other girl.

Then they saunter away, and just like that, it's over—the girls' lives, my Insight.

· · ·

I jolted awake and began to scream.

A hand clamped over my mouth.

"Kendra, shhhh!" Daemon knelt at the edge of my bed, smoothing back my hair, his voice low and comforting. "It's okay. You're going to be okay."

I encircled his wrist with my fingers and guided his hand away from my mouth.

"How did you find me?" I whispered, glancing toward the

closed door of the guest bedroom. "How'd you get in? And should you be here?"

"So many questions." He tried to smile. "Larson's out cold on the other side of the house."

"We pulled an all-nighter."

"I think it has more to do with the sedative I put in his coffee. You mind?" He gestured that he wanted to lie down. I thought of Matt and felt guilty, but I moved over for him.

"What happened this morning?" I asked quietly. "I saw the footage of the shooting, and it didn't make any sense. You weren't really part of killing all those people, were you?"

"Of course not," he said. "I was trying to stop the shooter."

"Were your people the ones who were initially going to assassinate Rhodes?"

"We were," he said. "I'm sure now you understand what that was all about."

"Were you in the governor's office when I was talking to Lacy Rhodes, or did you get away?"

"I was there," he said. "She's a piece of work, isn't she? We knew she was going to corner you and take you to his office, but we didn't know what she was going to say, so it was extremely helpful that—"

"Wait, you *what?*"

"One of our people had an Insight about what was going to happen in the hallway."

"And you let it happen?" My blood boiled. "You knew Matt was going to get shot like that, and you let it happen? Lacy Rhodes was going to kill me! I felt it! I saw it in her eyes! How dare you just let it happen?"

"We weren't letting it happen," he said. "That's why I was there, to protect you if necessary. We had tear gas ready to be sprayed in case we needed to get you to safety, but you handled things quite well on your own. We're all real happy with how you handled yourself."

"Yeah, well, now they've got my mother. God, you're such a jerk. You're all such jerks." I pushed him. "Get out of the bed."

He did, but then he sat back on it.

"You need to think of the big picture, Kendra, the end goal. We're trying to save your mom's life here, aren't we? We're trying to stop an attack that's otherwise going to kill millions of people. To do that, we need information, and your meeting with Lacy Rhodes gave us lots of information. For instance, did you know her father was a big player in the eugenics movement back in the thirties and forties? He made his money in copper, which he used to further the eugenics movement."

"Eugenics," I said, sounding out the word. I'd heard it before, of course, but I wasn't clear on what it was or why it was important.

"It's an attempt to breed out certain genetic qualities from the population and purify it. Hitler and the Nazis were into it, of course, but a lot of Americans were, too. Famous people like Teddy Roosevelt and Helen Keller and Alexander Graham Bell and Charles Lindbergh. Francis Crick, the guy who discovered DNA? He believed in eugenics. So did Winston Churchill. It had a ton of supporters back in the day until Hitler came along and gave it a bad name, but there still are plenty of people who believe in it, only secretly, and Lacy Rhodes is one of them."

"You're kidding."

"You know that work she did back East? It had to do with trying to identify intelligence genes based on people's DNA—not only looking at whether certain races are genetically wired to be more intelligent than others, but even within a race, can you ascertain someone's range of intelligence based on their DNA? It turns out you most likely can. At this point, scientists are in general agreement that about seventy-five percent of a person's IQ is coded in their genetic profile, so in the nature-nuture debate, nature actually wins. The research is one thing; it's what people do with the research—how they apply it—that's the scary thing. It invites people to play God. And do you know what she used to do before she did that?"

I shook my head.

"This is very well covered-up or her husband would never be in office, but back in the day, she was associated with a group accused of illegally sterilizing women from low-income neighborhoods. They offered a free immunization clinic, but they also gave the women a second shot containing something that caused them to lose their ability to get pregnant. They did this for years until someone involved grew a conscience and reported it."

I felt sick. "She wasn't arrested?"

"Nothing ever came of it, and the whistleblower was found dead of an apparent suicide shortly afterwards. Makes you wonder, huh?"

Blame it on my mediocre genetic makeup, but I had to ask, "Makes you wonder what?"

"What she's got in store for us."

"Us? As in you and me?"

"No, as in the world," he said. "If she's involved in this massive plot to wipe out half the world's population, don't you think she'd want to make sure it's the so-called lesser half who dies?"

"How could she do that?"

"We don't know—yet."

"How bad is it that Mrs. Rhodes can read Insights?"

"It's not entirely unexpected," Daemon said. "We know the other side goes after people who have Insights or who get killed in Insights, and this explains why—they want them just like we want them for the information they can provide. Often, it's a race to get there first. Like with you. In your case, Ridgeway got there first, and so we won."

"Except they have my mom."

"They took her because they know it works," he said. "They know what you did last time when Gardiner took her, and they're expecting you to do the same thing this time."

"Speaking of Gardiner, you should know he might not be all bad. I don't think he knows what's really going on."

"I'm sure he doesn't know everything that's going on—only a very few people would know everything—but what makes you say that?"

"Because when Lacy Rhodes was reading my Insight, I was reading hers, and in hers, the outbreak happens, and you show up with the vice president at the Denver airport, and Gardiner's there, and he pledges his loyalty to the vice president, who he'd thought was dead."

"I was there? You weren't?" Daemon looked confused. "That doesn't make any sense. And the outbreak *doesn't* happen. You stop it."

"Maybe not. Destinies can be changed, remember?"

Before we could talk further, we heard approaching sirens. Daemon started toward the bedroom door.

"Daemon, wait! You've got to put me on the Underground Railroad. I'm ready to go without my mom."

"We need to keep you out," he said. "Things are changing rapidly, and—"

"You promised!"

"I know," he said. "And I'm sorry, but I also promise you're going to be okay."

"You can't promise that!"

"I can," he said, halfway out the door. "I do."

"Wait, listen! I had another Insight! You need to see it."

The sirens kept getting louder. Daemon rushed back to me, grabbed my hands, and pressed his thumbs into my palms. When he pulled back, his look was troubled.

"That happens tonight," he said. "Like, imminently, and we need those girls to live. You're going to have to tell Larson, because I don't think I can get there in time, not with everyone trying to hunt me down. Plus it's a great distraction for when the cops get here. Keep them busy with your Insight and don't let on I was here."

"You can't leave." I nearly cried. "You promised you'd help."

"Meet me later tonight, okay?" he said. "Meet me in the—"

"I'll come with you now."

I got out of bed, but he shook his head.

"Meet me in the cemetery at midnight," he said. "Meet me at your boyfriend's grave."

"Why there? Did someone have an Insight about it and you're setting me up like you did last night? Because I'm not going to let you use me like that again."

"Just be there, Kendra."

"I notice you didn't deny it."

"Just be there."

"No," I said as he headed out the door. "Just no."

HOURS LATER FROM MY PERCH ON DETECTIVE LARSON'S LIV-
ing room sofa, I watched him speed up to the house and slam on
his brakes. Heart sinking, I rose and met him at the door.

I'd been in the house alone for a while, although a patrolman
was parked at the curb. After Daemon made his earlier escape—
a.k.a. abandoned me—two Brookview patrol cars arrived, sirens
blaring, but thankfully Daemon wasn't their target; Larson had
asked them to protect me.

"What happened?" I said. I'd told him about my newest Insight,
describing the woods as best I could. He'd been out ever since trying to stop the attack from happening.

"There's been an attack in the woods." He looked at me grimly.
"I need to take you to the crime scene."

"No," I disagreed. "I don't need to see that."

"The police chief's insisting on it," he said. "But there's some
good news: The girls are alive."

"Is there bad news, too?"

"I'll tell you on the way," he said.

He drove fast with his siren flashing, and whenever we came
up behind cars in the road they pulled off to the side to let us pass.

It gave me flashbacks to the night of the accident when Adam was driving just as obnoxiously.

"Can you please slow down?" I said. "And maybe tell me what happened?"

Larson pulled to the side of the road, put the patrol car in park, and faced me. "All right, here's the deal: Daemon Godwin took a machete and single-handedly plowed down three men in the woods north of town."

My stomach lurched. "He *what?* Are you sure it was him?"

"It was him, and all three men died. The girls witnessed the whole thing and said Daemon was absolutely brutal, attacking with intent to kill. He wasn't merely trying to scare them off." He gave me a long look. "My question to you is how did he happen to be in the exact right spot at the exact right time?"

"Ummm . . ." *Because he was at your house and in the bedroom with me after drugging you.* "I'm not sure about that."

"Not sure, or not sure you want to tell me?"

"Exactly." My eyes sank closed as I visualized what must have happened. Having seen how brutal the men had been in my Insight, I understood exactly why Daemon acted the way he had. "Had they attacked the girls?"

"They'd started to. The men approached wielding a gun and knives, and things continued on from there exactly as you described in your Insight, until Daemon showed up and put an end to things."

"How far had it gotten?" I asked. "Was the one girl raped?"

Larson shook his head, no. "He got there in the nick of time, apparently. The other girl said Godwin dashed out of the woods like a madman, waving the knife around to get their attention, and then went after the one choking her friend and hacked him up something good. Got him right in the jugular. Then he sliced and diced the other two and ran off again."

"They deserved to die. Daemon was only defending those girls."

"But the public doesn't know that, and couldn't he have defended the girls without killing the men? To most people, this looks premeditated, and don't forget, he's already wanted in connection with the shooting earlier today."

"You know that's a setup."

"What I know is that one young man against the full power of the law isn't going to get very far or last very long out on his own, and you should be prepared, Kendra: Very likely, he's not going to be brought in alive."

"He's not going to be brought in at all." I slumped in my seat and stared out the window. There was a trail of flashing red lights snaking up the ravine and into the woods. "I saw it in an Insight. He lives."

Did I really believe that?

No. I believed either of us could die at any time.

Larson got back on the road and we followed the trail of red lights. When we got to the crime scene, Commander Gardiner was there—waiting for me.

I glared at Larson. "You didn't tell me he was going to be here."

"He wasn't here when I left to come get you."

Gardiner yanked me out of the car. "Where is he?"

I hated him so much I couldn't reconcile my hatred with my knowledge that he'd do the right thing in the end. "Do you remember the oath you took to defend the country against all enemies, foreign and domestic?"

He shoved me against the car and held me there, his elbow in my neck. *"Where is he?"*

His eyes were full of power and fury, and although I found him highly intimidating, I'd also seen a better side to him.

"Governor Rhodes is planning a coup, and his wife's in on it, too."

"Let go of her," Larson said, coming around to my side of the car. He put his hand on his holster, and the instant he did several of Gardiner's men aimed their weapons at him. Meanwhile, Gardiner maintained his grip and stared at me. I could have sworn I saw a flicker of doubt, which I took as a good sign.

"I'm trying to help you," I said quietly. "What did Russell Hendricks do, anyway? What did he do that was so bad you were supposed to kill him instead of questioning him or arresting him? I know what he did—you want to know? He heard something he wasn't supposed to hear, that's all."

"I'm a soldier," he spewed. "I follow orders. That's all I do. It's not my place to question."

"They're taking advantage of your loyalty. You're being used. You took an oath to defend the country against all enemies foreign and domestic," I said again. "Sometimes that means you can't follow the orders."

Still holding me against the car, Gardiner aimed his pistol at my head. Oddly, I felt no fear.

"Where's Daemon Godwin?" he said, as if our entire conversation had not taken place.

"You'll never find him," I said. "You won't see him until he comes to you in Denver, and then you'd damn well better listen to what he's got to say."

Just then a flood of lights from television cameras blasted us.

"Commander Gardiner!" a reporter called. "Is this a suspected accomplice?"

"Is the ITB spearheading the manhunt?" asked another.

"Who's this girl?"

"I'm Kendra Sinclair!" I called out. "And Governor Rhodes is trying to overthrow the government!"

Gardiner laughed and let me go. "Now you've done it. They're going to think you're crazy."

"I have Insights!" I said. "I had a premonition about this attack, and I reported it to the police. The man who killed them is a hero, not a murderer! It's Governor Rhodes who's the killer—he's responsible for the deaths of those people at the rally!"

From their laughter, it was obvious the reporters thought I was nuts.

Larson took my arm. "Come meet the girls from the attack."

He led me to a barricaded area. Inside the barricade was a police car, and inside the police car were the two girls from my Insight. I stopped short at the sight of them, and then a strange thing happened: One of the girls saw me and pointed and her mouth dropped open in shock.

"I can't believe you're here," she said. It was the girl who would have been raped if Daemon hadn't saved her.

"How do you know who I am?" I asked.

"Kelly, this is the girl!" she told her friend. "This is the girl I was telling you about!"

The friend's eyes widened. I got a horrible feeling in the pit of my stomach.

"Do you know me?" I said.

"No," she said. "All I know is you're supposed to be dead."

● HONESTLY, NOTHING SURPRISED ME ANYMORE.

"Explain why I'm supposed to be dead," I said to the almost-raped girl.

"Well, when that man was choking me, I was losing consciousness," she said. "And I started hallucinating about this girl being beaten and tortured by these military types, and—"

Oh no, I thought. *This is not good.*

"Were the military types similar to those guys out there?" I asked, pointing to Gardiner's men.

"Yes, and you were the girl. I swear I'm not making this up."

"I know you're not," I said, reeling from the prospect of being tortured.

"I was passing out," the girl continued, and I thought, *No, you were dying.* "I guess I thought it was just a hallucination, but now . . . you *are* here, aren't you?" She reached forward from the back seat and touched my arm. "This is real?"

"It's real," I said, feeling awful for her. I remembered asking the same question after my first Insight about Maddie Meyers when I was in the hospital.

The girl's name was Melanie. She and Kelly were going to

be seniors at St. Andrew's, the private high school in Brookview. Kelly's boyfriend was going away to college in a few weeks, and she wanted to give him a framed picture of herself, so they'd been doing a photo shoot in the woods. *Such innocence,* I thought. *Gone forever now.*

"So in the, uh, the hallucination you had about me, did I, um . . . what happened to me? Oh! You know what? Would you mind if we tried something?"

"I guess not," she said, glancing at her friend for affirmation.

"All I want to do is take your hands for a minute and try something," I said, reaching for them. "It won't hurt, I promise." But then I zapped her and had to quickly apologize. "I'm sorry! I forgot about that. It's okay now, right? It doesn't hurt anymore? That zapping only lasts a couple seconds."

I pressed my thumbs into the palms of her hands, and when her expression softened, I knew the waves of relaxation were washing over her like they did when Daemon read my Insights. I closed my eyes and visualized my chest expanding, opening, making way for something to float into it, and suddenly I was in Melanie's Insight, circling it with the view of a raised movie camera, capturing it from several angles.

She was right: The men were military types, the kind who'd seen war, who'd killed and learned to like it. You could see it in their bloodthirsty eyes as they knocked me around.

My ankles were tied to the wooden chair I was sitting on, while my hands were tied behind my back. At the point I came into the Insight, my lip was bleeding and my right eye was swollen shut. One of the men smacked me so hard the chair fell over, and he smiled as my head hit the ground.

He hauled me back up. *Are you going to tell us, bitch? Huh? You going to tell us?* I couldn't have talked if I'd wanted to, but hanging from his neck, hitting my teeth, was a chain with the tell-tale gold-bullet pendant Russell had told me about, so I spread my jaw and captured the vial in my mouth, then clamped down on the chain and yanked as hard as I could.

The other guy was on me in an instant. He shoved one hand against my jaw so I couldn't move and with the other, he grabbed his partner's chain and held it steady. He, too, wore a chain with a bullet-shaped pendant. Once he had the other guy's chain gripped tightly, he pulled out a gun that had been tucked into the back of his pants and held the barrel against my temple. I immediately released the vial. Once he had it back, he smashed the gun against the side of my head, and I began to lose consciousness.

Go back, I instructed myself. *Go back before this moment.*

I did, and it was earlier that same night. I was running through woods so thick I couldn't see the moonlight through the canopy of trees. I kept tripping, and there were dogs chasing me, barking, happy-to-be-on-the-hunt dogs, and behind them a posse of men with guns. A few shots rang out, but they were either warning shots or they missed, and I kept running. The night was cool, and I kept running deeper into the woods. But the dogs were bred for hunting, and they tracked and out-ran me. One wolf-like dog leapt and knocked me over, while the other locked his nasty-jawed mouth around my ankle.

I buried my face in my hands to protect it and kept it buried even when the dogs were called off. Like a little kid who thought if she couldn't see the monsters, then the monsters couldn't see her, I willed myself to be invisible. One man slid a thick hand through my hair, grabbed it at the roots, and arched me backwards for the other men to see. I opened my eyes and understood how completely screwed I was. Four men surrounded me, all of whom appeared quite competent with their guns and all with the same bullet-shaped vials around their necks. One pulled a syringe from his camo-pants side pocket, fiddled with it, and injected me with something.

Again, I watched myself lose consciousness. The man who'd later take such pleasure in beating me handed off his gun, hauled me up and over his shoulder, and hiked out of the woods. He tossed me in the bed of his massive shiny-black pickup truck and pulled its cover down over me. He flicked the lock, trapping me, and sped off down the middle of a dark dirt road, the lead in a caravan of big-redneck-boy vehicles. Although I was locked in the bed of the pickup truck, I heard the phone call he made. He said just four words: *Governor? We got her.*

My eyes bolted open, and I dropped Melanie's hands.

"I need to get out of here," I said. "Will you guys help me? How did you get here—did you drive?"

"I did, yeah," said Kelly.

"Which one's your car?"

She looked at my outraised hand uncertainly. "It's that grey Jetta over there. Why?"

"I need to borrow it."

"Will I get it back?"

"Of course," I said, although I knew returning her car would be the last thing on my mind. I kept my hand out until she put the keys in them. "Thank you. But try not to let them know I took it, okay? Seriously, every second you stall and cover for me will help me more than you'll ever know."

"We will," Melanie promised.

"I'll tell them I drove my dad's Mercedes, and maybe that'll slow them down a little, too," Kelly said. "That way, they'll be looking for the wrong car."

"You guys are great," I said.

"Why would they torture you like that?" Melanie said.

"No good reason."

"But how weird you just showed up," she said.

"Melanie, I hate to tell you, but there's no such thing as coincidence in your life anymore," I said, remembering when I'd been on the receiving end of that statement. "Listen, I don't have time to get into things with you, but your life would be a lot easier if you didn't tell anyone about your hallucination. You're probably going to have more, but I highly, *highly* suggest you keep them secret."

"What do you mean I'm going to have more? How do you know? You have them, too, don't you?"

I got out of the car and then leaned back in. "You know that hardware store on Hammerhill Road? Ray's Ace Hardware?"

"I know it," she said. "I got paint from there a couple weeks ago. A really cute guy helped me."

"That's my friend, Matt, and he's the son of the owner. He knows what's going on, so if you can possibly connect with him, that might be really helpful . . . only he's in jail right now, and he's probably going to be watched when he gets out, so you've got to be really careful, okay? But tell him you met me and tell him your Insight, and then, uh . . . I don't know. I don't know what happens next. I can't offer you any advice. Sorry."

"Why's he in jail?" Kelly said.

"For protecting me."

I scoped out the situation. Gardiner was now holding a press conference with Chief Baxter, which was perfect because everyone was watching them and had their backs to me. Gardiner and Baxter were focused on answering the media's questions. Gardiner's men were nowhere to be seen, probably off hunting Daemon in the woods. Larson was part of the press conference, standing on stage behind Gardiner and Baxter, but his eyes were on me.

"Okay, I'm going to go," I said. "I think Detective Larson's one of the good guys, by the way. Watch what he does, and we'll see for sure. He's that guy standing behind the police chief, the one looking over here. If he's one of the good guys, he'll let me sneak away. And if he doesn't, I'm screwed."

I slinked as unobtrusively as possible to Kelly's car. I slipped into the driver's seat, closed the door silently, and looked back over at Larson. He was focused hard on the police chief, deliberately not watching me leave, and a rush of gratitude came over me.

I started up the car and slowly rolled out of the parking lot. I kept the headlights off and didn't brake so there'd be no taillight until I'd driven around the first curve and out of sight of the people left behind. I drove steadily home, never speeding, planning what I'd do once I got there. In light of Melanie's Insight, it seemed best to disappear immediately, even if it meant leaving my mom behind, so I'd make it quick, just grab some food and money and pack a bag and go with Mr. Swanson to his cabin up north. I'd have to trust that Daemon and his people would get my mom to safety.

I parked a few houses down from Mr. Swanson and stopped at his place on the way to mine. I always entered his house through the back door, but when I got to it I found a note taped on the window: *Gone Fishing.*

In the middle of the night?

I didn't think so.

Something must have happened that forced him to leave.

Earlier, he'd given me verbal directions to his off-grid cabin, but I couldn't remember them now. All I knew was to head north, but that wasn't nearly enough.

He'd also left a military-type backpack propped against the door. I unzipped the top and found it stocked with cash, a wool blanket, a windbreaker, a flashlight, granola bars, a toothbrush and toothpaste, bottled water, a box of bandages, a tube of antibiotic ointment, plastic handcuffs, pepper spray. On top of it all was a gun.

For years, my mom and I had joked behind Mr. Swanson's back about his survivalist tendencies. He believed the shit could hit the fan at any moment; I'd thought it never would.

I should have left right then, just taken the backpack and headed north. I didn't *need* anything from my house; it was nostalgia as much as a desire to grab some clean underwear and my favorite sweatshirt. I wanted the framed picture of my mom from my nightstand.

Nostalgia can lead a person to do some really stupid things.

I went around to the front door of my house, unlocked it, and went inside—and then I screamed, because Governor Rhodes was sitting on the couch in complete darkness.

"Sorry, I didn't mean to startle you." He stood and gestured for me to come further inside, as if he owned the house and I was the guest.

"What are you doing here?" I asked, even though I already knew.

He was waiting for me.

I FELT LIKE LITTLE RED RIDING HOOD: GOVERNOR RHODES was the wolf, about to devour me.

But Little Red Riding Hood tricked the wolf, I reminded myself. *And she survived.*

I entered the living room, clutching Kelly's keys in case I needed to use them as a weapon, not that they'd be much use in that regard.

"How did you get in?" I said.

"Your mother gave me a key." Usually very dapper, that night he looked rumpled, like he'd had a long day or had finally let down his guard. His suit jacket was folded over the back of one of our reading chairs, and his dress shirt was not tucked in well. But mostly, his eyes revealed his weariness.

"My mother didn't give you anything," I said. "You took it. I know you're holding her against her will."

"What's gotten into you, Kendra? I'm doing no such thing!" His expression was a show of righteous surprise, but I was sure that's all it was, a show.

"Then where is she? Why isn't she here?"

"Because you told her to stay at our house. That was the arrangement you made with my wife."

"No, it's not. Can we stop the games?" I said. "I really don't—"

"Kendra, I'm not playing games. Why don't you have a seat?"

He gestured toward the couch as if it was his house, not mine. I didn't take the bait. Sitting would trap me. By staying where I was near the front door, I had better access to go back through it, or down the hallway to my bedroom, or through the kitchen to the back patio door.

"Why don't *you* have a seat?"

"Okay." He sat back in the same spot he'd been in when I entered. "You were acting strange at the charity event last night, and you're acting strange now. I'm concerned about you."

"How am I supposed to act when people are trying to kill me?"

"You really think people are trying to kill you?"

I laughed, couldn't help it. "Yes, Governor, I really think that."

"Do you have any idea who?"

I pressed my lips together so I'd not snap and say—scream— the sarcastic things I wanted to. My purpose wasn't to confront him. It was to escape him.

"Why are you here?" I said.

"Your mother said she's been unable to get hold of you ever since you left the Capitol last night. I told her I'd come get you."

"Well, that's really interesting, because I've been trying to call her like crazy, and she's not picking up, so you either took her Butler or did something worse, like hurt her. Which you'd better not have."

"Why would I hurt your mother, Kendra? I adore your mother."

"Adore?"

He reddened. "I adore her cooking." He paused. "And she's a breath of fresh air in my normally very stuffy political world."

Compared to your wife, you mean.

"So let me call her," I challenged him.

"That's fine. Of course."

My heart quickened at the prospect that maybe my mom was okay. I plugged in the wall Butler.

"You always unplug it?" Governor Rhodes asked as we waited for it to warm up.

"Just lately."

"Where's your new watch, Kendra?"

I turned to him. "People tell me you can be spied on through them. It didn't seem like a smart time to be wearing one."

I expected a mocking reply, but he nodded, unfazed, and held up his own Butler-less wrist. "That's why I don't wear one. People have no idea how little privacy's left in the world. I think it's one of the most significant issues of the day. People who don't care about privacy don't know their history, plain and simple. If they did, they'd be a little more careful."

"What do you mean?"

"Imagine if the technology of Butlers had been available to Hitler," he said. "Imagine if the Nazis knew everyone's location, reading material, shopping habits. Buying kosher? Good to know. Doing daily Torah study? Also good to know. With today's technology, there'd be no hiding for the Jews. I thought about it after watching you activate your new Butler watch the other day and submitting a pinprick of blood. Irrefutable proof of one's Jewishness is embedded in one's DNA, you know. Maybe we shouldn't rush to have that fact stored in a database somewhere."

"Are you Jewish?" I asked.

"No." He raised an eyebrow. "Then why do I care, are you wondering?"

"No, I—"

"Everyone should care. My wife thinks technology's wonderful. I'm not so sure." He squinted at me. "What's wrong?"

"Nothing. Butler's ready. *Call Mom*," I instructed it.

User not available, I was told.

I yanked the cord from the wall before turning back to him. "See? Not available."

"I don't know what to say. I was just with her. She's fine."

"You're holding her against her will."

He stood again. "I'm bothered you'd even suggest such a thing."

"And I'm bothered you let six innocent people die this morning!"

He drew back like I'd punched him in the gut. "I hate that they died, too, but I didn't *let*—. Have you seen the news? I took down the shooter! Yes, I wish I could have—"

"You *hired* the shooter! The whole thing was a setup! Six innocent people died so you could get your name splashed all over the news. You make me sick!"

"Good Lord, Kendra." He looked utterly confused and alarmed. "*What* are you talking about?"

"Never mind," I said. "So why are you really here? And don't say to bring me to my mom. You could have sent anyone to do that."

"I'm here because I wanted to talk to you privately."

His words hung heavy. "Where's your bodyguard?"

"Waiting in the car out front. You didn't notice him when you came in?"

"Yeah, I noticed him." I hadn't, though, because after I'd parked the car a few doors down from Mr. Swanson's house, I'd cut through neighbors' backyards to get to his back door. From there, I'd gone to my front door but hadn't even looked to the street. *Note to self,* I thought, looking around for escape possibilities since leaving through the front door was no longer an option. *Pay better attention.* "What did you want to talk to me about?"

"You're so jittery," he said. "Would you please have a seat?"

I sat on the edge of our ottoman. He moved closer and sat in my mom's favorite armchair, resting his arm on her cashmere throw.

"Have you learned anything more about that biological weapons attack you told me about the other day?"

"Why?" I said. "Did *you* learn something?"

"It turns out the prison illness I told you about the other day moved beyond the initial victims," he said. "Several family members of the prison guards have fallen ill, so we believe it's able to spread with some virulence—which means it's got the potential of getting out of hand fast. What's worse, there's a second outbreak. Several of our wounded warriors at Walter Reed in D.C. are exhibiting the same symptoms, and the president just visited there yesterday. He physically touched each of the men who are now ill. We're hoping to God he doesn't come down with it. He's in isolation and being monitored, of course, but—" He shook his head as if there were no words for what he was thinking. "It could prove to be a very bad situation."

This is how it starts, I thought. *This is how the coup starts.*

"Has any of this been on the news yet?"

"Absolutely not," he said. "Can you imagine the panic it would cause? An experimental vaccine is being rushed to production, and we've got some on hand for the president in the event he becomes ill, but every day we can delay the public finding out, we're one day closer to having the vaccine ready, so we're just trying to buy some time."

"When will the vaccine be ready?"

"Unfortunately, probably not fast enough to stop the first wave of the outbreak, but hopefully in time to stop the second. Pandemics usually come in waves, you know."

"My mom's going to die," I said. "My Insight's going to come true."

"Didn't you say they can be changed?" he said. "Maddie Meyers wasn't kidnapped, after all. You changed that Insight by the actions you took, right? Well, I promise you, Kendra—you and your mom will be safe. You'll go with my family to our cabin up north. Guards will be posted out front, and once you're there, no one will be allowed in or out until it's over. We've got a year's supply of food and a truck is being stocked right now to follow you there with even more. You'll be absolutely safe there."

"Where's your cabin?"

"Near Lake Vermilion. And it's more like a lodge than a cabin. We've got a whole compound with acreage up there, so you'll have your space. We have an outbuilding you and your mom can stay in if you don't want to stay in the main house. It's got its own bath, but you'd still have to go to the main-house kitchen to eat. No one really cooks when they visit us."

I thought of what I'd seen in Melanie's Insight—thick woods, isolation. I'd gone camping with my Girl Scout troop near Lake Vermilion and knew it fit the bill. Going to Lake Vermilion with the Rhodes family was *not* an option.

"Will you be there, too?"

He shook his head. "I'll stay here. We can't have our leaders appear to be running and hiding; that doesn't instill confidence in the masses."

"How much time do you think we have before it starts to spread?"

"I think it already has," he said grimly. "The CDC is tracing everyone who's been in contact with the families of the prison guards and the patients at Walter Reed, and I have every expectation we'll have more illnesses showing up from those groups soon. Clearly, it's airborne, so if it spreads to one—which it has—there's no reason it won't spread to a million. Or many millions."

My head pounded from the implications of what he said.

How, I wondered. *How the hell do I stop it?*

You're there at the end, Daemon had said. *You defeat the bad guy. You're the hero of this whole damn thing.*

In that moment, I knew what I had to do.

I had to kill Governor Rhodes.

A CERTAINTY CAME OVER ME. A CALMNESS, A RIGHTNESS OF purpose, as if this was the moment I'd been building toward all along. My job was to kill Governor Rhodes, and I had to do it now while it was just the two of us because I might never get the chance again.

"We should get going," I said, standing. "I need a few minutes to pack."

"Need help?" I shook my head. "Take your time." He sank back into the chair, idly smoothing his fingertips over the cashmere throw. "It's quite peaceful here. I could use the break."

With his back to me, I walked from the living room to the kitchen and pulled out the sharpest knife we had. But just like that, the calmness that had overtaken me disappeared, and I started shaking uncontrollably looking at the length of the blade. I felt sick thinking what it would be like to stab him. To press the tip of the blade against his skin. To see the first splash of crimson blood. To have to push the knife deep into sinew and bone and flesh and twist it. To do the most damage possible. To kill.

I didn't think I could do it, despite my unwavering resolve that he needed to die. A knife was too intimate. The gun in the backpack Mr. Swanson had left for me would work much better; that way, I wouldn't have to get too close. I could shoot him from a distance.

I put the knife back in the drawer and silently slid it closed.

"Want a glass of water?" I called, mostly to explain away why I'd gone to the kitchen instead of my bedroom.

"Sure," he called back.

I brought him a glass—no more shakiness, I was relieved to note. He took a sip and flexed his neck from side to side, cracking it. He loosened his tie, and upon further thought removed it altogether and unbuttoned the top button of his true-blue dress shirt.

"I feel like I've lived an entire life since I woke up this morning," he said. "I hope I never have another day like today."

You won't, I thought, and then choked back a gasp when I realized he was wearing one of those bullet-shaped pendant chains Russell Hendricks had described. If I'd doubted his involvement before—and I hadn't, not really—seeing that pendant was all the proof I needed. Inside the twisty-off part must be some sort of pill to protect against the virus. It was the only thing that made sense.

I needed to get my hands on it and get it to Daemon. I guess I *would* be going to the cemetery at midnight after all.

"I'll go pack," I said, forcing myself to take slow, calculated steps down the hall to my room, hardly believing he'd really let me out of his sight—but he did.

Once in my room, I flung open a drawer loudly in case he was listening and then turned on the water in the sink in my bathroom. I closed the bathroom door, stepped into the shower, and raised the opaque glass window I'd crawled through numerous times over the years to sneak out and go to Nora's house when I was supposed to be sleeping. We'd meet up in her tree house and think we were getting away with something, but I'd learned later that our parents had figured out what we were doing early on and decided to let us have our little thrill.

Once out the window, I ran to Mr. Swanson's back door, opened the backpack, grabbed the gun and other items I thought I might need, and retraced my steps, crawling back in through the same window. I left it open because if all went well I'd be going through it again in the very near future.

Before returning o the living room, I paused long enough to understand how the plastic handcuffs worked, and I took the cap off the pepper spray so it would be ready if I needed it. I stuck both in my back waistband. Then I gripped the gun with my right hand, cocked it, and walked carefully back out to the living room, pointing it in front of me until I came into view of Governor Rhodes.

And then I pointed it at him.

GOVERNOR RHODES STOOD AS SOON AS HE SAW THE GUN, but instead of putting his hands up like people are supposed to when someone points a gun at them, he turned his palms upward in a questioning way.

"What do we have here, Kendra?" he said, calm as anything.

"A gun, obviously."

I kept it aimed at him and stepped a few feet closer. When I shot him, I didn't want to miss.

"And what are you planning to do with a gun?"

"I'm going to shoot you, of course," I said. "This is my destiny. This is how I'm going to stop the outbreak from happening."

"This isn't your destiny," he said. "And whoever says so is misleading you."

"Put your hands up."

"Why? You're not going to shoot me. It would be a huge mistake for you to shoot me."

"I'm not only going to shoot you—I'm going to kill you," I said. "I'm going to stop the coup by killing you, because if the coup can't happen, then the outbreak doesn't need to happen, either."

"What coup?"

"You know perfectly well what coup," I said. "You're killing off the president from this disease, and then you're going to try to kill the vice president, only it's not going to work, but in the meantime, you're going to make it so you're the next in command, and you're going to seize power. I saw it all in an Insight."

Your wife's Insight, I thought but didn't say. I'd already said too much. I shouldn't have mentioned the vice president survived; it had been an amateur mistake and it might get him killed.

"That's ridiculous." Rhodes laughed with incredulity, but quickly stopped when he saw my stony face. "For a couple reasons. First, *there's no coup being planned.* Flat-out, it's not happening. I'd never agree to something like that. Second, it's not terribly difficult to get elected. You simply outspend the other guys. It's how I became governor. I outspent my opponent three-to-one. If I wanted to be president, I'd do the same thing. I'd run on my own merits, which are considerable, and my wife's money and that of her billionaire friends. No one needs to kill anyone, much less manufacture a pandemic, to make that happen. It's not that hard for people like me to get into office. The world belongs to people like me."

"The world belongs to everyone." Even so, his words had a ring of truth to them, and my resolve faltered the tiniest bit—but *just* the tiniest bit. "Give me that necklace you have on."

"This? Fine." He pulled it off and tossed it to me. I didn't attempt to catch it but let it fall on the ground because I didn't want to give him an opportunity to rush me while I bent to pick it up. "I have one for you, and for your mom, too. They're back at the residence. We got them today from the CDC. They contain a sort of . . . antidote, I believe . . . or something that buys us a little time if we need to get to where the vaccine can be administered."

"I'm not *going* to the residence. Now go over there and get on your knees." I gestured to the wall that separated the living room from the kitchen. Once he did as I ordered, I tossed him the hand-cuffs from a safe distance. "Put those on."

He did so awkwardly, slipping them loosely around his wrists.

"Make them tighter," I said.

"You're making a mistake," he said as he did what I asked. "I'm on your side, Kendra. You seem to be very confused in the infor-mation you have. You either don't have all the facts, or you're being deliberately misled, so you need to ask yourself why. Who told you to kill me? Who stands to gain if I die?"

"The whole world stands to gain if you die."

"Kendra, I'm not involved in any coup."

"I know all about your wife." I scooped up the chain from the carpet. "I know she used to sterilize poor women so they couldn't have children, and I know your people released the virus at the prison and the hospital on purpose, and I know you're planning to take over as president once the pandemic hits. You know how I know this? *Because I read your wife's Insight while she was reading mine.*"

A stunned silence followed, during which his face drained of all color.

"My wife doesn't have Insights," he said, his voice hollow.

"Oh, yes, she does."

"Kendra, I'd know if my wife had Insights."

"I know you'd know! That's my whole point! And while I was reading her Insight in your office last night, she was reading mine, which just so happened to be about you being assassinated at that rally, and the next thing you know all those other people are dead instead of you, and you're being called a hero. The whole thing was staged so when you take over as president everyone knows who you are and thinks you're awesome." I practiced my aim. "Well, I'm not going to let that happen."

Governor Rhodes sank back on his heels. All his energy seemed to drain out of him. He shook his head over and over, as if trying and failing to make sense of what I'd said.

"I guarantee you this is the first I'm hearing of any of this," he said finally, giving me a plaintive look. "I don't know what my wife's been up to, but I've not been a part of it. We've always lived very separate lives."

Nice try, I thought. "There's no way you could be married to someone and not know they have Insights."

"We've always slept in separate bedrooms," he said. "She's an insomniac and keeps her own room. She barely ever sleeps. We're not a close couple. We're the quintessential marriage of convenience."

I scoffed. "You have, like, five children."

"Through surrogates," he said. "They are ours, biologically, but my wife was unable to carry them on her own. Or unwilling, I don't really know. But there was no sex, no love, involved in the creating of our children. We've both found those things elsewhere. Or, at least I have. I assume she has, too."

I put the chain around my neck. "Do you believe your wife's a good person?"

He let out a breath. "The better question is whether I believe she's capable of what you're suggesting."

"And do you?"

"Let me go, and I'll find out." The arm holding the gun fought to lower it against my will. It was as if my arm believed him . . . but I didn't. Even so, he saw my wavering arm. "I'll help you, Kendra, if what you say is true. I'll be the best advocate you have. I'm in the perfect position to help. If something's going on, I'll stop it."

"Do you think it might be true?" I said. "Do you think your wife could be capable of what I'm suggesting?"

"Yes," he said, and the pain in his eyes seemed real. "I believe my wife is capable of such evil."

"And what about you? Are you capable of such evil?"

"I think everyone's capable of evil, given the right circumstances," he said. "Perhaps the difference between my wife and me is that I've always turned away from it. You have plenty of chances in a life of politics to go down the wrong path, but given the choice, I've always turned away. If I'm involved now, it's unwittingly—and unwillingly. And if you let me go, I'll do everything in my power to help you."

I shouldn't have let him talk, I realized. In doing so, I'd allowed him to confuse me thoroughly. I sat on the edge of an armchair, keeping the gun aimed at him. Now I had to think the whole thing through again.

"Option one, I shoot you. I kill you," I said. "Maybe that stops the disease outbreak, maybe it doesn't, but it definitely stops the coup, so that's a good thing."

"In that scenario, though, what happens to your mother?" he said. "What happens to your friend, Matt? I immediately put in a call to have him released after hearing from your mom he'd been arrested. I didn't know anything about that."

"How could you not know? You were right there."

"Apparently a lot of things have been happening right under my nose without my knowledge," he said.

"So if I call Matt right now I'd be able to reach him? Because that would go a long way toward me believing you, if you really got him released."

"I don't know if he's released already," he said. "I just put in the call on the way over here, so I'm not sure how long it'll take. I'd say it's probably fifty-fifty whether you could get hold of him or not. I'm just being honest with you."

"It's worth a shot." I got up and started to plug the Butler back in.

"Is it, though?" he countered quickly. "If you try, someone will know you're trying, and then if you end up shooting me, they'll think the two of you were working together to kill me, and they'll lock Matt away again and hunt you down for the rest of your short life. Option one's a bad option, Kendra. It doesn't free your mother, if she's indeed being held against her will; it doesn't free Matt; and it may or may not stop the outbreak, so it's not a guaranteed success. Plus, what about the sound of the gunshot? That'll get my guard running in here, and you won't have much chance of escape. A better option is to leave me here, all tied up, and make your getaway. I won't fight to be found; I'll wait here quietly. I don't know how much time you'll have, but certainly more than if my security guard hears a gunshot."

He was right about the gunshot. I hadn't even thought of the noise it would make.

"If I leave you and make my escape, then what?"

He smiled. "Then I become the best ally you've got."

IN THE END, I COULDN'T DO IT. I COULDN'T MAKE MYSELF fire the gun.

I'd wanted to, I really had. The Insight I'd just read in which I was tortured on his orders was never far from my mind, no matter how convincingly Governor Rhodes spoke otherwise. And he *was* convincing. The things he said made good sense, but everything depended on his being innocent, and the facts I had available to me didn't point to that conclusion. So I planted my feet firmly on the ground, aimed for his heart, and intended to squeeze the trigger at the same time I squeezed my eyes shut so I wouldn't have to see what I was about to do.

But I couldn't.

I just couldn't do it.

If I was going to—in Daemon's words—be the hero of this whole damn thing, it would have to happen without me killing anybody.

I opened my eyes and glared at Governor Rhodes. "I'm going to let you live, but you'd better help me."

"I will," he promised, smiling encouragingly as if we were in it together now. "And you'd better run."

Leaving him handcuffed and kneeling on the floor, I climbed through the bathroom window yet again. I ran to Mr. Swanson's back door, shoved the gun into the backpack, and strapped it on my back. I took off through the backyards, retracing the same route I'd taken to Nora's throughout my childhood. I tried to leap over the row of bushes at the edge of her property as I usually did, but I didn't clear the bushes because I hadn't accounted for the weight of the backpack, and I crashed to the ground like a complete idiot.

I scrambled back up, noticing a light was on in Nora's bedroom. I raced over and tapped on her window. She peeked out and did a double take.

"Kendra! I *just* got home! How did you know I was back? And how *are* you? I've missed you so much!"

It seemed like a lifetime since I'd last seen her, even though it had only been a few weeks. Sadly, it was not the time for chitchat.

"I've missed you, too," I said. "But I don't have time to talk. I need to borrow your car. Governor Rhodes is tied up on my living room floor and—"

"He's what?" The look on her face was priceless. "Did you hear about the shooting near the courthouse today? Gosh, that—"

"I heard about it," I said. "Can I have the keys to your car? I'll have it back in a couple hours."

I wouldn't, but I figured she'd be more likely to say yes if she thought I would.

"You don't look so good, Kendra."

"Like I said, I've got Governor Rhodes handcuffed on my living room floor."

"What do you mean by that?"

"It's not a metaphor, Nora. He's literally tied up in my house, and people are going to be after me any second. There are people who want me dead right now."

"I'm not going to lend you my car, Kendra."

That did it.

"Matt got arrested for me, and you won't even—"

"Matt got arrested?"

"Just LEND ME YOUR CAR. Or, you know what? Never mind. I should have known I couldn't count on you."

I turned away. There was a lot I would have liked to say, but staying alive was more important than having it out with her right then.

"Wait!" she called. "I was going to say I'm not going to lend you my car, but I'll drive you wherever you want to go." I turned back. "I felt awful abandoning you when I left for camp, and I only did it because my parents made me, but I promise I'm not going to do it again. Let me grab my keys and I'll meet you in the garage."

"I—you can't, I—" Matt was already in jail because of me. "I don't want you to get in trouble."

"Get in my car and lay down on the floor," she said. "I'll be out in two seconds."

"Seriously?"

"Seriously. Now go."

I ran off, ducking low until I'd passed the kitchen and living room windows that faced the backyard. I slipped through the side door to the garage, tossed my backpack into the back seat of her car, then headed over to her dad's disorganized shelves and grabbed two sleeping bags, a tent, a wool blanket, a cooler, and a box of miscellaneous camping supplies. I threw it all into her car and worked my way down the row of shelves, frantically grabbing a flashlight, a jerry can of gas, an axe, a hammer, and a case of water.

I shoved everything in the back seat, and I got in the front passenger seat. I pushed the seat as far back as it could go and then got down so I was kneeling on the floor, hidden from view. Really, I should have hidden in the trunk, but Nora would need me to tell her what to do. She'd have no idea, whereas I did. I'd watched every single episode, after all, and some of them more than once.

Nora and I were going to make a run for it.

We were going to get Lost in America—and try like hell not to get caught.

To see what happens next, read Episode Four,

available as an e-book,

or sign up for my newsletter to be

informed when Book Two is available.

ACKNOWLEDGMENTS

The author would like to acknowledge The Editorial Department for its comprehensive support of the author and manuscript. In particular:

Ross Browne, for content and developmental editing. Also for the many years of all-around advice and friendship.

Morgana Gallaway, for the perfect project management, interior design, and inspired plot assistance.

Oceana Garceau for the gorgeous cover design.

Julie Miller and Molly Gallaway for their eagle-eyed copy editing.

Jane Ryder and Liz Felix for encouragement and administrative support.

Q&A WITH THE AUTHOR

Morgana Gallaway, author of *Suffer a Witch* and *Discordia*, sits down with Laura Fitzgerald about her new series *Lost in America*.

Several aspects of *Lost In America* have a ripped-from-the-headlines feel to them. Is that deliberate?

Definitely! The story takes place in the near-future, which gives me license to think ahead and invent things and not use the names of real people or real companies, but readers should be able to read about my near-future story almost as if it was taking place in real-time. The capability of Butler watches, for example, isn't too far ahead of where smart watches are today. The mysterious outbreak and the role the fear surrounding it is going to play is similar to the recent outbreak of Ebola in the U.S.

I wanted all the surface things to feel disconcertingly familiar so the below-the-surface things do, too. The plot is so evil and so diabolical, but it's not too far from the realm of possibility. Giving the story a ripped-from-the-headlines feel helps make the conspiracy that much more real and scary.

What are we supposed to think of Daemon Godwin? What does Kendra think about him?

For the most part, Kendra represents us, the common person. She is everywoman, someone who just wants to live her life but gets caught up in something larger than herself. Throughout the novel, she struggles to understand whom can she trust. The bad guys are charismatic, well-respected people that society has largely judged to be good guys. Visionary. Even heroic.

Not only does Kendra have to contend with that, but also she's forced to wonder: Are the good guys really good? They kill people, after all. Daemon killed her boyfriend, so how can she ever think well of him? At the same time, he's fighting a heroic fight knowing he's going to die at the end of it, which is unquestionably admirable. Not to mention, he's older and handsome and mysterious, which is a potent combination. Kendra is definitely attracted to him at the same time she's repulsed by him, something Matt has quite rightly picked up on.

In future episodes, we're going to learn a lot more about Daemon. Life was not destined to be easy for him, but he acts honorably in spite of that.

You're writing this as a serial novel, publishing new episodes almost immediately after you write them. Do you have the whole story plotted out, or are you making it up as you go along?

I know absolutely how the story ends, very specifically, scene by scene. I know who lives and who dies. Sadly, several good people must die throughout the course of the story. Other things I'm far less clear on. For instance, I know where Kendra needs to arrive now that she's fled her hometown, but I'm not sure how she's going to get there or what's going to happen along the way except in a very general sense.

The first three episodes took a long time to write, edit, and polish to make sure the story is set up properly. All three episodes were done before the first one was released. From Episode Four on, it's a race to the finish. I'm committed to have a new (E-book) episode out every few weeks, so the story is going to have to be carried by the strength of the plot, not by the beauty of the language (which isn't a strong suit of mine in any case). It's a scary and invigorating way to write. I used to be a newspaper reporter, so I'm used to publishing stories minutes after writing them. Newspapers are thought to be the first draft of history, while a book feels like such a permanent thing … but it's fiction. Must we take ourselves so seriously?

In the end, all I'm shooting for is to present a great story, told well enough.

Out of all the potential stories you could have told, why did you choose to tell this one?

It's every writer's dilemma. We're blessed/cursed with active imaginations, which leave us with more story ideas than we'll ever have time to write. Before I start a novel, I find a question or issue I want to explore that can hold my interest for the year or longer it will take to write it. I then build the plot around that question.

My burning issue these days is privacy. It annoys the hell out of me that in order to use technology to the everyday degree I do, I have to surrender my right to privacy. It *is* a right—the Fourth Amendment says in very clear language, "The right of people to be secure in their persons, houses, papers, and effects, against unreasonable searches and seizures, *shall not be violated.*"

And yet … my smart TV can record every conversation that happens in the privacy of my home. My cell phone provider knows where I am at all times. My email provider sells information about me to the highest bidder.

It's not just companies. Every telephone conversation, email, online chat, Facebook post is automatically recorded, stored, and accessible to the government now and forevermore. The NSA captures something like 1.7 *billion* pieces of communication every single day, not necessarily just those of known or suspected bad guys, but also those of ordinary, every day citizens—people like you and me.

When she reads this, my teenage daughter will roll her eyes. "I have nothing to hide," she always says. "Why should it matter if all this information is collected?" It's highly frustrating!

Lost In America was born out of that frustration. The question I'm exploring is this: What's the absolute worst thing that could happen as a result of our privacy being lost, stolen, or carelessly given away? It's a fascinating question with a terrifying answer.

So … what happens next? (Give us a hint, anyway!)

We've got Kendra on the run being hunted by people who want her dead. We've got a terrible disease about to be let loose on an unprepared and unsuspecting population. We've got a conspiracy yet to be figured out. As the hero of the story, Kendra's got to be the one who figures it out and stops it, and yet at the end of Book One, she largely still wishes she could just run away and hide. She's not as committed to the cause as Daemon and the others are, so something's got to happen that gets her to commit. You'll just have to check out future episodes to find out what that is.

What I've enjoyed the most writing beyond Episode Three is how I've been able to expand the scope of how the story is told. In the first three episodes, it's mostly told through Kendra's eyes, with the occasional bad-guy point-of-view so the reader gets a sense of the true stakes of what's going on. Going forward, however, we'll hear some of the story from Daemon's point of view, Matt's point of view, Lacy Rhodes' point of view, and Maddie Meyers' point of view. Not only has this been fun to write, but I feel it's going to deepen how the reader experiences the story. That's the hope, anyway! Please tell me if I'm right or wrong, because since I'm writing and publishing this story in real-time, I can be influenced by what people say and potentially even change the course of the story. Who should Kendra end up with, Daemon or Matt? (Just kidding. I already know the answer to that question.)

I'm best reached through my website at laurafitzgerald.com.

Anything else you want to say?

Yes! I'd like to thank my loyal readers for being willing to stick with me as I write a new sort of story, and to invite people who like my work to get in touch with me in one or more of the ways listed below. I have several new creative ideas I intend to explore in the next couple years, and some of them will be shaped by the involvement of my readers, fans, and friends.

Oh! And if you're enjoying the story, please take a moment and review it on Amazon and/or Goodreads. Reviews help tremendously when people are deciding whether or not to give a book a chance. Thank you in advance!

CONNECT WITH LAURA

www.laurafitzgerald.com

Facebook Group: "**Laura Fitzgerald Fan Club**"

To Friend on Facebook: **writer.laurafitzgerald**

Goodreads: **Laura Fitzgerald**

Twitter: **@FitzgeraldLaura**

Instagram: **writerlaurafitzgerald**

Tumblr: **LostInAmerica-TheBook**

All social media websites are managed directly by the author.